The Conch Killers

Best wishes,
Chip

Live slow; sail Fast! Chip Giles

Order this book online at www.trafford.com
or email orders@trafford.com

Most Trafford titles are also available at major online book retailers.

Printed in Victoria, BC, Canada.

ISBN: 978-1-4269-2563-4 (soft)
ISBN: 978-1-4269-2562-7 (hard)

Library of Congress Control Number: 2010900504

*Our mission is to efficiently provide the world's finest, most comprehensive book publishing
service, enabling every author to experience success. To find out how to publish your book, your
way, and have it available worldwide, visit us online at www.trafford.com*

Trafford rev. 01/20/2010

 www.trafford.com

North America & international
toll-free: 1 888 232 4444 (USA & Canada)
phone: 250 383 6864 ♦ fax: 812 355 4082

Acknowledgements

I would like to express my gratitude to several important people who were instrumental in the development of this project. To LTC Art Durante (ret.) and SFC Jimmy King (ret.), you are great Americans, great soldiers and great friends. To Bert and Kathy Ward, you guys are the best! You are great friends and important to have around in a tight spot. To Ms. Uluwehi Hopkins, thank you for the valuable advice on Hawaiian culture and language. The book would not have been the same without your input. To Tim Dorsey, thank you for your gracious advice that helped me start and finish this book. I hope I can return the favor some day. The biggest thank you goes out to my wife, Kelly Giles, for being there always and putting up with me. None of this would be possible or meaningful without you.

Chapter One

Blood exploded in a bright red spray when the brown, barnacle-covered shell smacked loudly into the man's head. THWOCK! The man's eyes rolled back into his head and a big gash just above his temple revealed his skull, glistening with a patina of blood. None of the people watching were paying much attention to the dying man with a big hole in his head. Their attention was focused on the other man standing next to the dead guy.

That would be the guy with the shell.

Snapping out of his stupor, Tad stumbled down into the gin-clear shallow water, the bottom visible even at night. "Ramon, I think you beat him to death with… that shell. That's a new one, even for you."

"Not just any shell…," he continued, "…a Queen Conch shell. Definitely not just any shell. The shell most associated with the Florida Keys and this Shangri La called the Bahamas. It stirs the imagination and fires the passions. It'll also hold a door open, but that's another story. Can you hear me, O'Brien? Are you listening? Conch – rhymes with conk – like what I just did to your head."

O'Brien heard nothing. His head was six inches under water and no bubbles were emanating from within. No input from O'Brien.

"Shell, I proclaim that you are a killer. You have killed Mr. O'Brien, who needed to be killed and hence is such and done is the deed. You and I have become one. We are brothers of the molluskial dark arts."

Murphy looked at Tad impatiently. Tad replied, "You know how he is. The spirit moves him."

Murphy grumbled, "Something better move us all."

A red stain spread around the vicinity of O'Brien's cabeza muerta throughout the water.

Murphy cleared his throat and said, "Ramon, you know the difference between killers and murderers? Killers are the ones that have not been caught yet. And we have not yet been caught. Murderers have been convicted. We have not and I would prefer to keep it that way. Now, please pull your head out of your fourth point of contact or we are going to be stuck in a Bahamian jail with Jamaican drug runners using us for blowup dolls. We have to go, Ramon. Tad, you and Ramon get to the boat and we will get to the sea plane."

"Ah, yes," Ramon said, "There's that. Time to leave," he said slowly, "…but the shell comes with us. It's all about synergy. Working together. Man and nature. Mano y Shello."

Tad exhaled in a measured breath nodded, "Goes on the mantle. Let's go home, Conch Killer."

"Conch Killer? I like it!" Ramon said. His face brightened as he washed the blood off the edge of the shell. "Time to go."

It was then that they watched the big Morris Yacht motoring swiftly out of the channel and headed toward the Gulf Stream.

Their way home was leaving without them. Great. What now?

Chapter Two

(Alexandria, Virginia) The smell of pizza wafted through the night air, assaulting the senses of the throngs of people on the sidewalk. Don Vito's was a favorite spot, just five blocks from the waterfront on King Street. The young couple walked down here from their brownstone, just like many nights before. The handsome young man nodded at the busy cashier and called out, "Hey Vinnie! Give us the usual. Try not to screw it up again."

The dark, hairy man was throwing dough into the air. He feigned outrage, "That's right. Keep it up. I'm *this close* to putting in a call to Lenny Two Fingers. Then - Bada Bing! You – at the bottom of the Potomac... and then your woman, she'll be mine. That's right, keep it up." He smiled as he wiped his hands on his flour and sauce-covered apron and began to ladle pizza sauce onto the dough.

The young man walked behind the counter and gave the man a hug. "How you doing, Vinnie?"

"Fine, Johnny, just fine. How's that beautiful fiancé of yours?"

"Jesus, Vinnie! You know we're not engaged. Why do you keep embarrassing Elizabeth like that?"

"Why do you keep embarrassing the family? And yourself, you putz. Put a ring on that girl's finger. Don't wait too long. Now go sit down. I'll have it out soon."

Johnny kissed the elderly Italian woman at the cash register on the cheek, and went to his girlfriend.

The couple sat and chatted. They talked about whatever young people talked about when they were in love. The future was certain, the stars were in their proper alignment and all was right with the world.

The girl's eyes sparkled as she stared into Johnny's face. He leaned over and whispered a private joke in her ear, causing peals of laughter. Johnny was sure he had found the woman with whom he would grow old. He had slowly allowed their relationship to grow, not rushing it. He was careful. He had to be. He was her bodyguard.

But on this night, fate was fickle and Johnny was paying more attention to Elizabeth the love of his young life rather than Elizabeth, the subject he was guarding. And that was bad.

Johnny had come to let his guard down more and more. When he looked around, he saw the world through the eyes of a goggle-eyed fool in love rather than through suspicious, probing eyes. He knew he would marry Elizabeth in time, but for how he enjoyed her company. In fact, it was all he craved. He was losing his edge. No, losing is not the right word. He was *shedding* his bodyguard skin and trying hard to be a good boyfriend.

Never had Johnny made such a big mistake. He had become complacent. And tonight, Elizabeth would pay. Dearly.

• • •

"What a handsome couple," the old lady thought. Edna Stribling had lived in Alexandria for forty-six years. Each night Edna would walk down to the Potomac River and back. She would carefully make her way up the sidewalk to King Street and turn right. The night air was pleasant and she enjoyed the ambience.

She had seen a lot in her seventy-eight years. Edna was what you could call a "spunky old bird." She had been in New York when the boys come back from the Big War in '45. *"That was a hell of a party,"* she thought, *"the good old days."* She was twenty years old, and one good looking broad. At least that was what here soon-to-be husband told her. Plus, Benjamin liked her ta-ta's.

Benjamin Stribling was a Marine captain who had successfully led a company of Marines at Guadalcanal. He was a handsome devil, a decorated war hero and best of all, awfully rich. Benjamin's father, Ernest Stribling, had built a thriving company from the ground up.

Edna did not know exactly what they did, but it had something to do with selling mechanical parts to the military and other government agencies.

Edna met Benjamin at a USO dance. After seven dances, four gin martinis and two hours in the sack, Benjamin was convinced he had found his dream girl. Six months later they were married. They had an exciting and fulfilling fifty-one years of marriage, until Benjamin's heart gave out while sweeping off the front walk.

Edna had lived the last five years alone in their Georgetown brownstone, making the most of each and every day. That's why she liked to walk at night – because it made her feel *alive* and *young*.

As Edna watched the young couple come out of the pizza parlor, she smiled. Young people in love always had a distinct glow – an aura of wonder and promise that radiated from the way they smiled and held each other. Benjamin held her like that fifty-six years ago on this very street. Edna silent wished the unknown couple fifty-one years together as they made their way to the waterfront.

• • •

Elizabeth and Johnny had a very non-traditional start, as a young couple in love. Usually on a campus, boy sees girl, boy meets girl, boy and girl decide they kind of like each other, and they end up in the sack for two months. If they can stand each other then, the relationship has real promise. Liz and Johnny had a different story.

Liz was a junior at Georgetown, majoring in economics. Liz's father was Bradford Wallington Forbish, IV, CEO and majority stockholder of Forboco Petrochemical, Incorporated. Their family fortune was substantial and they lived at an old Virginia plantation house named Knottywood.

"If you don't have a name for your spread, you ain't shit." Forbish liked to give the image of the rough and tumble oilman rising to the top of the ranks, but sadly it was not true. Forbish was not much more than a flaming ass and a bumbling fool. He inherited the petroleum company from his father fifteen years ago. Old man Titus Forbish, on his deathbed, debated on whether to flip a coin to decide who gets the fortune – his asshole son or some goddamn cat foundation. Fortunately for Bradford, the old man croaked before finding any loose change that he could reach.

The Forbish's enjoyed the perks of the elite upper crust of the great American society. Bradford and his wife, Bootsy, raised four children with the help of seven full time servants, two child psychologists, an assload of prescription medicine, and one mistress. The medicine was for Bootsy; the mistress for Bradford.

In the world of high finance and petrochemicals, Bradford fancied himself as a hard bastard. Everyone in his social circle knew him to be a buffoon, but he had far too many millions to prevent anyone from pointing this out to him.

The Forboco Petrochemical Building was located in Dallas, staffed by eighteen hundred men and women who dutifully managed the business, mostly in the absence of its owner. Bradford had an enormous teleconferencing system set up in his office at Knottywood, allowing him access to all the Forboco executives at a moment's notice.

The wonders of modern communications technology practically negated the necessity of him ever going to his own corporate headquarters at all. Despite this, Bradford periodically flew out to Dallas under the auspices of board meetings, networking and briefings from the underlings. What really happened was quail hunting, expensive liquor and high dollar whores from the chemical pimps that wooed Forbish's business.

Mostly, Forbish spent his time in Northern Virginia. Texas made him nervous. Those Texans seemed to look right through a man and spot bullshit from a mile away. Around Northern Virginia and D.C., *everyone* was full of bullshit. The city ran on bullshit. Bullshit was not only tolerated, but was at certain levels to be admired. That is, so long as there was some money to back it up. So Bradford Wallington Forbish, IV was in his element, as he was as full of shit as a Christmas turkey and rich as a sheik.

Bradford had attracted the attention of most of the prominent men and women in society. Powerful men and women snickered when he entered rooms. He sat on several prominent advisory panels. He was ridiculed at society soirées and in Capitol Hill cloakrooms. He had arrived.

He was just about on top of his game, when disaster fell on the Forbish household.

Forbish received an urgent call from Phillip Dixon. Dixon was the Chief of Security for the vast Forbish Empire. Forbish was entertaining two senators and a handful of government executives from the EPA at his manor. It was amazing what a few cans of Beluga caviar and a little personal attention could do to help block an obscure environmental bill.

A small Pilipino servant wearing an immaculate white uniform brought out a phone and handed it to Forbish. "Sir, its Mister Dixon."

"The tray. goddammit, bring out the goddamn phone on the goddamn tray. Shit." he hissed. But he didn't hiss too long, because when Phillip Dixon called, he knew to stop what he was doing and listen. It was seldom good news, but always important.

"Go ahead, Phillip. What is it?"

"I'm on the way to the big house. Be there in fifteen minutes. We need to talk. It'll take the rest of the day."

"Knottywood. The name of the friggin' house is Knottywood. Will you stop calling it the Big House! (pause) All day? No sh…You want to tell me what this is about?"

"Fifteen minutes." And he hung up. Most people wondered how Dixon could get away with talking to the old man like that. After all, Phillip Dixon was only five feet, six inches tall. He was in perfect shape, though. He graduated from the top of his class at MIT, and went on to serve six years in Marine Corps Force Recon. He excelled in martial arts and enjoyed competing in ironman competitions just for fun.

Phillip was recognized early as a talented man, and Bradford was looking for just such a man to help solve a few "problems" in his ranks. And Phillip Dixon was black, very black. This made him quite unique in an industry that still was lily white.

Dixon quickly rose to take over all of Bradford's security operations, including Knottywood. He was bright, effective, and best of all, feared. Bradford enjoyed boasting of how intensely loyal Dixon was, but privately he wondered. Hell, Bradford still got heebiejeebies when Dixon entered his office with that penetrating gaze. Dixon was the Obi Wan Kenobe of corporate strata - awful quite when calm, but a sonofabitch when you piss him off.

Bradford took the senator from the great state of Virginia off to the side, and said, "I'm sorry, but I just got a call from my office. My man Dixon is coming over with an urgent matter. I need to cut the meeting a little short."

"Ah, yes! Dixon. How is he? Isn't he the one who watches over your corporation? Capable man, eh?"

"Capable? Oh, yeah. He's a real badass. When he shows up, someone's ass is about to hit the fan."

The Senator blinked a couple of times as his scotch-addled brain processed the mixed metaphor. Nothing like passed the day like mixing drinks and metaphors. He cleared his throat and said, "And here he is showing up at Knottywood. What fun!"

• • •

The two guards at the gate of Bradford's estate watched a new jaguar glide up the road. They knew exactly who was in that car, because Dixon had personally selected each of the eighteen guards that provided security around the clock. Two at the gate and two were roaming, around the clock, in all weather. Bradford had no illusions about the vulnerability of his cherished estate, and relied on Dixon to make it secure ("Get this damn place tighter than a frog's ass, Dixon!").

The British sports car growled as Dixon downshifted, swinging into the driveway. The massive double wrought iron gates stood passive before him, blocking the driveway. The first guard walked smartly to the driver's side while the second guard remained in the doorway of the stucco guard house. The first and most important rule of manning the gate was "Never open the gate before confirming who they are. Never. Period. Don't even think about doing it."

And they didn't. Not even for Bradford, who would launch a broadside of profanity at the guards that would make a sailor blush. But the rule held, mostly because they were far more afraid of Dixon than the old man. One day last November, Bradford came home to the usual closed gate. His chauffer, Jules, was blowing the horn long before they got to the gate. The younger guard, Sonny, looked at the other guard, "Beau, he's blowing this time. What do we do?" The older guard cracked a small smile and said, "Screw him. We're checking that limo out. Procedures are procedures." They prepared to visually inspect the interior of the limo, hidden by the darkened windows.

These guards had been at the gate all day long, with cold rain and sleet sliding down their necks. They were tired, pissed off and not at all in the mood for old man Bradford's attitude today. So they performed their job exceptionally well today (translated – they took their sweet time) as they walked up to the rear window and knocked.

The rear window rolled down, and Bradford stuck his head out. "Open the friggin' gate you moron. Now…Open it… I gotta…"

The two guards looked at each other. Something was wrong. The senior guard, Beau, leaned further in the window. "What's wrong Mr. Bradford? You don't look so good."

Bradford clenched his teeth and winced. It looked like every muscle in his body was tensed up. Perspiration was beaded all over his forehead and his skin had a pallid tone. Sonny hollered out, "*His heart. He's dyin' right here, Beau - on our shift!*"

Bradford slowly turned to the guard, staring into the man's eyes with a pained look of desperation. Veins bulged from his temples. "God, Beau…I… gotta…take a …crap." His face twitched momentarily, and ceased. And then the old man collapsed and the darkly tinted window began to slowly roll up.

The Bentley sat in the driveway, idling quietly. The massive gate swung open, and the Bentley cruised slowly up the long, pea-gravel driveway. The next day Bradford made a call to Dixon, demanding the guards be fired, but he would not say why. (*"You get rid of their asses before I run them off myself!"*) Dixon made some calls, and had a word with Jules. Beau and Sonny, the two guards received a raise. The two guards became somewhat legends among the security staff.

And now here was Dixon, making an unscheduled visit. Beau greeted Dixon and thoroughly checked the Jag.

"Nowhere for anyone to hide in there, Boss."

"No, there's not. How are things?"

"Fine, Boss. Anything we need to know about going on?"

"Maybe. Keep an extra close eye out for anything out of the ordinary. I need to go in now to talk to the old man." Dixon gave the security guard a nod. Take care of the troops. Keep the morale up. He learned his leadership habits in the demanding environment of military special operations, and some habits just do not die.

The big gates swung open, and Dixon drove up the same driveway where only five months ago one of the richest men in Virginia had shit his pants.

• • •

James, the small Pilipino butler, met Dixon at the immense, white door. "Mr. Dixon, always a pleasure, Sir."

Dixon smiled and approached the small man. "How are you, James? And how is your wife, Evelyn? Is she well? How are the eyes?"

A mixture of pain and relief swirled in the eyes of the little man. "Ah, Mr. Dixon, she is fine. Your doctor is making her no longer be in pain. And I know you will ask about Evita. She is now at the University of Virginia. In one more year, she will graduate and become a teacher. My family sends their love."

A year ago, Dixon discovered that Bradford's butler had a wife who was suffering from diabetes. Her eyesight was diminishing, and her general health was declining. While Bradford was completely unaware of a problem, Dixon did what he did best. He fixed the problem. He made a phone call, and by the end of the next day, the little Pilipino lady was sitting in the office of one of the top diabetes specialists in Northern Virginia. From that day, James was fiercely loyal to Dixon. He was also the top source of information of the comings and goings in the Bradford household. James had the ability to capture intelligence and pass it on to Dixon in a manner that would make the Mossad jealous.

Dixon entered the study and began to survey the room. It was decorated in early Marlin Perkins, with a distinct pseudo-Dickensian overture. Animal heads stared down from around the room. Cape buffalo, kudu, gazelle and others lined the walls, dress right dressed on the dark cherry and each gazing placidly into the spacious interior. In the corner, there was a magnificent action scene of a male lion killing a springbuck.

Bradford loved to show off the room to any male who entered the palatial manor Knottywood. It had kind of a high-octane, testosterone-laden feel to it that made him want to dress up like Hemmingway and go shoot something. Of course Bradford didn't have the stones to go to Africa and shoot anything. Old man Titus had killed all these animals, but the younger Forbish kept them around. Once, when Forbish kept Dixon waiting too long, Dixon took a bottle of liquid paper from the desk and put white dots on all the glass eyes of the animal heads. It gave the room a creepy feel, but Forbish did not say anything to Dixon. He did not make Dixon wait any more, either.

Forbish was sitting in an overstuffed leather chair when Dixon entered the room.

Normally Dixon would have jerked him around a little, making up some story to agitate Forbish. Forbish had actually come to enjoy the unusual relationship between himself and Dixon. Dixon was the only one Bradford Forbish trusted. Forbish knew he needed him, and quite frankly, he missed Dixon when he was not around.

"Dixon, what in the hell is up?" He expected the usual banter, but only received a penetrating gaze that betrayed no emotions at all.

"It's Elizabeth. They've kidnapped her, Bradford. This is for real."

The bluster and superiority immediately drained out of the sixty-year-old man. He closed his eyes and leaned back for about ten seconds. He then buried his head in his hands and sobbed loudly. "Oh, God. Not Lizzy. Not again. What do we do?"

Phillip Dixon pulled a matching chair up to Forbish's chair, so that they were facing each other. "I think this time it may be different. Here is what we are going to do . . ."

• • •

The couple had only walked a block from the pizza parlor when they walked past the white van. Johnny looked up and saw two men walking toward him, talking to each other. Warning bells went off. Something didn't look right about these two, and grabbed Elizabeth and steered her toward a recessed doorway of a closed down electronics shop. Just then, he felt something slam into his side, causing him to arch back. Something else slammed his shoulder, spinning him around.

Shrieks and screams came from all around, as panic registered on his brain and the metallic taste of adrenaline filled his mouth. He tried to get the concealed .40 caliber semiautomatic from his holster in the small of his back. His right arm was not responding at all. Most of his body, as a matter of fact, was not responding. He felt something cool on his face. He looked up and saw it was the sidewalk.

As he lay on the cool pavement, he saw the two guys dragging Elizabeth away from the closed storefront. *"No,"* he thought, *"This cannot be happening."* He tried to turn his head to see where they were taking his true love.

Each man had a hold of an arm, and the girl was shrieking, "No! Not this! You killed him!"

The van came into focus, and Johnny saw the two men throw Liz in. He swiveled his head to see the person approaching. "You shot me, you bastard. If you hurt her I will find you and kill you." As he focused, he saw two people walk up to him, and squat down. It was a man and a woman. Both had pistols with silencers on them.

The woman had long, auburn hair and dark sunglasses concealed her eyes. She leaned down and put the end of the silencer in Johnny's ear. Johnny thought, *"That thing is so cold. So this is what death feels like."* Her mouth curled in a small smile, and she said, "Poor baby. I think your killing days are over, Jonathan Ancio Perecci."

Johnny faced his executioner and thought, *"Don't look away. Don't give them the satisfaction. If you gotta go, go like a man. Hey wait! How the hell does she know my name?"* He waited for the shot that would end his life, but it did not come.

The man and woman calmly walked to the van and got in. The van drove off, signaling to enter traffic and turning left at the next intersection.

People ran to Johnny, but did not touch him. The wail of the sirens got louder, and soon Johnny was being loaded onto a stretcher, unconscious. Back at the pizza parlor, Vinnie got word it was Johnny that had been shot, and was trying to penetrate a ring of police officers to talk to someone in charge.

The police officers were trying to make sense out of the whole scene. After all, abductions were not something that happened every day, especially right next to the nation's capitol. Drive by shootings? Dime a dozen. Abductions? The excrement was surely going to hit the oscillator and the cops in charge were covering all the bases.

"Hey lieutenant," the paramedic called out, "this guy's got a gun on."

The plain clothes policeman walked over and examined the gun. He turned to the sergeant, who also shopped from the Al Bundy collection, and said "Jeez. It's a Smith and Wesson forty caliber semi. Sweet. What the hell's this kid doing with this?"

The sergeant nodded, and said "Drugs. He's not just her boyfriend. He's her drug dealer. It's a drug deal gone bad and they got his woman."

Vinnie finally pushed through the scrum of younger officers, who were doing their best to keep the crowd back. "He's not just her boyfriend, you idiots. He's her bodyguard. Her bodyguard! You want me to spell it out? B-O-D-Y . . ."

Two young officers grabbed Vinnie, one around the neck and the other putting him in an arm lock. They were dragging him off when the lieutenant held his hand up in the international cop hand signal that lower ranking officers recognize as *"let him go – for now. We'll beat him later."*

"You are that guy who owns the pizza place, Don Corleone's, right?"

"It's Don Vito's, you dipshit, and yes. This boy is my nephew. He is, WAS, her bodyguard. And her boyfriend. It's complicated."

The lieutenant thought for a minute, waiting for that moment of clarity. The epiphany didn't come. "OK, I give up. Who is the girl? Brittany Spears? Christina Applegate? Who?"

"Nope. She's Bradford Forbish's daughter."

The lieutenant closed his eyes and stood in a frozen pose for a full fifteen seconds. He turned to the sergeant, who was also absolutely still and had a deadpan expression.

"OK, this is bad. This is real bad. Sergeant, get this site secured, get the crime lab boys here, NOW! I gotta call the Chief. Oh God, not again. Not here."

• • •

The van pulled into an abandoned warehouse. The door opened and everyone bailed out. Elizabeth was sitting in the corner, eyeing the people around her. An auburn-haired woman peered in at her, staring intently. Obviously satisfied at what she was looking at, she turned and walked off without a word. The two men who drug Elizabeth off stood outside the van.

Elizabeth screamed, "You killed him! I can't believe you killed my Johnny!" The woman looked at the man who had shot Johnny. He was not just a foot soldier; he and the woman were the leaders. "Why did you do it? He's a sweet boy! You killed my Johnny."

The man looked at his partner and smiled a cruel smile. In voice that was thick with Irish brogue he said, "Sweet like sugar. Now he's dead. Took a bullet in the head. Nothing else to be said." The two walked off while the two foot soldiers remained. Elizabeth screamed.

• • •

Chapter Three

The two men sat in the shade of the ficus tree. The tall, blond haired man dug around in an old styrofoam cooler, making the ice rustle. His hand emerged with first one, and then another can of beer. He was wearing dark shorts, the kind you saw fishing guides wearing. His t-shirt was faded purple and sported a crew of green sea turtles drinking at a bar. He wore an old pair of boat shoes that had seen their better days many moons ago. The two men sat in the shade, and drank an ice cold beer. Life was just so good.

A blonde girl came around the back of the sailboat, walking toward them. Her hair spilled down over her tan shoulders to the middle of her back. She was wearing a halter top that had parrots all over it. The top was generously filled, though her right boob was significantly larger than the left one. Her yellow shorts revealed two long, tan legs that stretched down to her bare feet. Her toenails had parrots on each big toe. Her body screamed *"look at me,"* while her attitude hissed, *"I'm a vortex of social maladjustment waiting to suck you into the limitless depths of my dysfunction."* Twenty-two years of hard living from one trailer park to the next. She was marked as surely as if she had a scarlet "WT" branded on her forehead.

She marched over to them and stopped. "George wants to know when you want to move this thing back into the water." The Cuban man winced, much as if someone pinched the skin on his left nad. "Mi Dios, Hefty Leftie, you farm girl. Or is it Mighty Righty? Whatever. Anyway, it is a sailboat, not a *thing*. It is referred to as a "she." Try it again. Say 'when do you want to move *her* into the water?' Come on, say it. Can you believe this peasant girl? This simpleton? Tad, I command you to remove her from my presence."

The girl put one hand on her hip and gave the two a very convincing you-gotta-be-kidding-me look that bordered dangerously near her eat-shit-and-die look. She sucked her teeth making a loud *thhhhttt* and said, "Hey Ramon, you are absolutely right. Here, let me get you another something cold to drink. Hey! Here you go! How about a nice twelve ounce can of blow-it-out-your-ass! No, wait, what's this? Uh-huh! Just the thing! Let's supersize that with a twenty ounce bottle of shut-the-hell-up! Uh-huh! I'm going back to the office. Away from you losers. Wait until I tell George about you, Ricky Retardo."

She went to kick the cooler over, but only knocked a chunk of Styrofoam off of the top of the cooler. She grabbed the chunk and threw it in the general direction of Ramon.

The two men turned and looked at each other, each waiting for the other to make the next comment. Ramon nodded and said, "Tad, that girl – She digs me."

Tad turned up the can, emptying the contents, and said, "You know, she is the marina owner's girlfriend. This is where we live. More or less."

• • •

"Tomorrow? You want to move it tomorrow? OK, no problem, Tad. You know how to operate the lift. Don't screw it up. And don't hit that Island Packet! That friggin' boat would cost me an arm and a leg to fix if you hit it. And do you think you can leave BethAnn alone? Do you enjoy seeing me get my wrinkled ass chewed every single time you want to bust her chops? Can you not see I am an old man and I deserve some consideration from you two hooligans?"

George's current girlfriend was laying in an Adirondack chair outside, perpetually working on her tan. She sucked hard on a Camel, while adjusting the position of the chair two degrees to the left. When her body was in perfect sync with the solar rhumb line, she settled back to work on her melanoma farm. BethAnn Honeywell, the darling of Two Egg, Florida, was in her element.

George Giani was the owner of the Conch Island Marina. He moved to Key Largo from Trenton, New Jersey in 1979, looking to get away from the fast lane. He inherited his father's Greek restaurant, and was making a pretty good go at it before running afoul of some local wise guys. They wanted a piece of the action, and made him an offer he couldn't refuse. He made them a counter offer – catch me if you can.

He sold the place to an unsuspecting Haitian who arrived in country with a duffle bag full of drug money. Two weeks later, George was gone and the two wise guys paid a visit to the new owner. The ensuing shootout left one wise guy dead, one with his jaw blown off, three patrons with non-life threatening gunshot wounds, and everyone wondering where the new owner had disappeared to. Life is funny that way.

So George escaped to Key Largo and bought the dilapidated Flamingo Bay marina. His first act of renovation was to change the name to Conch Island Marina. He renovated the docks, added hardstand for boat storage, and improved the marina store. It was a *functional* marina, but definitely not a touristy marina. It was also cheap and well-maintained, and that is what attracts and keeps his clientele of locals. George was in his sixth-third year and living life much like most twenty-three year olds dream of.

The two young men stood in the air conditioned marina store, which doubled as an office, drinking area, impromptu picnic spot, and general forum to tell fishing lies and war stories. War stories are the ones that always start with, "This is no shit…"

Ramon said, "Hey George, this is no shit, I think your woman don't like us. And you, she's going to kill you one day. An old man like you with that young banshee. I give you three weeks – a month on the outside. The coroner's report will say that you came and went at the same time. 'Oh yes! Oh no! Ughh.' Don't worry, Tad and I will take over. The powerboats are the first to go. Want me to go start clearing them out?"

Tad smiled, and then glanced at George. You were never quite sure how he would take Ramon's incessant wit. Today was a good day, though.

George ignored Ramon as he rummaged in a cigar box. "Ah-Ha!" He produced a key that was attached to a tan foam rubber cutout of a bare foot. "Here's the key to the lift. You need me to show you again how to operate it?" Tad often wondered why the key had a flotation foam foot on it. The boat lift was a monstrous device that stood twenty feet tall,and twenty-five feet long. If the lift was in water when you dropped the key, you had a much bigger problem that finding the key.

George tossed the key on the counter. The foot landed right side up and said, "Sister Allison's Psychic Connection and Manatee Mailboxes. Little Torch Key." Go figure. That was the Keys for you. Anything and everything went. Then Tad went for the key ring.

Tad had been operating the boatlift for George since the third day he moved in. The truth was that George had almost no idea of how to lift a boat, move it around and put it up on boat stands, if necessary. George bought the lift from another boat yard in Tavernier, but did not know how to use it well. He tried for about six months to learn, but only succeeded in beating up the gel coat on several boats.

Tad had long ago learned his way around a working marina, and he offered to help George use the lift. "Nah, George." Tad said, "I think I remember. Hey, I might be able to get around to replacing the hose on the diesel pump this week. Let me know when it comes in." Tad had somewhat assumed the role of handyman around the marina. His other roles included security, advice-giver, beer-drinking neighbor, and surrogate son of the aging Greek owner. Tad took immediately to George, like the second father he didn't need. Tad was drawn into the strange relationship much like the player-to-be-named-later who shows up perplexed in a strange locker room.

"That's good. Tad, you're a good boy. Ramon, you are a pain in my tired old Greek ass. But if Tad can put up with you, so can I. Watch yourself. Don't make me come across this counter. Now get out of here. You're running off the customers." George publicly acted like he could not stand Ramon. In truth, he loved the banter between Ramon and himself. It reminded him of his younger days in New Jersey. Good old times when all the young Greek men in his crowd talked loud, chased women without shame, and generally raised hell. Ramon understood George better than anyone else in Key Largo had. Ramon wasn't a pain in the ass, he was *sentimental therapy*.

• • •

Tad and Ramon lived in two separate apartments that were on top of their boat shop. Each apartment was an efficiency, having minimal living space, a functional fridge and a flushable toilet.

The shop below was spacious, but did not afford them room to work on what they cherished the most, sailboats. There was plenty of room for storage, and to work on parts and components of sailboats. The two had met eight years ago in the army, and found out they had many common interests. Sailboats, island life, avoiding regular jobs, and adventurous living. These combined to help launch their venture, Conch Island Yacht Service.

Tad was born Thaddeus Spencer Hunter in San Diego, California. He grew up doing what most California boys do best, surfing, sailing, diving and chasing girls. He learned to dive when he was in his freshman year of college at UCLA, but sailing remained his first and foremost love. He graduated from UCLA with a degree in mechanical engineering, and dedicated himself to the demanding task of avoiding responsibility.

He actually went to a couple of job interviews, but the problem with most mechanical engineering positions that were offered was that they lacked salt water had the presence of heinous elements. Heinous elements include buildings that block the sunlight, white shirts, ties, a desk with a nameplate, and worst of all, a boss.

In an exemplary act of irresponsibility, Tad stood up an interviewer and signed on as a deck hand delivering a 52' Beneteau cutter rigged yacht named Seraphis from La Jolla to Key West, Florida. The skipper hired to deliver the boat was a friend of the family. Tad's father thought it might be a good idea to get Tad out of town for a little while. Do something to clear his head. Tad was obviously not happy in his quest to avoid a meaningful career.

The route took Tad down the western coast of Mexico and through the Panama Canal. Tad was doing what he loved best – sailing and traveling. The skipper helped hone Tad's navigation skills, as well as teaching him how to run a boat. They talked about boats, women, boats, foreign ports, boats and life in general. They also talked about boats.

After stops in Cozumel, the Cayman Islands and Cuba, the boat cruised into Key West Harbor thirty-six days later. After getting the boat properly docked, the skipper called the crew together. "Boys, you are now in Key West. There's no place like it in the world. There's an excellent place called Captain Tony's right around the block. It was Hemmingway's hangout a long time ago. You all meet me there at nine o'clock, and we'll celebrate this auspicious occasion. Tad, here's a hundred dollar bill. Pay for the rounds until I get there."

Tad and the other crew walked around the harbor, marveling at the many boats. Key West Harbor had it all – massive motor yachts, big sailboats, dive boats, catamarans, large tour boats, schooners, dinghies, trawlers – you name it. Tad felt like a kid in a candy store looking at all the boats. Boats were his passion and he couldn't pass them up without drinking them in with his eyes.

They walked past an old turtle cannery and continued on down the dock. They passed the schooner Western Union and turned into the Schooner Wharf Bar. The Seraphis crew threw back a few cold beers, watching the day go by. An old Cuban man rolled cigars in the bar and sold them to tourists. There were three girls at the table next to Tad's. Each girl was smoking a cigar. *"Strange place,"* thought Tad.

They paid for their drinks and left, eager to see the rest of the harbor and island. They wound around the dock and turned left next to a market. They walked to the corner and surveyed the area. Basically they were clueless as to where to go. Everywhere looked rather inviting.

A thin guy with glasses walked out of the store on the corner. A boating goods store. Cool. "You guys lost? You look like you're crewing on one of the boats, right?" the guy asked.

"We're not exactly lost since we don't know where we need to go. We just pulled in from LaJolla. Long trip. We're hungry. Any recommendations?"

The guy said, "No problem. Right behind you is B.O.'s Fish Wagon. Best grouper sandwich around. Come see me after that and I'll tell you anything you need to know."

They ordered conch fritters, grouper sandwiches and draft beers. Life was good. Later, Tad and his band of merry mariners stumbled onto Duval Street. The street was alive with people coming and going. Music blared from open air bars and pubs. It was a festive atmosphere. The Seraphis crew high-fived each other and headed toward the nearest bar. Tad thought, *"Hmmm, I could live in a place like this."*

• • •

Later that evening, Tad and his friends were throwing back plastic cups of draft beer in Captain Tony's, listening to the band do their worst Simon and Garfunkel. *"Mama pyjama rolled outta bed, she ran to the police station. When the cop found out, he began to shout, he started the investigation.*" Tad overheard a group of guys at the next table talking about diving. Since Tad was a diver, he listened in on the conversation, quietly evaluating the men.

Two hours and six Miller Lite drafts later, Tad struck up a conversation with the men. The chance meeting of Thaddeus Spencer Hunter with this group of men changed his life forever and plotted a course of adventure that Tad could have never imagined. By the end of the night Tad was drinking beer, and trading diving stories with seven guys who were members of the United States Army Special Forces. They were instructors at the army diving school, which was located on Naval Air Station Key West.

Two other guys were there, but they were not military. Tad asked what they did. "Oh, this and that, kind of like consultants."

"What kind of consulting?" Tad asked.

"We make the locking mechanisms that go on the plastic portapotties that the military uses."

"Really?"

"No, not really."

One of the soldiers belted out, "Hey Thad, you say you sailed here from California on that boat, Sarah Puss? That what you do for a living?" the short, stocky one asked. His name was Baker and he looked like he bench pressed Volkswagons for fun.

"Yes. Well – no. It's not Sarah Puss, it Seraphis. Actually, I'm working on some things right now. Kinda like evaluating my options. And it's Tad, not Thad." Tad explained.

"Ah-Ha! Options! You got options like the Pope has a trophy wife. You don't got a frickin' job, do you, Chad?" This came from Arnie, the tall, thin soldier.

Tad crinkled his face, trying to process the hopelessly mixed metaphor in his beer-soaked brain. "Well, actually I have a college degree. I just don't know what I want to do with it. Something will happen. And it's <u>Tad</u>."

One of the soldiers leaned across the table. He was clearly the group leader. He had a drooping mustache that could not possibly meet any army's regulations. His skin was wrinkled and pocked. He had been around the block a few times. He had been there, done that, got the scars. Everyone at the table shut up when he spoke.

"Listen Scad. They're just pointing out the obvious. Do seriously intend to be a shitbird yacht monkey the rest of your life?"

Those ice blue eyes bore into Tad, testing him. Tad took a deep breath, controlling the rising anger. He met mustache man's stare, and held it for a few seconds.

"I'd rather be a yacht monkey than wear that Rip Taylor moustache. The name's Tad, got it?"

Instantly the table fell absolutely silent. Every eye was looking directly at Tad with a deadpan stare. Tad thought, *"Oh shit. What have I done? I'm a dead man now."*

He tried to make it better, "I meant *'Got it, Sir?'*"

The table exploded with howls of laughter. Baker said, "Hey Chief, you got his name now?" Mustache man smiled and sank back in his chair. They drank beer, hooted and howled until very early in the morning. Tad stumbled to the dock, flopped down in his berth, and didn't dream at all.

Chapter Four

The next day. 1100 hours. Sun up. Head hurts.

"The hatch! Goddammit watch the hatch, you pinhead! What's the matter with you?"

Tad's head felt like it had railroad spikes sticking in it from six different angles. The Key West sun was brutal. He was dangerously close to swearing off alcohol forever, as he hosed down the deck of the Seraphis. He had accidentally hosed down the interior twice, by not paying attention to what he was doing. The skipper was pissed, and was not quiet about it. He had bitched at Tad and the other crew members all morning about laying out all night. "If you are going to hoot with the owls all night, you got to be able to scream with the eagles the next day!"

From a few slips away, someone hollered out, "Fucking-A! Hoooah!"

The skipper, Tad, and the other crew members turned to see two men approaching the Seraphis. Tad recognized them as Baker and Arnie from the drinking spree last night. *"Oh, crap. This can't be good."* Tad thought. Baker and Arnie looked bright and cheerful, not at all like two men who had tried to do their part to drink Duval Street dry last night.

The two men studied the skipper and the skipper studied the two men. Baker offered, "Seal Team?" They seemed very interested in the skipper's tattoo on his leg.

"Yep. Seal Team One. Vietnam. 1968. You?"

"Fifth Special Forces. Dive School instructor. A little of here and a little of there. Can we borrow young Thaddeus for a while? We promise not to break him, nor fold, spindle or mutilate too much."

The skipper looked at Tad with a raised eyebrow. "Tad? You need to go with these guys?"

The butterflies were swarming his stomach. His head was exploding. "I…I don't know. Uh, where are we going?"

The stocky man smiled, looking extremely pleased with himself. "Rip Taylor…I mean the Chief wants to talk to you, Tad. Now go take a shit or something, and let's go. You look like hell."

The skipper looked at the young deckhand. "Better get going. These desperados mean business."

"You know about this?"

The skipper smiled, but remained quiet as he went about his business.

They loaded up in an old Jeep Wagoneer and careened around the island, breaking several laws belonging to both the State of Florida and Issac Newton. *"Great,"* Tad thought, *"No air conditioning."* Tad felt as thought his stomach was full of Cream of Wheat and battery acid. Two massive bags of laundry occupied the driver's side of the rear seat, as well as gallon-sized jugs of detergent and little boxes of dryer sheets. "Watch the laundry. Me and Arnie been doing laundry this morning while you were dickin' around on the Sarah Puss."

The radio was blaring out Talking Heads and the two comrades were singing at the top of their lungs as the Jeep bounced off the curb turning onto Catherine Street. *"Take me to the river! Drop me in the water!"* It was like being on Space Mountain while in advanced stages of Ebola. *"…Hug me, squeeze me, love me, tease me . . ."* Arnie couldn't carry a tune in a bucket but Baker was having some success. As the bile rose, Tad thought, *"Oh God, let me die. Now would be OK."*

They swerved around a family of Japanese tourists who were taking pictures of chickens and accelerated into a neighborhood. "Hey Tad! This is going to be great! Did you fart? Jesus, did you fart in my truck? My laundry is back there. Did you fart on my laundry? No wait, that was ME! Whew! S-B-D! Stank you very much."

The eggfart assault and exhaust fumes put Tad in the final stages of death by hangover. The Jeep screeched to a halt in front of a two-story key lime green house. A thin, bearded man in thick glasses was pruning palm leaves off of a tree in the yard. Massive hedges prevented Tad from easily exiting the vehicle, but he managed to squeeze out, ripping his shirt. He pulled off his boat shoes before stepping into a puddle of milky runoff water. He felt warm water cover his feet, and clumsily hopped out of the puddle. He felt spasms from his midsection, much like the guy in Alien must have felt at the beginning of the dinner scene.

"Come on. Chief's in there. You OK? You don't look so good. Jeez, is that dog shit you jumped into? Arnie, he just stepped in dog shit. Can you believe this guy?"

The world reeled and warm dog feces squished between Tad's toes. Tad grabbed on to a nearby mailbox that was shaped like a cat as he briefly experienced tunnel vision. The next twenty seconds were a whirlwind of projectile vomiting, cursing his two compadres, and dirty looks from Japanese tourists. Both shoes dropped in the milky puddle and filled up.

Tad muttered, still leaning on the calico mailbox, "So this is it. *The End*. This is what it all comes down to. My head is throbbing. My stomach is … fission. My shoes are wet, and I just stepped in warm dog shit. It's still between my toes and it is… *warm*. For real, guys. Get me something to wipe my face, please. Napkins or something. I don't want the coroner to find me dead with puke coming out of my nose."

"No problem, Tad-O. Wait a minute." Baker rustled around in the Jeep for a minute, and trotted over to Tad. "Here you go, Sport. This'll work, I think."

Tad took the dry towelette and blew his nose, still holding on to the cat mailbox. He didn't trust his legs yet. He wiped his mouth and felt an acrid sensation in his nose and a funny taste form on his lips . . . "Wait a minute! What kind of napkin is this? Baker . . . what is this?"

Baker glanced sheepishly at Arnie and said, "It's a napkin, OK? … Alright, it's NOT a napkin. It's a dryer sheet. It's all I got. Let's go. The Chief is waiting."

"Arrrrhhh….you bas…Arrrrhhh…you son of … Arrrhh." Profanities blended nicely with dry heaves. One of the Japanese tourists eventually won a photo contest back in Tokyo with a photo entitled, "funny looking American with snot-chunks coming from nose while hugging cat on post." Click, whirrrr, click, whirrr.

"Ah, you're fine." Baker and Arnie drug the ailing young man into restaurant, smiling for the tourists and giving the two-finger V sign. The big wooden Indian outside the Cuban restaurant door silently judged the three, as they stumbled into the air conditioned building. The Chief was already at a table awaiting them.

"So Tad, I'll bet you wonder why you are here? Are you just the least bit curious?" the mustached man said. "I guess you know by now that I know your skipper. In fact, he and I did some work together a long time ago. Whenever he is here in Key West, we always throw back a few together. Hey, drink your Diet Coke. You look like hell. What's the problem?"

Baker piped up, "He stepped in dogshit, Chief! You should'a seen it! God, it was funny. First he…"

"I think I got it, Baker," the Chief said.

Tad sucked on the straw fiercely. *"God that's good."* "Well, Chief - that's who you are, right? I didn't know you and the skipper knew each other, but it makes a little sense, I suppose."

The Chief silently appraised the young man, seemingly choosing his words carefully. "Tad, I know your father and Benji are friends. Benji tells me that you are a young man with great talents, but absolutely no direction. That's what I want to talk to you about. Direction. You know what I mean?"

The portly Cuban woman arrived at the table, carrying four plates of pork, black beans, white rice, onions and fried plantains. Manna from heaven. No food in the history of food had ever smelled this good.

Baker and Arnie dug in like hound dogs on table scraps. Tad picked at the plate, still not trusting the tube that connected his mouth and his anus to process food in a one-way direction.

Tad thought, *"No. I have no idea what you mean"* "Look, I have direction. I have a college degree, right? Somebody's going to hire me, I imagine. I do have some skills. Sort of."

The Chief nodded sagely. "You keep telling us about your college degree, but I have been apprised of the level of commitment you have toward finding a regular job. Zilch. Let me tell you what I can do for you. Come spend the day at our office."

"Do I have a choice?"

"No. You'll be back by five. Your skipper knows you will be late. Eat up. Let's go."

Tad, Baker and Arnie piled back in the deathmobile, and took off. The Jeep's tires squalled as they accelerated down Margaret Street, narrowly missing a chicken and some guy dressed in black, wearing a coonskin cap and toting a sign that read "Tell Your Fortune." The radio blared again. Baker and Arnie howled like coon dogs under a treed raccoon. *"Saturday night I was downtown, working for the FBI..."*

"Baker. BAKER! Do you have to drive like this?"

"Cruising the booze along the west side for people who were doin' wrong... What? What you say? *Just about to call up the DA man..."*

Tad closed his eyes and sunk down in the seat. "Never mind. Let me know before we die in a fireball."

The old wagoneer followed a circuitous route and turned into the gate of Naval Air Station Key West. The guard checked their IDs and waved them through. Fighter jets roared like dragons as they flew over in formation, rattling windows across Key West.

"Hoo, boy! You hear that?" Baker roared. "That's the sound of freedom. Kickin' ass and taking names. That's what those boys in the fighters do."

Tad was in eyeball defilade, barely peering over the edge of the door. "That's what you all do? You do something with those jets? I thought you ran a dive school."

Arnie turned and looked Tad in the eyes. For the first time, he was very serious. "We do a lot of things. That's kind of the point. We do anything, anywhere. Now take that FA-18 there. He can drop a smart bomb and plug up the poopchute of any bad guy with amazing precision. The only problem is that when he does it, the whole world knows. We, on the other hand, can get to anyone, anywhere, and get the job done and nobody knows we were there."

"Get the job done - What is the job?"

"Killing folks, Tad..." Arnie said matter-of-factly, "...killing the bad man."

Tad spent the day with the soldiers. He dived using their equipment in their pool. They rappelled, ran the obstacle course and fired pistols at the range. By the end of the day, his hangover was gone and he was having a grand time.

"Hey Tad, Chief wants to see you." Baker said, and pointed his thumb toward a quonset hut. Tad walked over and knocked on the door.

"Enter!" The voice commanded. "Come in."

The Chief sat behind an aging metal desk. Behind him on the wall, there was a big poster of a blonde with enormous hooters scantily clad in a camouflage bikini. The text under her green high heels proclaimed, "Kill a Commie for Mommy."

"Here's the deal. Your skipper thinks you have what it takes to be one of us. Frankly, I might agree. But I might not. I'll tell you this; you are wasting your time - jerking yourself around. That's what you are doing. The United States Army Special Forces is my home. It's a hellava home."

"I'm in."

"OK, stop being such a pussy. You'll push yourself so far beyond your limits; you'll think you are going to die. You will have to exert every ounce of effort you have. You will have to use every bit of intelligence you can muster. Most of all, you will have to have the heart, determination and drive of a man possessed. That's the only way."

"Sounds good. Let's do it."

"Alright, let me finish. If you are not capable of total commitment to become one of us, you need to go back to your sailboat and grab a mop. With us, you will parachute from a plane at night, infiltrate enemy territory using scuba gear, shoot over a hundred weapons and learn them like the back of you hand. You will assemble and dissemble them blindfolded. You will learn to use classified communications equipment, learn more first aid than the average EMT and learn another language."

"I'm in."

"Shut up and listen. You will become a silent killer, learn hand-to-hand combat, learn to fight with a knife, a machete and other sneaky weapons. You will master demolitions, both conventional and homemade. You will baddest, most well-trained soldier in the entire world. Either that or you can go back to your boat and grab a mop. What's it going to be? What do you say?"

Tad thought a minute, but not too long. "Two questions - Can I still be around the ocean and what do I need to do to sign up?"

The Chief smiled.

• • •

Ten months later, Tad was Private First Class Hunter. He has successfully completed his basic training at Fort Benning, Georgia. His MOS (military job) was 11B (infantryman). Translated - grunt who carried a rifle. He spent three more weeks at Airborne School getting screamed at by rabid trainers who wore black hats. In fact, they were creatively known as Blackhats. He made his fifth jump on the Friday of the third week, and graduated that afternoon.

Four days later, he found himself in Fort Bragg, North Carolina. He felt like a million bucks. He had pushed himself to the limits of physical endurance running up and down those sandy hills of Georgia. He could do pushups like an Olympian. He stepped out of the cab, and surveyed the old two story barracks. He shared the cab ride with a Latino soldier who was also hailing a cab at the airport. The Latino stood beside Tad, stared at the sign. He wailed, "I. . . . AM . . . the . . . MAN. United States Army Special Forces school, I shall conquer *you*. You will be my conquest. I will consume you, but only for the growth and development of my inner child. My inner child screams for you, it says 'I want my green beret.' I shall give my inner child what it needs. I will FEED my inner child. You will be mine."

Tad cut his eyes at the fruitcake, and thought, *"OK, it's official. He's insane. I am standing next to a maniac. A maniac who is insane. Is that possible?"* They both made their way to the orderly room. The Latino looked at Tad and smiled, "Ramon Garcia." He held out his hand. "I'm Ramon. What's your name?"

"Hunter. Tad Hunter." As Bogey might have phrased it, it was the beginning of a beautiful relationship.

The next six months went by in a blur. Tad and Ramon became the best of buddies. The sweated together, exercised together, suffered the misery of being perpetually tired together, and finally graduated together. Tad grew used to the strange ramblings of his comrade, still convinced that Ramon was a few bubbles off level. On the afternoon after their graduation, the two were walking by the orderly room where they first met.

Ramon turned to the sign that arched over the sidewalk. "Oh John F. Kennedy Special Warfare School. I have conquered you. I have taken your soul and I hold it captive in my heart, which is deep inside my body. I take your legends and sing them to myself in my sleep. I take your spirit and wear it like karmic armor. I am invincible. I am Ramon, Lover of Women, Drinker of Rum, Lord and Master of All I Survey."

Tad watched, "OK, Ramon. I've got it. You're trying to get out of the army, much like Klinger on MASH, right? You can't really be this insane. It's an act, right?"

Ramon turned to Tad with a slight smile. "That hurts. Now that really cuts to the bone, which is also deep inside my body. Get out of the army? No way, my gringo amigo. Now let's go see the First Sergeant about getting out of this place. You, my buddy blanco, and I are linked by some unseen force. We arrive here in the same cab, we endure this hellish endurance test together, and now we go to the same unit together. THE SAME UNIT! Can you imagine the odds? Actually, there are not a lot of special forces units, but you know what I mean. We go on from here, my brother, as one. You and I, yin and yang, Dale Evans and Buttermilk."

"Dale Evans . . . No way. You can be Buttermilk, I'm going to be Dale. Wait, that's not so good either. I think I'm supposed to be Roy. Screw it. Let's go. The future waits."

Ramon looked at the horizon, scanning about as if looking for bad guys to come hopping out of building windows. "No my friend. The future waits for no man. Archimedes said that. Or Miss Cleo – I forget. Never mind, let's go forth and seize all that waits for us. It is there. Can you see it? Can you feel it? Fate is stroking our hair with its silky fingers. We will be gods."

The friendship that was formed during six months of green beret training solidified as the two young men walked toward the bus.

Chapter Five

"Thank you for meeting with me. Can you give me a rundown on what happened?" Phillip Dixon asked. The police station was a lot nicer than one would imagine. Gone were the days of cracked paint, exposed pipes, giant rooms full of old wooden desks and poor lighting. The Alexandria Police Department headquarters was in an old brick building. The detective's office overlooked King Street. The hardwood floor was clean, and the office was generally neat. Dixon thought this might be an office at IBM headquarters. The ubiquitous certificates and photos hung on one wall, certifying that this man had done something. But who really reads those things?

Lieutenant Brannon O'Clary cleared his voice, and began. "Yes, Dixon, I can. That's your name, right? Dixon? First though, you mind telling me just what your relationship is with Mr. Forbish? I get a call from our chief saying you are coming and to cooperate fully, but I don't know you. That makes me nervous. I don't like to be nervous."

Dixon said, "Does being unemployed make you nervous?"

"Do I need to be nervous?"

"What did your chief say, O'Clary?"

"He didn't say anything about me being nervous."

"No – I mean when you said getting a call from your chief makes you nervous. Do you remember saying that?"

"When? You been talking to the Chief?"

Dixon stared at the man and said, "Work with me. I am the chief of security of Forbico Petrochemical, Inc. I also help Bradford Forbish solve certain problems. Like this one. As you know, my boss and your boss are acquainted with each other. That's not entirely true. My boss and your boss's boss know each other. What the hell, everyone knows Bradford Forbish. But let's get real, lieutenant, you want to do every thing in your power to help me. Know why? We want the same thing - to get Elizabeth Forbish back. The FBI will have this case by this afternoon. What do you have to lose? I can use resources that you don't have. Frankly, I can use resources you could never get. The Feds are going to cut you out of this case in about six hours and you are going to look like a bumbling fool that dropped the ball. Just like that - boom - out. Just tell me what you have. Let me talk to the witnesses. I know you have some. Jesus, a kidnapping on King Street on a Friday night? Gotta be some witnesses. And ballistics also. I need it now, right damn now, if I have any chance of getting that girl back alive."

The lieutenant eyed Dixon carefully. "You know who did this, don't you? It's the same people, isn't it? Those nutcases that zapped her sister. It's them. They called you? Is there a ransom?"

Dixon leveled his gaze on the disheveled police officer. This guy had been up all night, working the crime scene. Dixon did not want to bust the guy's balls too much. Policing was a thankless job and paid a miserable paycheck for the work put into it. Even for cavemen.

"I'm going to the hospital now. Room four twenty-eight. I'll be waiting." And Dixon walked out.

$$\bullet \bullet \bullet$$

Dixon walked into Johnny's room holding a brown grocery bag. He took off his coat, and laid it on the chair. He walked to the side of the bed, and surveyed the broken lad. "Johnny, we have to talk. I think you need to start from the beginning."

Johnny nodded, not able to hold the gaze of the man before him.

Johnny ran through the story, excluding nothing. He knew Dixon hired him to be a bodyguard, not a boyfriend. But that's the way life goes sometimes. You can't pick and choose with whom you fall in love.

"Mr. Dixon, I swear to God, we didn't mean to start a relationship. I mean, it just happened. I'm going to propose to her in a couple of months. I even have the ring on layaway."

Dixon pondered the information. Elizabeth came from a family that redefined dysfunction, and here this young man was, ready to marry her. A solid kid, a good kid. Forbish would pop a gasket, but what the hell; no one would meet his standards for his daughters. Not any more.

"Mr. Dixon, they wouldn't hurt her, would they? I mean, they want money to give her back. A ransom, right? Have they called her father?"

Dixon took a deep breath, and closed his eyes. What to tell this young man? How much is enough? Dixon realized that Johnny had as much invested in this as anyone – probably more.

"Johnny, it's complicated. And it doesn't look good. Here's the story."

Dixon inhaled deeply again. "You probably know by now that Elizabeth was not Bradford Forbish's only daughter. He, in fact, had three more. Elizabeth is the youngest. Almost two years ago, twenty months to be precise, something happened at their mansion. Elizabeth ever mention any of this?"

Johnny shook his head, "Not much."

"Alright, it went something like this. One afternoon Elizabeth's big sister, Katherine, was out by the pool, sunning herself. This is broad daylight, on Saturday afternoon. The butler, James, comes outside with a pitcher of lemonade for Katherine. She's gone. She just vanished from the face of the earth, or at least from her home."

Johnny's eyes were growing hard and narrowing. "Kidnapped. She was kidnapped."

"Right you are young John. She was kidnapped. Forbish received the ransom call three hours later. It was a group no one had ever heard of. They claimed to be the Earth Eco-Liberators. Their agenda was completely unknown. They demanded the usual nonsense – Forbish sell all his stock in Forbico. All petrochemical research facilities be closed immediately. Public admission of all sorts of ecological devastation – some real and some fictitious. They also wanted two million dollars. Good old fashioned greed was alive and well, even with the idealists. The old man was livid."

"He called the deputy director of the FBI at his house that night raising hell. By morning, his mansion, Knottywood, was swarming with Feds. He thought he was smarter than these two-bit ecoterrorists. He was wrong. He was very, very wrong."

"At seven o'clock, Katherine's body was found behind a convenient store with an ecological manifesto. There was also a note chiding Forbish for sacrificing his daughter. The terrorists knew he called the FBI. They killed Katherine and dumped the body. Once the FBI became involved, the game was up. Bang. Now Forbish only has three daughters. Three daughters, and you, YOU Johnny, were hired to protect the youngest."

Tears formed in Johnny's eyes. "Screw you, Dixon."

"Yeah, screw me. So now it's just Dixon. Well Johnny, we're all screwed. After the first kidnapping, Forbish brought me on board. Now we have to unravel this thing fast and act quickly. Within the hour, the FBI will be here to talk to you. They will want to make up for their failure two years ago. You will not, repeat, will NOT help them get Elizabeth killed. You will be fuzzy about all the details. You were shot. You didn't see the shooters, or the ones who snatched her. Got it? Good. Now let's rehearse the story."

"Who's the group?"

Dixon thought a second and replied, "Earth Eco-Liberators – we call them EELs. They started being a bunch of whackos, until they mixed in with a couple of pros. There was a man and a woman who came out of nowhere. Phantoms. They took over leadership with the group, and the rest is history. The thing is, we just don't know much about them. We think they are small in numbers. Actually, very small in numbers. Otherwise, someone would have talked. Two students at UCLA were found dead last year. The FBI interviewed them after Katherine was killed. Two days later, they are dead. Signature hits. Two to the heart, and one to the head. Then the group turns to vapor. No one has seen or heard from them since. At least, not until last night."

"Who did they call?" Johnny asked.

"Me. They called me on an unlisted cell phone number that only the old man has. So you see why we cannot let the FBI step in too deeply. We can't keep them all the way out, but we can damn well make sure they don't get too close."

"What's the ransom?"

Dixon thought a moment and said, "That's not for you to know."

"What do you mean? Are you going to pay it? Give me that much!"

"Yes. Of course we are going to pay it. I just need to try to get some intel on these guys first. We need to have a contingency plan. That's what I am doing here. I need to piece together what happened, get a lead, a description, something…"

"Hey Dixon, I know a guy. He can help."

Dixon's face read skepticism. "You know a guy. Sure. We all know a guy."

"No, really. He was with us overseas. He dealt with this sort of thing. He was a consultant."

"A consultant for who?"

"You know. He was Y.G.A."

"Y.G.A? What's that?"

"Yuppie Government Agent. That's what we called him. He was a spook. No offense."

"Why would I take offense?"

"Because you're…uh…you know…"

"Because I'm black?"

"Yeah. That's what I mean."

"So this guy was black?"

"No, he was a white spook."

"I'm not following you."

"You're doing this on purpose, right?"

"Absolutely. What was his name?"

Johnny eyed Dixon suspiciously. "If I tell you, am I in?"

"In? What do you mean in?"

"Screw you again, Dixon. You came here to fire me, didn't you? Tell the truth! I can hook you up with someone who might be able to help, but you have to promise that I stay in the loop. I mean all the way in, too!"

"OK, you're in. But that is contingent on how much your Y.G.A. spook can help. So who's the guy? And how do you contact him?"

The old ways were coming back to Johnny fast. The honed instincts of the hunter. The burning desire to seek and destroy the bad guys. Find the wicked and smite them. The need for violence. Except that this time it was personal. Johnny knew he was going to find who did this and kill them. "Murph. His name is Murph. Please hand me my wallet and the phone."

Johnny dialed the number. The room was quiet, oppressively quiet. Dixon thought, *"Please let this boy not be full of crap. Please."*

Johnny spoke, "Murph, this is Bushmaster Four." He rattled off a ten digit cell phone number. "It's important to me, and probably important to you."

Johnny looked out the window, staring into the distance. "He'll call, Mr. Dixon. It may take a couple of hours, but he will definitely call."

Dixon said, "We'll see. In the meantime I will start running down these eyewitnesses to the incident." The incident. Yeah, that really sanitized it for both of them. Not a kidnapping or abduction, an incident. Perfect.

• • •

Dixon rang the doorbell to the brownstone, and stepped back a pace. He could see someone eyeballing him through the peephole. The door opened, and an elderly lady peered out. *"No chain,"* Dixon thought, *"brave old bird or stupid."* This was the only witness that the police had found and passed on to Dixon.

The old lady said, "I was wondering when you would come. Come right on in. My, you G-Men sure look just as handsome today as you did forty years ago."

"G-Men . . .? Oh, yes, well thank you, Mrs. Uh…?"

"Edna Stribling. I may have been here before electricity, but I surely am not too blind to see what happened to that nice couple. May I offer you some coffee, Special Agent…What did you say your name was?"

"Dixon. Phillip Dixon. No thank you. Could you please just tell me what happened last night?" No need to clarify the misunderstanding right this second.

"Oh, yes! I was out taking a walk. It's so beautiful on King Street at night. The lights and people just make it magical. You know some of the seniors who live here don't get out at night. Scares them."

"Can't imagine why. Shootings and all."

Edna droned on and on. Dixon let her. Never interrupt a witness when they start talking. She would eventually work her way around to the story.

"…then I saw the couple walking out. I knew they were lovebirds. He looked at her just the way my Benjamin did back in 1945. Then the white van opened up and those two men came out. And the couple behind them. At first I thought they were those sort of police officers that dress like regular people, you know like in Miami Vice. They pulled out guns, but they shot the boy. I was mortified."

Dixon coaxed her on. "What did the people look like?"

"Well, they looked quite normal. The man had on khaki slacks and a golf shirt. You know the kind that used to have an alligator on it? You don't see the alligators much now, I am sure it was like an alligator shirt. Except it had a whale on it. It was white and blue, I think. He had a beautiful leather jacket on. Not one like the Hell's Angels wear, but very stylish. I think he looked much like Marty."

Dixon cogitated on that one for a minute. "Marty? Who is Marty?"

"You know, the lieutenant from Miami Vice. He is major beefcake. Tall, dark and handsome."

Dixon nodded thoughtfully. "Of course. Marty from Miami Vice. What about the girl?"

"Well, you know, she was tall and thin. But not too thin. She had nice legs and a great pair of boobs. You know what I mean, Agent Dixon. That's what first made Benjamin look at me, my boobs. Back then, I had a rack that would turn every soldier's head…"

"Excuse me?... Edna, focus. What else about the woman?"

"Oh yeah, well she had a light complexion, and dressed very well. You know, some women just know how to dress for their man. She certainly did, in her cashmere sweater, showing off those boobs. You know, I can almost tuck mine in my belt."

"TMI Edna! TMI! Help me out here. Throw me a bone. What else about the woman, not counting her . . ., well you know?"

"Her walk. She went to a finishing school, I'm sure. She came from distinct breeding. She had a composure about her that screamed class and confidence. I could pick her out of a crowd anytime. Say, Agent Dixon, you are not writing any of this down."

"Uh, well Edna, they train us at the academy to remember all of our notes in our head."

Edna nodded, eyes wide. "Oh goodness, I read about that. You have a photogenetic memory, right?"

"Photogenetic memory…YES…yes, I do, Edna."

"That's nice – and it's also a crock. Who are you? You are not an FBI agent. Are you here to rape me? Is that what you want? Some old lady nook-nook?" She eyed him suspiciously. Or was that gleam in her eye something other than suspicion?

Dixon closed his eyes and took a looong breath. He had been doing that a lot lately. That image stuck in his head was causing brain pain. "No Edna, I'm not here to rape you. Sorry. My own death might be preferable. I'm here to find a girl who has been kidnapped. In a couple of days she will be killed. That boy with her, the one who got shot, loves her. If I don't find her before the FBI gets too involved, it's all over. Her father hired me. If you will help me, maybe I can prevent a tragedy. Their family has suffered too much already. Will you help me, Edna?"

She studied the young, handsome black man. "Well of course, Dearie. Why didn't you just say so? What can I do?"

Dixon questioned her for another forty minutes before his cell phone rang.

"This is Dixon."

"Mr. Dixon, you know where Murphy's is?" It was Johnny.

"Wait a minute. Edna, where's Murphy's? You ever heard of it?"

Edna smiled sweetly. "Of course, dearie. Two blocks up. Will we be going there?"

He ignored her. "Yes, Johnny. What's up?"

"Be there in thirty minutes. He will meet you."

"He? He who?"

"He HIM."

"Him, who?"

"HE him, that's who."

"You mean HIM as in HE? Murphy?…Why are we talking like this?"

Johnny lowered his voice to almost a whisper. "Someone is standing outside the door."

"Who?"

"They look like FBI guys."

"Well, why in the world would you not want to say Murphy's name around them? They probably know him."

"Doubt it, Mr. Dixon. Just go to Murphy's."

Dixon mused, "Perfect. I'm supposed to go to Murphy's to meet Murphy. This is working out so well, I'm tinkling on myself. And how, pray tell, will he know who I am?"

"He'll know you. You'll stick out."

"Stick out?"

"Like a turd in a punchbowl. Trust me on this one."

Exasperated, Dixon said, "Whatever," and hung up. How white people survived, he would never understand.

Thirty minutes later, Dixon walked through the front door of Murphy's Irish Pub on King Street. He took a seat in a corner, and a waiter walked up to him. In a terribly fake Irish accent, he cheerfully asked, "Top of the day to you laddie! Welcome to Murphy's! What'l it be today? A Guiness to whet the whistle? A Bass Ale for ye?"

Dixon ordered a Harp, just to get the man off of his back. As he was staring at the relics nailed to the wall, a man sat down at the booth with him.

"Phillip, Jesus, how are you, old boy? It's been ages!"

Dixon surveyed the man. "Sonuvabitch! You are Y.G.A." About six feet, a bit on the thin side, yacht club hair cut and the perfect tan. He looked like an ad for L.L. Bean.

"Y.G.A.? You did *not* just say that. It has surely been twelve hours since I have heard that line. Let's get out of here, and go see the others." The preppie man leaned down and whispered, "Walk with me. Don't talk outside. Let's go."

So the two left, and walked a swift and circuitous route around Georgetown. Dixon recognized the tactics. Murph was looking for a tail. They cut into stores abruptly, exiting from side doors. They crossed the street and reversed direction. They sat on a bench for a while. After almost an hour of walking, they arrived at the waterfront.

They walked into a marine chandlery near the waterfront. Murph wound his way though the brass and stainless items, turned left at the wall of various colors and sizes of polyester lines, and walked up the stairs to a loft. Dixon followed. Finally, they entered a run-down looking room in the rear of the loft.

Murph motioned for Dixon to sit in a folding metal chair and then plopped in an old fighting chair that once was on a fishing boat. The chair was bolted to the floor. The chair swiveled, and was a good two feet higher off the floor than the folding chair. Dixon thought, *"He's doing this on purpose. He wants me off balance. Well screw him."*

Murphy sat back in the fishing chair like it was the Lazy-Boy in his own den.

"Alright, Murph. Here we are. What now?"

Murph ran his fingers through his hair, much like a fashion model would on the runway. He spoke. "Phillip Dixon. MIT class of '85. Upper ten percent – nice! United States Marine Corps, Force Recon no less. Achieved the rank of Captain. Hired by Bradford Wallington Forbish to solve some security issues. Quickly ascends to the top of the security department. Right hand man to Forbish. One hundred and fifty-five thou a year. No serious political party ties. Heterosexual, probably. Black belt in Yoshukai Karate. In absurdly good shape. Type A personality. That about cover it?"

Dixon looked into Murph's eyes, trying to uncover clues. There were none. "You could not have acquired that much G-2 on me since Johnny called. What gives?"

Murph broke out in a dazzling smile. "Ah yes! G-2. Intelligence. Take the man out of the military, but not the military out of the man. We have looked at you before. Closely. You might come in useful to us."

"Who is us? CIA? NSA? Military Intel? Cub Scouts?"

"There you go, Phillip! Cutting right to the core! The piercing questions that penetrate the veil of unknown our relationship currently possesses. Actually, a little mystery in a relationship is good for longevity, don't you think?"

"I think you didn't answer my question."

Murph crossed a leg and examined his fingernails for something suspect. Nothing there, thank goodness. He then turned his attention back to Dixon.

"Phillip, is this really necessary? You know exactly what I mean when I say the phrase, 'need to know.' You don't have a need to know. You just have a need, and a pretty big one if I read young Jonathan correctly. How is he?"

"How in God's name does Johnny know you? And yes, he is fine, I think. Maybe getting out in a week."

"Phillip, he's checking out now as we speak. I think he will be a little difficult for members of a sister organization to find and question in the future. He will be nearby, so worry not. Jonathan Ancio Perecci was a member of an army special forces A-Team during a recent military incursion into Middle Eastern and Persian countries. He distinguished himself many times over. I met him in Iraq, and had a chance to work with him. I was a consultant there, as you may have gathered. When Jonathan was discharged, I kept up with him. His call to me was not entirely unexpected. Once a man is in special ops, it dogs him for a long time. It's sort of like a black bag gravitational force. For what it is worth, he is a good man. Solid."

"Solid, huh? He's so solid, he got his principal kidnapped."

"Yes, Phillip, but do you not think you have asked a little much of him? Do you know who he was up against? I think you do. This means that this entire predicament falls on your shoulders. You failed to take the appropriate security arrangements, knowing who was gunning for your employer."

"You bastard. Of course I know who done it. The Earth Eco-Liberators. Who else? They killed Forbish's other daughter. They are a bunch of nutcases who screwed the pooch on the first attempt. Now they are taking another shot."

Murph got up and paced the room, becoming more animated. "Oh yes! The EELs again. Can't you just see their secret hideout? 'Back to the Eel Cave, Robin!'" Murph was enjoying himself immensely. "Those damn slimy EELs. Dash it all! They tricked us again. Hard to get your hands on that bunch."

Dixon rose from the folding chair. "I don't need this." He headed for the door.

"Phillip, forgive me. Sometimes a moment of levity is essential. There's another group involved. You should know about them. I thought you did."

Dixon was almost to the door, "Yeah? Who are they? The SALAMANDERS?"

Dixon froze as Murph said softly, "Hardly. The IRA. You have heard of them, right?"

"Quit messing with me. They've all but folded, right? Let's talk."

"What's the matter Phillip? Didn't like the folding chair? Try my fighting chair. I once landed a four hundred pound blue marlin in that very chair."

"I don't believe you."

"Well, somebody probably did. Or should have. Who knows? I do know this – you have received a ransom from the EELs and you want to catch them before the drop happens. Am I right?"

Dixon knew there was no benefit to lying to this man. "You're right. Twenty-five million in a variety of accounts. I deliver an encoded CD disk; they let the Forbish girl go."

"Mr. Forbish will pay this, will he not? I think so. Where is the swap?"

"Florida. Don't ask me why. OK, Murph, I came clean. What's this about the IRA?"

"Florida you say? Key West, perhaps?"

"Yes. How? How could you know?"

"Phillip, really. The miracles of electronic surveillance."

"Bugs. You're bugging us. I should have known. Back to the IRA. Why them?"

"Mr. Douglas put it best – 'Greed is good.' It's all about money. The IRA could really care less about a small potatoes group like the EELs. Then someone in Belfast wised up and saw the earning potential for environmental terrorism. There's nothing like a foreign terrorist organization to get the FBI, CIA, NSA and everyone else in a frenzy. That is, if the group operates on good old American terra firma. Especially in this modern day of post-911 mentality. The old boys of the Provisional Wing of the IRA are no longer tolerated. Not politically correct anymore. But domestic ecoterrorists are far more warm and fuzzy. So they trash a few labs. So they pour sugar in the tank of a bulldozer. They are basically a bunch of college rejects with their panties in a wad."

"But, Phillip, enter the pros. A couple of operators show up, seemingly sympathetic to the environmental cause. This fledgling group is crying for leadership, and so they shall receive. These two operators organize the few EEL members into a team. In the first case, it was a snatch-and-grab team."

"Ever wonder why they didn't hold out a little longer? No, Phillip? I mean, everyone on the fruited plains knows that the FBI would be involved at some point. Wonder why they killed Katherine so quickly? Amateurs would not have done that."

Dixon nodded. "Of course we wondered. There are twenty good theories. Pick one."

The handsome man picked up an ancient sextant, and gazed through it, sighting in on a light bulb. "The first one was to set up this one. Plain and simple. It was not a snatch and grab, per se. It was a hit squad. They do it to get Forbish's attention. Now, my friend, I can assure you they have his attention. They never wanted the two million two years ago. They want twenty-five million now. And I have a sneaking suspicion they will get it. Am I correct?" Murph wiped off dust from the lens, and sighted again.

A stream of possibilities flooded Dixon's thoughts. "You sure about this theory? How do you prove it?"

"Good Heavens, man. How does one prove anything in this line of work? I can offer you a saving grace, though. They will not kill her. At least not until they have the money. So that presents a problem, does it not? Do you follow Bradford's instructions and pay up, thus giving the bad guys the green light to kill the girl? Or do you hold out, trying to get a toehold in catching them, thus buying some time. Hopefully, that is. I do not envy the man who has to make that decision. Do you?"

"You are holding out. There is something not yet spoken, Murph, or whoever in the hell you really are. Why am I here?"

"Let me help." Murph spread out his hands, palms up. "I have the resources. We really would like to rid the planet of these two operators. The other members of the EEL, you can have, if they exist. We want the male and the female."

"Who are they and what do you want to do with them?"

"The man is Michael O'Brien. This is a fictitious name. He was a rising star in the Provisional Wing of the IRA. He hooked up with the girl, and dropped out of sight. The girl calls herself Catherine Hayes. Another fictitious name, but this one has some significance. Catherine Hayes was a famous early nineteenth century opera singer in Ireland. How it is significant, who knows? But the two have taken a foolish bunch of college kids, and turned it into a killing machine. They offed two of the kids at UCLA after the first Forbish daughter was abducted. And you know what? I think they killed the rest of them also. Every single one. I think those idealistic young friends of the environment have been replaced by a handful of trained killers. So that is what you face. You pay them the money, they finance terror across Europe. It would be so nice to stop them. So pleasant. That is my angle, Phillip. That is my motivation."

"How is this going to go down? Do you have a plan?"

"A plan. YES, I have a plan! A fine plan. The wheels are in motion already. I know these guys in Florida . . ."

• • •

The two men talked for an hour. Murph's plan was basically sound, but Dixon helped fine tune it. "*This might work. It just might work.*" Dixon thought, as he strolled up the street. He entered Don Vito's and spotted Vinnie immediately. He approached the counter. "Vincent Perecci? Can I have a moment?"

Vinnie eyed the fit black man. Dixon thought Vincent had M-U-R in his right eye and D-E-R in his left eye.

"How long you want, cop? A moment to pick yourself up from the concrete? A moment to stop your broken nose from bleeding? A moment to pull my size twelve from your . . ."

"Vinnie! That's no way to talk!" The elderly Italian woman shuffled to the counter. "Forgive my son. He's a little shook up. A member of the family just got . . .well, let's just say is in bad shape."

Vinnie poked a meaty finger in the air at Dixon. "Yeah. Why don't you just go and find his killer. Well, not his killer, 'cause he ain't dead, but he could be. Or might be. Hell, you know what I mean. And find the girl. That's my future second cousin, twice removed. I think. Why don't you go to the hospital and tell Johnny how you are finding the killers. Not killers, but . . . you know what I mean."

Dixon checked his anger. This was becoming a trying day. "I am not a cop, Vincent. Now, you got a place to talk? In the back, quiet like?"

Vinnie wiped the flour off his hands and looked at his mother. She nodded. The two men went into the back room. Vinnie opened the great silver door to a walk-in freezer. Vinnie gestured for Dixon to enter. Dixon entered, though reluctantly.

"You have to be kidding. Tell me you are kidding."

"No I am not kidding, Mister I-am-not-a-cop-but-I-still-am-not-telling-you-much-about-me. It's great for meetings with people that you want to make sure no one can overhear."

"Vinnie, what kind of people meet in freezers to avoid being overheard?"

"Don't make me say it! This is family you're messing with! Family like as in F-A-M-I-L-I-E…No wait, …L-Y!"

"My apologies. I thought it was just family. I didn't realize it was FAMILY family."

"Yeah. So as I was interjecting, as we converse, you can talk in here and certain members of the community whom might have a professional need to listen in cannot do so in which."

Dixon surveyed the boxes of pizza components with feigned interest. "Here's the scoop. I'm Johnny's boss. The people I work with are out for the shooters and guys who snatched his girlfriend. We have a line on them, but we need to make sure the FBI does not get in the way. To do this, we had to make sure Johnny is dead."

The big Italian's eyes went wide with rage. "Dead! You killed him? You killed our Johnny? I'll freakin' do you right here and now, your rat bastard." Vinnie shot up from sitting on bucket of frozen pizza sauce and launched himself at Dixon.

Dixon barely had time to react, as the giant, hairy Italian grabbed him around the neck. It was like a python had him, and was squeezing until his head popped right off his body.

"Nooo . . . aaahhhgggg . . . heeeth . . .heeeth . . . naaah . . . deeehhh . . ." Dixon pleaded.

The massive man did not relinquish his grip. Dixon was beginning to seriously lose oxygen. He thought to himself, *"Focus. One time. Focus."* He delivered a powerful open palm heel strike to Vinnie's solar plexus. Vinnie reeled back, tripped on a log of mozzarella and collapsed on the cases of parmesan. Giant spasms of vapor came from his mouth in the subfreezing cooler. He looked like an Alaskan Sasquatch with asthma. The look in Vinnie's eyes told Dixon that he was preparing himself for another offensive.

"WAIT, YOU LUMMOX. Johnny's not dead. Not really. We're making it look like he is dead. He's fine. He's in a house near here. We want everyone to believe he died, so the FBI cannot use him and the killers will not come back to him."

The breath slowly returned. Oxygen for both men. Blessed, blessed O2.

Giant spasms of vapor continued to emanate from Vinnie. "Dixon, what kinda game are you playing. You say Johnny's dead, but not really dead. He's near here, but out of sight. You ain't protecting him. You're using him again, just like you used him to protect Elizabeth. You want Johnny to find these guys, don't you? You know what he can do to them. He can do it to you too if you screw him over."

Dixon appraised the man. "For a big, hairy meatball, you are not as stupid as you appear. We're going to get her. Johnny is going with us. If I let you go, wouldn't you?"

"I would. You know I would."

"You and your family have to keep quiet. I figure in a few hours the news and radio will pick up Johnny's 'death.' I did not want you all to freak out, so I came to explain. For this to work, you have to play along. You have to be convincing."

"Like grieving. Yeah. Italians can grieve real good."

"Right. Now let's get out of this freezer. Vinnie, you ever really have any mobsters in this cooler?"

"Nah. It sounds good, though. Chicks dig it."

Chapter Six

Tad and Ramon had the sailboat in the sling, and lifted so that the keel was approximately twelve inches above the ground. The electric lift was a rather complicated and moody piece of machinery. Eventually, they coaxed the boat into the water.

"Let's back it in the slip stern-to." Tad said. The big Perkins diesel engine came to life with a rumble.

Ramon pointed to the east. "Hey Tad. We need to take this boat out there. Probably now. This is a special occasion, being our first complete renovation . . . Hey! What's this? Is this what I think it is? It looks like a cooler. And in it is . . . No way! An iced down twelve pack of Miller Lites. All yours Tad, if you only steer for the channel. Quite a deal for an indigent such as yourself. Where's your shirt? 'I will pilot sailboats for beer.' Let's celebrate and go for a cruise."

"You think I would take my responsibilities as a United States Coast Guard Captain so lightly? You think I would jeopardize all that I have built just to motor a sailboat around the coast while consuming alcoholic beverages? You think I would display utter contempt of the law by impairing my brain with beer? Mere freezing cold bottled beer? I am shocked and appalled. (pause) Gimme one. Let's go."

Ramon stood in the bow pulpit, leaning out over the water. He had a beer in each hand. "I'm the King of the World! Hey, did you see that movie? It really had a happy ending, with DaCrappio sinking to the bottom like that."

The two cruised up and down the Intracoastal Waterway for several hours. They did not raise the sails, mostly because the sails were folded up and stowed away in the forward berth. When they pulled back into the marina, the sun was sinking in the horizon. A cascade of colors decorated the bottom of the cotton candy clouds. Pink, magenta, violet, and other hues danced on the clouds, while millions of sparkles danced on the rippling water. Tad thought, *"Life is good."*

George walked up to the slip, as the boat gently nudged the dock. "Hey Tad. This guy called. He wants to pay you to do some work. He just bought a new sailboat. Big one. Maybe you should call him back. Here's his number."

Tad and Ramon both cut their glances at each other. Big, new sailboat equals big dollars. Tad took the number and dialed his cell phone.

"Speak quick before I hang up on your ass."

"Hello. I'm Tad Hunter. You called me."

"I didn't call you, fruitboy. This some kind of phone scam? You trying to make me switch phone companies?

"No. No, not that. It's about your boat. You called about your boat."

"No shit? What about my boat?"

"I don't know. You wanted me to help fix a new boat?"

"If the frickin' boat is new, what needs fixin'? You my ex-wife's lawyer? You'll never get this boat, you shitstain. You may have got the last one, but not this one. Go f . . ."

"HEY! You called me. This is Conch Island Yacht Service. Ring any bells?"

(Pause) "Yeah, Hoss! That's you? Sorry about that. You know how it is."

Tad didn't really know how it was. The man continued.

"I just bought of a fifty-two foot Morris. Good lookin' thing. I need you to put a few things on it. Radar, GPS, VHS, all that other shit. You can do that, right, Hoss?"

"Yes, we can. Please call me Tad. What's you name?"

The phone was fading out. Tad heard static.

". . .be there tomorrow . . . boat name . . . 'Who's Your Daddy' . . ." And the cell phone faded out.

Ramon looked at Tad. "A paying job? A paying job to fill the empty coffers of our business enterprise? Slap me down! Could it be?"

Tad smiled, and tipped his beer toward Ramon, who clinked his beer in a toast. "To paying jobs. Salud!"

The next day, Tad cancelled a supply run to Homestead. He and Tad sat out back of the marina office. BethAnn was padding down the dock, wearing a bright yellow thong, and a matching bikini top. In her left hand she had a paperback book, a bottle of Panama Jack tanning oil (SPF .5), and a pack of Camels. In her right hand, she had a big, pinkish frozen drink. She approached the two, looking at them as if they were something she scraped from the bottom of her shoe.

"You're in my chair. I always sit in that chair when I sit out here."

Ramon said, "My apologies, Dutchess. You sit here when you sit? Is that accurate? Am I hearing you correctly?"

The smell of coconut oil and sour rum breath floated delicately the air. "That's my seat. George bought that seat for me, not you. Now move! The sun ain't goin' to be up all day."

Ramon looked at Tad. "Oh ho! The sun ain't going to be up all day! Does Copernicus know about this? Please, Madam Gali-loser, enlighten us."

And so it went. Tad strolled down the dock, tidying up some of the errant lines and picking up trash. He made mental notes of electrical boxes that needed to be checked. He chatted with liveaboards as he made his way to the end. Ramon followed.

"Why do you do that with her? Can't you just leave her alone? George likes her, or at least likes having her around. Can you not be nice to her?"

"Yes, Tad. I could be nice. But if I was, she would not respect me. She does not respect George already. She's just sponging off the old man."

"Don't be so cynical."

"She's a predatory trailer park princess who is living the good life off a man who cannot keep his wrinkled eyes and wrinkled hands off her right boob. Left one too, probably."

"I think you are off base."

"Maybe, you putz. But am I not right most of the time?"

Tad did not answer the question. He did not have to. Ramon was a true student of human nature. Not much got by him. After meeting someone for the first time, he could give a pretty good summation of the person. Especially women.

Ramon clamped both hands on Tad's shoulders. "Thaddeus. Look in yon horizon. Gaze on that glorious sight. Our ship is coming in. 'Who's Your Daddy' is here. Can he dock it laden with heavy checkbook? This should be good. Let us render assistance."

• • •

Tad gazed at the yacht. It was a beauty, sleek and elegant. The brightwork gleamed on deck. There was a shirtless man piloting the vessel. He looked to be in his late forties. He was wearing lime green shorts and shoeless. He had no shirt on and his back was as hairy as a grizzly. His shoulders were bright lobster red, a sure sign that he would be in much pain soon.

He called out to Tad and Ramon, as he was making the turn into the slip. "Ahoy, there!"

Ramon looked at Tad, and said quietly, "Did he just say 'ahoy?' Let's get out of here. He said ahoy to us. Nobody says ahoy. We should run now." Ramon was about to call back something equally nautically inappropriate when disaster reared its ugly head.

Tad said, "I think he's going a little fast to enter the slip, Ramon." (pause) "He's definitely going too fast! He's going to crash that boat!"

The Morris yacht came steaming toward the slip, showing no sign of slowing down.

"Ahoy again! Help me catch her! Holy crap! This is harder than I thought! Ahoy! Ahoy!"

The boat entered the slip going a full six knots. The momentum of a fifty-two foot sailboat with a displacement of twenty-five thousand pounds had the potential to cut right through the dock. Suddenly, the boat kicked into reverse and the engines revved wide open. The diesels screamed in protest.

The bow was forty feet from the front of the slip. The water boiled behind the boat as the powerful diesels attempted to slow the forward progress. Tad was frantically trying to figure out how to help, but nothing brilliant came to mind.

Thirty feet, Twenty-five feet. The yacht kept coming. Ramon had sense enough to back out of the way, sensing the impending disaster.

"Goddammit! Help me stop this thing! It's going to crash!" the man screamed.

The people who lived on their boats were hopping up on the dock, trying to get a good angle to watch the new boat slam into the dock. There is not much a powerboater enjoys seeing more than a sailboat screw up. The same goes for sailors, just in reverse.

Fifteen feet, ten feet. The yacht's forward progress slowed to four knots. Still a lot of momentum. Tad held his hands out in a "What can I do gesture."

Eight, seven, six feet. The big diesels screamed in protest to the boat's forward motion. Blue smoke was boiling out of the water. On came the big Morris.

Five, four, three feet. The boat was down to only two knots.

Two feet, one foot. The diesels continued to growl. BAM! The Morris banged into the back of the slip, and the whole dock shook. The other boats, which were tied up to the dock, were shook. Masts were clanging, halyards were swinging and people on all the docks were hooting with laughter. The man at the helm cut the power.

The yacht had climbed up on the dock about a foot, and then slowly sank back into the slip. The dock had a chunk taken out that resembled a pie slice. The front of the sailboat had a two foot section that was somewhere between dinged and mangled.

The pilot walked to the edge of the cockpit and said, "You're the guy from Conch Alley Yacht Service, right?"

Tad said, "That's me. And this is Ramon. It's Conch Island… nevermind." Ramon gave the man a two-finger boy scout salute from the front of slip. "What did you say your name was?"

The man smiled and said, "Beauregard Jamison Jenkins, at your service. My friends call me Jimbo."

Tad played the gracious host and said, ""Jimbo? Nice to meet you… Jimbo."

"Let's get her tied off . . . Jimbo." Ramon said.

They quickly cleated the dock lines, and made coils out of the excess line. Tad, Ramon and Jimbo walked to the front of the boat, and silently surveyed the damage.

Tad thought, *"My God, what has he done to this beautiful ship?"*
Ramon thought, *"You sir, are an affront to seamanship."*
Jimbo thought, *"Not to shabby!"*
He then said "Hell's bells, boys. That was pretty good for the first time driving a sailboat! Who's Your Daddy? Me, baby, me! And here I thought driving a boat would be hard."

Tad invited Jimbo up to the marina office, which doubled as his office on the rare occasion when he needed to sit down with a customer. "Come on up... The air conditioning will make that sunburn feel better."

Jimbo crinkled his brow, "Sunburn? This is sunTAN, my man, not sunBURN. Seems you boys must not know a tan when you see one. Besides, I gotta go get the cargo first."

Ramon offered, "Don't worry about unpacking. We'll get that later."

Jimbo smiled devilishly at Ramon. "Boy, you won't be unpacking this cargo…or packing it either. Her name is Tiffani, with an 'I'."

The beet-red man hopped back aboard the boat, with all the dexterity of a club-foot water buffalo. When his lead foot landed on the boat, he slammed his little toe on a cleat. Inertia took charge and his forward momentum continued, while his left leg crumpled. Jimbo reached out for an emergency handhold, and found the global positioning system chartplotter, which was mounted on the navigation station. He promptly ripped it off, trying quite unsuccessfully to avoid crashing to the deck. His head bounced off the steering wheel, pinching his nose between the wheel and the pedestal.

While climbing to his feet, he let out a torrent of profanity. He then hopped around on one foot in a circle, not quite sure of the extent of the damage. When he calmed down, Jimbo limped toward the hatch, leaving little splotches of blood from the spot where his left toenail used to be and breathing in giant wheezing gasps. He had the marina liveaboards who were still on deck roaring with laughter at the second act of today's entertainment.

"Tiffani! Get your butt up here! Jeez Louise, bring me some peroxide and a bandaid! My friggin' toe is broke slam off. Good God, it hurts. *It hurrrrrts!*"

The girl emerged from within the yacht. She was in her early twenties, and had the girl-next-door look down pat. She had blonde hair, pulled back in a ponytail. Her eyes were ice blue and riveting. She was wearing a thin, gauzy white shirt open over a floral tube top, and wore matching shorts and boat sandals. She was carrying a small handbag, a clear plastic bottle and several band-aids. Tiffani saw the two men on the dock and smiled without comment.

"Tiffani, gimme the damn peroxide! I'm bleeding to death here. Hey! My toe looks like hamburger meat! Anyone hungry?" Jimbo's face was even redder than his shoulders, if that was possible. Everyone grimaced and groaned at the disgusting mental image Jimbo had created. He appeared to be on the verge of popping a gasket at any minute, blood vessels in his head reaching max PSI and internal gauges redlining while he tried to maintain some composure. He unscrewed the cap, and poured the clear liquid on his toe.

"OK, this will fix it right up and . . . Aiiyyyyeee! . . . Oh fu . . . oh . . . sh . . .sh . . . It *burrrrrrnnnnnns*!" Jimbo collapsed in the starboard seats of the cockpit, hands clenched in a deathgrip on nothing but air. He was grunting like a pot bellied pig and wheezing for breath. He momentarily lost sphincter control and farted. Tears rolled down his cheek as he shut his eyes. "Tiffani? Oh, darlin' Tiffani? (eyes still closed) Was that peroxide? Would you please check that while I lay here and expire from the frickin' pain? Tell me that was peroxide."

Tiffani turned the bottle so she had a view of the label. She then turned and met Tad and Ramon's eyes, and said, "Oh shoot! This says alcohol! That's OK, they're both clear. I guess I got all mixed up. You're not mad at me, are you Jimbo?" She gave the boys a smile. Tad half expected her to say, "*Aw, shucks.*"

Ramon said, "Aw, shucks!"

Jimbo struggled to regain his composure, tears trickling down his cheeks. "Alcohol. That explains a lot. Why didn't you just bring a blow torch? Burn the damn thing right off! Am I mad? HELL YES I AM MAD! Jesus God I'm gonna need a prosthetic toe. TAD! Cut that damn thing off!"

"Your toe?"

"NO! Not my toe, the thingie that I tripped on."

Tad looked at the dock between his shoes, trying very hard not to laugh. "Well, I would, except that thingie is a cleat and you will probably need it. Can I come aboard and help you?"

Jimbo snapped his fingers at Tiffani to come help him up. "Hell no. I can take it. You gotta learn to play through the pain. I look like a candyass to you? Here we go." Tiffani helped Jimbo step up on the dock.

A roar of applause and hooting came from all over the marina. Several people had their drinks lifted in salute to Jimbo. He saluted them with his middle finger. "Yeah, that's right. Screw you all too. Kick a man when he's down. I can make it, Tiffani. Lemme go."

She stepped aside.

Ramon said, "After you, Tiny Tim…and God Bless us All!"

Jimbo hobbled up the dock, thumping his left foot, trying to relieve the pressure. Tad followed closely, waiting to prevent him from tumbling into the water if something gave out. Ramon stopped next to Tiffani.

Quietly he said, "My name is Ramon. I am pleased to meet such a beautiful woman. You are Tiffani?"

"With an 'I.'"

"So I have heard. Allow me to escort you to the office."

Chills went up and down Ramon's spine. The little hairs on his neck and arms stood up, as he offered his arm. Tiffani smiled again, and started walking to the office. "I think I can find my way."

Ramon stood, transfixed, admiring the view as the view made its way to the office. His gaze was that of a wolf standing on a hill, staring down at a flock of sheep. He thought, *You are a goddess.*

• • •

Jimbo plopped down into an old office chair, near the air conditioner. Tad said, "Hey George, this is Jimbo. We're going to do some work on his boat. He's had a little accident, as you can see."

Jimbo gave George a little wave. "Good Lord Almighty! It's freezing in here! The only thing keeping me from losing my toe to frostbite is already losing it to that damn boat!"

George offered, "Well, that's because you got so sunburned. Why in hell didn't you put on a shirt, or at least sunscreen? This is Florida, man! That sun'll kill you."

"What is it with all of you? A man gets a tan, and you all want turn it into third degree burns! OK, you're right. I'm an asshole. It's sunburn. What do you do about it?"

George looked astounded. "You never had sunburn?"

Jimbo shook his head. "Not like this! I'm from Arkansas. This sun down here is like a frickin' microwave."

George motioned to Tad. "Get some of that aloe gel off the shelf and put it on him."

Tad looked at George like he was asked to massage a bucket of guts. Ramon was biting his cheek and coughing, trying to disguise his barely suppressed laugh. George was having great fun. Considering how quiet the marina usually was, this was a banner day.

Tiffani sensed reluctance on Tad's part to rub down Jimbo's hairy, sweaty back. She said, "I got it. Lean over, Jimbo"

She shook the bottle and fired a giant stream of green gel all over Jimbo's back and shoulders. He arched up like a .357 magnum round had slammed into him between his shoulders.

"WHOOOOOOO! . . . FREEZING! . . . Cold, it's cold, it's cold . . .Aiyiyiyiyiyi! Don't touch me! I'm in Eskimo hell. Oh, God."

Ramon and George could hold out no longer. They burst in to laughter, along with Tiffani. Tad was bewildered at how this big galoot could have such a beautiful boat and girl. Jimbo sat there with lines of aloe gel all over his back in big circles. It looked like a giant green snail had circumnavigated his back.

Jimbo whispered to Tiffani, "OK, its not so bad now. Spread it around. It feels pretty good actually . . .WHOOOOOOO! . . . IT'S COLD AGAIN! Stop spreading it!" Tiffani ignored him and continued to slather him in green goo. George and Ramon went into gut-busting laughter again. Tad shook his head, imagining his client taking his boat to some other place. The place that didn't break his toes, wreck his yacht and laugh at his sunburn.

"Jimminey H. Christmas! I'm glad you're enjoying this. Can't a man get a little sympathy around here?"

Tiffani immediately stopped, as if she had an important thought. Everyone froze in place, waiting for her to say something. "Jimbo, this reminds me of something! It's like - a joke!" She continued on, "Sympathy. Wait, let me get it right. Okaaay, I know. You're supposed to look in the dictionary. That's it! Then you'll find sympathy between shit and syphilis. There! That's it!" Tiffani beamed and hugged Jimbo, who jumped again. "That's it Jimbo! Wasn't that funny? That's where it is, between . . ."

"Yep! I got it, Muffin. That's funnier'n a fart in a scuba tank. Lemme me catch my breath. Between shit and syphilis. Sheesh!" The color returned to Jimbo's face. "Hey George! You're right! That stuff does work! Tiffany, Honey, get me a beer from the cooler over there. And get a couple of bottles of this stuff." He made a mischievous smile and said, "I'll bet there are a thousand uses for this!" Tiffani handed him a Miller Lite longneck. He drained half the bottle on the first swig.

"Alright! This is good, Tad, this is good!" Jimbo gave George a mock salute with the beer bottle. "This is great. To you George, and Who's Your Daddy!"

George's expression changed from mirth to malevolence. "What do you mean who's my daddy. None of your damn business who my father is."

Ramon tried to suppress a laugh, but coughed and blew a snot bubble. Tad raised his hands out in front of him, trying to calm George down. "That's his boat. Who's Your Daddy. He's not talking about you."

Jimbo raised his hands in mock surrender. "Nope. Not talking about you. That's my boat out there, Who's Your Daddy. This is a real classy place you have here, George. Real elegant."

As if on cue, BethAnn burst through the side door wearing her ubiquitous thong and scanty top. She had a lit camel in one hand, and a plunger in the other. "George, the damn toilet is stopped up. Fix it . . . Uh, . . . hello . . . George, who are these people? Gawd what a sunburn! You could get cancer! And your toe. I think it is bleeding."

Tiffani narrowed her eyes in a stare that might just melt steel. She looked at BethAnn like a cobra looking at a lab mouse. "Yes George. Real classy."

• • •

They talked for over an hour, going over all the details of what Jimbo wanted do on the boat. All the equipment was on the boat. Radar, Global Positioning System (now broken and on the deck), autopilot, marine VHF radio, Single sideband radio and more electronics. He had all sorts of accessories and miscellaneous items that needed to be installed.

Tad said, "Jimbo, I'm not being nosy or complaining. God knows, I appreciate your business, but you have a whole sleeping berth filled with stuff. Where did you get all this?"

Jimbo smiled a big, satisfied smile. "A man can't divulge all his secrets, son. Very expensive shit."

Tiffani said, "On sale at the Annapolis Boat Show."

A little miffed, Jimbo said, "OK, I got it at a boat show, but who the hell cares? You can still put it on, right?"

"Sure. No problem."

Jimbo hesitated, "There's ahhh . . . one other thing."

Tad and Ramon waited expectedly.

"Ahhh . . . I need you to go with me sailing."

"You mean go sailing one afternoon? To test out the equipment? We were going to do that anyway."

"No, not like one afternoon. I mean for several days. A week, maybe."

Tad swallowed, and looked at Ramon. Ramon raised his eyebrows in an *"I don't have a clue either"* gesture.

"You want to elaborate a little, Jimbo?"

He looked down at his feet, testing out his little toe see if it would still bend. He whispered, "I . . . uh . . . don't know how to sail."

Ramon leaned in from his perch by the beer cooler. "What did you say? I couldn't hear you?"

"I DON'T KNOW HOW TO SAIL! There, are you happy? I need you to teach me how to sail! I've never been on a sailboat until a couple of days ago."

Tad's expression never changed. Ever the stoic businessman. "Jimbo, you just paid over half a million for a boat you don't know how to sail. Hmmmmm. No problem. We can work out something." He was furiously calculating what a fair price would be to spend a week with Jimbo on that marvelous boat.

"Ten large." Jimbo interjected. "I'll give you ten grand to fix up my boat and take me and my girl on a cruise. You gotta teach me how to sail it, though. Five now, and five after you deliver. That's the deal."

Tad and Ramon were stunned. Speechless. Stupified. George, ever the businessman, had the presence of mind to say, "I think that's fair. They'll get started tomorrow."

Jimbo breathed out heavily, and started filling out a check. "Whew! Good. I thought you were going to take me for a ride. You know, jack up your prices, or something. Hey Ramon, if you don't mind, help me get the bags out of the boat? We're gotta find a hotel somewhere. Any suggestions, George?" He handed the check to Tad.

"Well sure. The King Kamehameha Motor Court is right next door. I'm sure they have something available. It's a very historic place. Nice, too."

In nineteen forty-eight, two brothers from Ohio built a motel in paradise. They took a very tiki-centric approach to the design and construction. The result was the luxurious King Kamehameha Motor court. Fresh water pool, and all. Seventeen tiny bungalows, each with a private bathroom. All the way through the Eisenhower years, the motel remained jam-packed with tourists, eager to get away from their homes. Many would end up in Miami Beach, but the adventurous ones would make the extra drive to Key Largo.

The King Kamehameha was painted pink, with palm trees lining the driveways and parking areas. The back of the motel property was a grassy lawn, leading back to the ocean. The mosquitoes were terrible, but the smart tourist always went to the office and bought one of those fancy mosquito coils, that looked like an oven eye and burned in a spiral. Paradise Found. The mosquitoes were still present, but the mosquito coils had vanished sometime shortly after the Tet Offensive.

Tiffani walked, Jimbo limped, and Tad and Ramon struggled under the weight of the five massive bags of luggage. The Gill bags were new and jammed packed with clothes.

As the group exited the marina and made a hairpin turn into the motor court's parking lot, Jimbo said, "What kind of shithole is this? This is the historic motel you were talking about? Jeez Louise, I'll bet the cockroaches are bigger than cocker spaniels."

Ramon tried to help. "I can guarantee you there are no cockroaches here. Not one. If you see a cockroach, you let me know. I'll eat him. Wait, I take that back – I'll squish him."

There were still seventeen bungalows. The fresh, pastel pink color of the walls disappeared with the Nixon administration. Potholes punctuated the crushed shell drive, leaving an ankle-twisting minefield to navigate. The once-manicured lawn that sloped gently to the ocean was long neglected, overgrown with bushes, trees and mangroves at the water's edge. The pool was fenced off behind the office. The concrete was cracked and aged, but it still held water. There were seven or eight dangerous looking people splashing around in the pool. Several more stood around the ancient tiki bar, drinking beer out of aluminum cans shrouded in Styrofoam can coolers. The King Kamehameha was a tired old monarch, but he still lived on. Long live the King!

They approached the front office door. The door was guarded by two massive tiki gods. The seven-foot tall, wooden idols watched down on all who entered, playing the role of Polynesian gargoyles. Jimbo said, "Well, would you look at this! The gods of cockroaches."

"Ki'i" Tad explained. "Hawaiian idols. In Tahitian they are called Tiki."

Tiffani opened the door to the office, and moved out of the way for Jimbo to limp in. A tiny elderly Hawaiian woman shuffled in. She was not an inch over five two and bore a strong resemblance to Granny from the Beverly Hillbillies. Her ponytail was tied up with a black bandana with little skulls all over it. She had on a black T-Shirt that said, "Southernmost Harley Davidson, Key West, Florida" on the front, and on the back it said, "If you can read this, the bitch fell off."

"Well, it looks like you desperados need a place to hole up. Room for four?"

Jimbo piped up, "No. Room for two. Anything not condemned?"

She smiled and sweetly. "Well! You're in luck. We're running a Horse's Ass special, and you seem to qualify. Let me check to see if we have anything open." The nameplate on the front desk said, "Annie Taneikaika - Owner."

"Here we go. You're just the lucky one again! The Captain Cooke suite is open. How many nights, guvnor?"

"Uh, I don't know. Let's start with three. How much is that?"

"Two hundred, seventy four dollars and thirteen cents. That's including tax. Will that be cash or credit card?"

Jimbo's face was starting its fade to scarlet again. "How much? Good God, woman! Nevermind! Just . . . give me the key. Here's my card."

Jimbo filled out the registration card, and gave it to Annie.

"Thank you, sir! Oh wait, did you want to use the phone?"

"Why? Do we have to climb the pole? Of course we want to use the phone."

"That will be an additional twenty dollars deposit."

"You have my credit card! Why do you need an additional deposit?"

"And how about the television? There's a ten dollar deposit on the remote."

"I won't use the remote. I'll change it myself."

"It won't work without the remote. I'll add the deposit."

"Jiminy H. Christmas! I cannot believe this. You are the Bonnie Parker of the Pacific, aren't you? You shanghaied a ship, killed the crew, and plundered the coastline until you settled here. That was sometime during the Jurassic period, right?"

"And towels. I know you will want them also. That's a ten-dollar linen deposit. The total is three hundred fifty nine dollars - even."

Jimbo was livid. Ramon and Tiffani were amused. Tad was thinking about the towers of Budapest. "Pay the lady, Jimbo. Let's get settled in our little love-nest." Tiffani's suggestive pleas soothed the savage lummox.

Jimbo stepped closer to the desk to retrieve his credit card, and slammed his hurt toe into one of the luggage bags. "Ahhhhh! Oh my God. See what you did, woman!"

The sliding glass door opened on the side of the office. A mountain of a man stepped in. Not a regular mountain, either. A big mountain. A mountain that was bald headed as a melon and had a silver skull dangling from his left ear. He also had twin hoop earrings on each ear. His eyes were set way too close to each other. He wore a Harley Davidson shirt also, but his had the sleeves cut off. His arms rippled with muscles the size of cantaloupes. Elaborate tattoos decorated his arms from his wrist to his shoulder. "Momma? Is everything OK? I heard voices."

"Everything is fine, Kama. Be a good boy and show Mr. Jerkoff to his room."

"That's Jenkins! Jenkins!" Jimbo interjected, as he signed the credit card authorization.

Annie studied the card closely. "Oh yes. I am so sorry. My mistake. They are in the Captain Cooke suite. Show them their room, would you please?"

Tank studied the group very, very carefully. "How you doing, Tad? Ramon?"

Ramon answered, "Not too bad, Tank. How's life?"

"Clean and green."

His dark Hawaiian eyes never left Jimbo. He grumbled and said, "This way."

Tank led Jimbo and Tiffani to their room. When the door closed, Ramon smiled at Annie, "Ah, Annie. What a vision of loveliness you are. The days that pass without visiting you are without sunshine, meaning and purpose."

Annie smiled at Ramon. "You, you Cuban scoundrel are, how do you say… full of shit! Yes, I believe I captured that colloquialism. Tad, how are you, my boy? Still hanging out around that degenerate, George Greekopolis?"

"It's Giani. Still there, both Ramon and me. How's business and such?"

A gleam came in the old Hawaiian's eyes. "Not too bad. Tank is finishing up dental school next year. Then he can take care of an old lady."

Ramon piped up, "Old? Thaddeus, do you see anyone *old* here? I don't see anyone old. And Annie, you can take care of yourself. When Tank sets up his dentist practice, you can sell this joint and move in with me. Wear my letterman jacket. I like café con leche for breakfast. Learn to make that."

Annie's smile only got broader. "Tad, take this pervert and leave. Come back and visit more often. And thanks for that charmer you brought to me. What are you hanging out with someone like that for?"

Tad shrugged. "It's a job. He's a client. You know, business."

"Hooboy do I ever know. Now go, Kamalei, and tend to your business. As we say back on the big island, aloha pumehana."

Chapter Seven

Tad and Ramon rose early the next morning. Ramon was pulling out equipment from a forward berth of the Who's Your Daddy, while Tad took inventory on a yellow legal pad. By eight o'clock, they had a pretty thorough inventory in addition to a timeline for installation. Four days of uninterrupted work should do it. They got right to it.

At nine fifteen, Tad's cell phone rang. He and Ramon were preparing a wiring harness to connect instruments from the cockpit to the interior navigation station. Tad set down the equipment, and answered it. "Hello? Conch Island Yacht Service."

"Hello Thaddeus. Good to hear your voice again. It has been a while, has it not?"

Ramon surveyed Tad's face, as it visibly darkened. "Who is it? The IRS?"

Tad held the phone against his chest, muffling the speaker. "Worse. It's Murph."

"Murph? Like as in Murph?" Tad nodded. Ramon said, "Well, talk to him. Tell him which part of his body to stick up which orifice. Here hand me the phone. I will."

Tad put the phone back up to his ear. "What do you want, Murph? I hope this is a social call."

"Are they all not social calls in some small way? Really, Thaddeus, after all we have endured together. If I did not know better, I would say you are not happy to hear my golden voice."

"Again, what do you want? I'm getting ready to hang up. One Mississippi…"

"I need you to do a job. Quick and easy. Very lucrative. What do you say?"

"Murph, I say no. Nothing associated with you has ever been quick or easy. Two Mississippi..."

"Alright Thaddeus, I appreciate your time. By the way, the payout is twenty-five thousand dollars. Goodbye."

There was a pregnant silence on the phone. "Thaddeus, did you hang up? Go ahead and hang up. You first. No wait, we'll hang up on the count of three. One Mississippi…"

"Did you say twenty-five thousand dollars? Is that what you said?"

"Yes, my young protégé. I believe that is what I said."

"I am not your protégé. It's bad work, isn't it? I am not going to associate myself with any more of that. I got out a long time ago."

Patiently Murph said, "No, Thaddeus. It is a simple job. All you have to do is carry a person to a locale nearby yours. There you have to help make a swap. That simple. It should take you less than a day. You will receive for your trouble twenty five thousand dollars. Something similar to a consulting fee. Twelve five for you and twelve five for Ramon. And how is he? He is standing next to you, is he not? Please give him my kindest regards."

Tad's mind was swirling at cyclone speed. "Murph, listen. I don't know. I just don't know. We are out of the business. I told you that a long time ago. Out!"

Murph patiently lectured. "Thaddeus, in this business, you are never really out. You know this to be true. Think about it. I need an answer soon."

"OK. The answer is no."

"No? Well let me add a detail. It's Johnny. He has been shot, wounded and his fiancé has been kidnapped. I need you to make the payoff and get his girl back."

"Johnny? Our Johnny?"

"The one and only."

"Is he alive?"

"Yes he is, but he's still somewhat incapacitated."

"When do you need to know?"

"Now. Talk to Ramon. I'll call you back in five minutes."

Tad and Ramon went into the boat and settled in the dinette. Tad gave Ramon all the details of the conversation. "Let's analyze this." Tad said.

"Nothing to analyze. Johnny needs us to come through. Period."

"True. But you know Murph is using us for his own means."

Ramon nodded. "True. But this is not about Murph. It's about Johnny."

"What about our current customer? We have his check. A bird in the bush is better than doing something with your hand."

"You are right. But one day, Tad. He said it would only take one day. Don't tell me this doesn't intrigue you even a little bit."

"Yes, Ramon, it does intrigue me. The money intrigues me. Been kinda boring around here, except for listening to you and BethAnn act like juvenile delinquents. Do you really want to get into the game again?"

"No. Not the game we were in. Maybe this is a different game. Different place. Different rules. Different people."

"It's all the same. It doesn't matter if it is Afghanistan, Iraq or Miami. It's all the same when you are playing games. And besides, Murph never lied to us. Not once."

"No he did not. OK, Tad. I'm in, but only to watch your gringo backside. If it gets too hairy, we walk away. That is the condition."

"I agree. If it gets too hairy, we E&E out of there."

Ramon's expression was a portent of doom. "Bad things. That's what Murph brings - bad things."

A minute later the phone rang. Tad answered, "What's the job?"

Murph countered, "Are you in? Both of you?"

"Yes."

"Welcome back, laddies. Here's the plan. A Fedex package will arrive today. In it is a smaller package. You will deliver the package to a rendezvous point in Key West. You will call me from there and we will meet. You will trade the package for a person. You deliver the person to our team, who will be waiting nearby. They give you the money. You go home. End of story."

"When?"

"Three days from today at twelve o'clock. High noon, just like the movie. You can be Gary Cooper."

"How do we know the person we are retrieving is the right person?"

"No problem. I am sending someone to help. She is the sister of the person you are picking up. Her name is Sandy. She will make the ID. But Thaddeus, this is important: Don't bring her into this more than you need to. Don't discuss operations with her. Don't tell her the plans until the last minute. This family has already lost too much. Don't bring this girl into our world. Protect her and keep her safe. She's is quite capable, I assure you, but keep her distant."

The smugness in Murph's voice was gone. He was speaking in earnest. Tad said, "No problem, Murph. When does she arrive?"

"I'm surprised she's not already there."

"You knew we would be in, didn't you? How?"

"Like I said, Thaddeus. Once you walk in the dark side, you never really leave." The cell phone clicked off.

Ramon queried his friend, "Well, what's double-oh-septic have to say?"

Tad filled him in with the details.

"What about Jimbo?" Ramon said. "We can't just run off and leave him."

"I've got an idea. Follow this." And Tad explained the plan. The details seemed to flow out of him like he had thought it out last week, revised and revamped the plan, and memorized the sequence of events. Planning for operations was a gift Tad possessed. It had got them out of a sticky situation more than once.

"Sounds good, Tad. Crazy enough to work. We better go talk to Jimbo."

"Yep. First we'll let George know if a female shows up, to send her our way."

• • •

"You boys want to do what?"

Tad explained. "We want to go ahead and make the shakedown cruise. We'll install some things on the water. That's no problem, really. Today's Wednesday. We'll leave tomorrow morning at eight o'clock. We'll make Marathon by afternoon. By Friday afternoon, we will be in Key West. We will stay there for a day or two, and make our way back. By then, we will have spent much time delivering personal instruction and honing your navigation and sailing skills. Additionally, we can individualize much of the equipment installation according to your specific needs and desires, as only can be done on the water."

"A maestro of BS at work here..." thought Ramon.

"This is great!" said Jimbo.

Tad was like a football coach, pumping up the team. "Well, alright! We're on! Ramon and I will prepare the boat! You two show up at the marina office at seven thirty in the morning! And about dinner. How about dinner tonight at eight? We know a little place."

"Oh goodie. We get to leave the Four Seasons." said Tiffani, with more than a touch of grouchiness. She was clearly not appreciative of the historic nature of her present accommodations.

Tad and Ramon were walking by the marina office, when George leaned out the door and said, "Hey, you two schmucks. Come here. This came from Fedex." He was holding a small box. "I signed for it. Parts I guess."

Tad took the box warily. "Thanks, George. Parts, yeah." The box was light. George said, "One more delivery. She's in here."

Tad and Ramon looked at each other. Neither seemed to know exactly what to say, so they walked into the marina office. Sitting in the same chair where earlier Jimbo received the aloe arctic blast was a woman. She turned to study the two.

She had deep green eyes that were magnetic. They had flecks of gold in them. That was the first thing that caught Tad, the intensity of her eyes. She rose to meet them. *"This is it,"* thought Tad. *"This is the big one. I'm in love."*

She was nicely proportioned and moved like a jungle cat. Tad stumbled over his words, "Uh, . . . yeah . . . I'm Tad. That's me. And this is Ramon. We've been expecting you. Our . . . Uh . . . mutual friend said you would be here today. So here you are."

She offered her hand, and Tad grabbed it, a little too eagerly. He shook it up and down a couple of times, staring into her eyes. Then he just stopped, waiting on her to say something. She did not.

"OK, I am a complete ass. Say something, stupid." "So, your name is Sandy. That's with a 'Y,' right?"

And then she spoke. "I should say so. Tad, we need to talk. Can we go somewhere?" Her voice was husky. A good kind of husky in a

Kathleen Turner sort of way. Chills raced all up and down Tad's spine, accompanied by a vicious swarm of butterflies in his stomach.

"YES. Yes, we should. Please, let's talk on the boat. It's right out here. The Who's Your Daddy. After you."

Sandy exited the office and made her way down the dock. Tad was about to follow as Ramon stopped him and said quietly, "Well Mr. Smoothie, not bad. But she didn't rip your clothes off, did she? I was watching and I am sure she did not rip your clothes off. Not even like a sock or something. Shameful."

Tad was about to reply, when she turned and said, "Good news for Tad - the day is still young, Ramon. My hearing is better than your humor." And then she turned and continued to stroll to the sailboat.

Ramon smiled. "Ahh! A tigress. She will chew you up and spit you out. You, Thaddeus, are a dead man. Doomed. Save yourself. Give up now and let me take over. It's your only way out. I'm only saying this for your health and welfare."

Tad was getting the focus back in his eyes. He took off down the dock. "I'll take my chances. Let's go meet the mystery woman."

They went over a sanitized version of the plan with Sandy. This was a customer's boat, taking them on a shakedown cruise to Key West, yada yada. They decided to tell Jimbo and Tiffani that Sandy would be the significant other of Tad, as well as a pretty good sailor. Sandy would be there as crew.

Sandy asked them, "Where's the money? Is that what we are giving the kidnappers?"

Tad cleared his throat and prepared to lie. "Hmmph. Ah, money. Well, someone will deliver the money to us in Key West. Then we make the switch." Sandy nodded pensively and said nothing else.

Ramon said, "We gotta get going. We have to have, at a minimum, the VHF and GPS installed before we leave. It would be nice to have radar, but that ain't going to happen."

Tad concurred. "Right you are. Sandy, would you like to go up to our place and rest a while? It's over in the corner of the boat yard, where all those sailboats are up on boat stands."

Sandy rewarded Tad with a smile. "Why yes I would, Tad. How sweet of you."

Tad beamed. "The door is open. My apartment is the last one. There's extra towels in the closet. You can rack out in my bunk. I will stay on the couch. We're having dinner at eight." and thought *"Eight – wow, that rhymes with cohabi-tate."*

"A shower and nap would be marvy. Thanks. See you boys later."

They watched her glide down the dock. Graceful and sleek. BethAnn was coming out of the office, holding her Camel and suntan oil. She froze in her tracks, and stared at the woman coming down the dock. She looked as if she was about to say something, then ducked back inside. There was a new alpha female at Conch Island Marina, and it was not the bottle blonde from Two Egg, Florida. Sandy peeled off her course, left of the office and continued on toward Tad's apartment. She glided like an F-15 across the hardstand, disappearing behind a Catalina on boat stands.

Ramon snapped Tad out of his stupification. "Yeah boyo. You want to ride the tiger? Literally and figuratively? You may not be man enough. *I* may not be man enough."

"Stop being juvenile and chauvinistic."

"I know you are but what am I?"

The rest of the afternoon was spent installing electronics and communications systems. Tad and Ramon drove to the local supermarket, and provisioned. Just the basics for a five-day cruise. Water, food that did not require cooking, snacks and of course, beer.

Tad favored Miller Lite, while Ramon liked Corona. To each his own. Case, that is. They also factored the Jimbo variable into the shopping list, and bought two extra cases of beer and three extra boxes of Little Debbies.

The boat all provisioned, and the radio and GPS working, it was time to take a break. The two sat out on the dock, by the water, working on a cold, cold beer. A hundred pound tarpon Ramon had named Jaws was working the water between the boats and docks. They watched him slowly swimming, searching for prey. The dorsal fin would break the surface, much like a shark. Every now and then, the giant silver fish would break hard after something, probably a menhaden or other small fish. It was mesmerizing to watch the struggle for life that continually went on in the marina waters. Tad could not help but wax philosophical. "There he is again, Jaws. You know, he is like us.

We used to do just what he does. He never changes. He is here every day. He hunts down his prey, and takes them out. But, he has become so accustom to this place that we can hand feed him. Is he still the predator he was designed to be? Are we, Ramon? We've been out for three years. That's a long time with no training."

The sun was slowly retreating across the water. Another spectacular sunset in the Keys. The colors danced across the water. The clouds were a spectacular pink and periwinkle.

"I think some things never leave you. I think also that sometimes you get a little antsy for the excitement that we used to have. You think you can get a little taste of it again, without having to make a substantial commitment. I don't think it is the money at all drawing you into this. I think a small part of you, deep down inside, misses the action. Am I right?"

Tad sat quietly for a few minutes. He had asked himself similar questions for the last year. Did he miss the action? Was he chasing his dreams, working on sailboats? "Yeah, you are right. I do miss it a little. But I absolutely do not want to go back. I like the course we have charted for our lives. Like it a lot. What about you? Ever have any second thoughts about going back? You need a little excitement also?"

Ramon smiled. "Hey Chico, that I do. I always liked the excitement. I just don't like what I became when we were on missions. It took a while to get out of the mode. I'm not eager to get back into operational mode."

"I know what you mean. I know exactly what you mean. Well look on the bright side. We're going to make thirty-five grand over the next two weeks. We're going to help someone go home, who otherwise might not ever get to. We're going to get to go sailing on a better boat than either one of us has ever been on. Live is good."

They clinked beer bottles. "Yes it is, Chico. Life is good."

• • •

Tad and Ramon walked back up to their apartments. As Tad entered, the smell of shower steam was in the air. The bathroom opened, and Sandy stepped out, wearing one of Tad's Conch Island Yacht Service t-shirts and a pair of his boxers. She was combing out her long, brown hair. "Oh. Sorry, didn't know you were coming back. I hope you don't mind me borrowing some of your clothes."

Tad swallowed hard. Real hard. Ah, crap. Didn't all go down. Swallow hard again. Close enough. His face felt flush and he had a stirring feeling in the southernmost regions of his body. "No, of course not. We're going to eat soon. I hope you will join us?"

"Sure. Give me twenty minutes." She smiled and disappeared into his room. The door to Thad's room swung closed. Click. That sucks.

Tad walked next door to Ramon's apartment. Ramon was in the back, so Tad turned on the stereo, and pushed the button on the CD player. The room filled with Jimmy Buffett, as it should be. *"Looking back at the background, tryin' to figure out how I ever got here. Some things are still a mystery, while others are much too clear."*

"Thaddeus," Ramon quietly said as he entered the small den. "Let me see it."

"See what?"

"The brand on your backside. The 'S' with a circle around it. You have been selected. Darwin is alive and well."

"You're crazy."

J.B. continued, *"And mobile homes that smother the Keys, I hate those bastards so much!"*

Ramon acted like he was cracking a whip and quietly said, "Whoooosh-crack! That's you boy! I'll bet every pair of your underwear now says 'If found, please return to Sandy.'"

"Shhhh! She's going to hear us!"

"Well go to her, Big Man! Go back there and ravage her. Make her think a Florida panther attacked her."

Buffett - *"They're ugly and they are square. They don't belong there. They look a lot better as beer cans."*

"Ramon, I swear to God. Just shut up! Give me a break, OK?" Tad's face was turning three shades of crimson.

"Whooo Hoooo! Have a beer, Romeo! Gonna have fun tonight! We haven't been to the Mandalay in a month! I hope Angela is there." Ramon was doing his special version of some Latin dance moonwalk that Tad could not identify.

Buffett - *"I got a Caribbean soul I can barely control and some Texas hidden deep in my heart."*

Ramon had a unique ability to make everyone around him feel great. Absolutely great. Ramon had been keeping Tad's spirits up for years. Tad had, in turn, kept Ramon grounded, when he needed it most. They had an unusual, symbiotic relationship.

Tad gathered his courage and slinked back to his apartment.

When Sandy came out, she looked great. She had on a floral print shirt, khaki shorts and a pair of sandals. She wore a white bandana to pull here hair back. "Your turn," she told Tad. Tad emerged wearing parrots on his shirt. They all filed down stairs to meet up with Ramon, Jimbo and Tiffani.

Jimbo was standing out front of the marina office, looking down into the water. Tiffani was behind him. Tad and the group approached. "Hey Jimbo. You ready?"

"Hell yes I am. How we gonna get there? Cab?"

"No! We walk. It's right down the road. Five minutes, tops."

"Great. I got an Italian sausage for a toe and you want to walk. Let's get going. This the girl who is crewing tomorrow? Glad to meet you honey. I'm Jimbo and this is Tiffani."

Jimbo shook her hand and moved so Tiffani could do the same. Tad noticed that Sandy's eyes hardened immediately, but softened just as quickly. "Hello, Tiffani. I'm Sandy. Nice to meet you."

Tad thought, *"Why do women have to be like this?"*

Tiffany took here hand. "You too! That sure is a pretty shirt. Jimbo, I need some more shirts. You know, *island shirts*, while we are here."

"Sure honey. Sure. Let's go."

And they all headed off down US1 to dinner.

They arrived at the Mandalay, a local's paradise. Combination marina, outdoor restaurant and tiki bar. No hotel or outside restaurant in the Keys is official unless it has a tiki bar. They chose a table under the canopy that overlooked the small marina. The restaurant also overlooked Rodriguez Key, a small island about a quarter mile off shore. There were a dozen sailboat anchored in the lee of the Key.

Eight small dinghies were nosed up on the beach next to the tiki bar. These were the water taxis for the cruisers who were anchored offshore. The dinghies varied from inflatable Zodiacs and Avons to "hard" dinghies, made of fiberglass. There was even on curious boat that actually folded up flat, yet still floats when unfolded. Amazing.

The people hovering over beers and colorful drinks in plastic cups had a distinct look to them also. Tad explained that you could pick out the tourists from the locals and cruisers. It was as if everyone had a sign around their neck. "The tourists wear bright, clean, new clothes. Lots of tropical designs. The yuppie dad or husband often wears a light-colored polo shirt. Usually the visitors wear walking sandals or boat shoes. They all had a bright, scrubbed look to them. Tourists spent a lot of time looking around, doing what tourists do - taking in the sights. And, of course, there are the cameras. Lots of cameras. 'Waitress, do you mind taking our picture? No? Great.'"

"The locals looked somewhat scruffy and eccentric. Who wouldn't? The Keys are filled with expatriates from the Great American Society. It is as if you have entered a foreign country when you leave the city limits of Florida City on US1. As you head south, off the Florida mainland and cross Jewfish Creek, it does not take long to realize you are in a different kind of place."

"There are different kinds of locals, also. There exists a rare breed of person who was actually born in the Keys and lived there their whole lives. These people are called Conchs. No one has ever actually met one of these people and documented cases of meeting them are slightly fewer than Yeti sightings. More common are those who escaped their existence and moved to the Keys. If you have lived there for seven years, you are a Fresh Water Conch."

"The last group of locals is the refugees. They are the ones who are not really here permanently. They are really not anywhere permanently. They like the weather and, hey, the Keys are a pretty bitchin' place to hole up for a while. Key West draws these people with a magnetic intensity. Many of these people live on sailboats and houseboats around the islands, moored in the lee of mangrove islands, trying to find a little independence."

"Any let's not forget the cruisers. These people are the nomadic sailors who use the Keys as a temporary oasis. They show up, hang out until enough is enough, and move on to Costa Rica, the Bahamas, the British Virgin Islands, or if they are feeling adventurous, Venezuela. You can spot them a mile off. They motor in on small dinghies that look like a child's pool toy. Look at those three dinghies at the beach, the fiberglass ones. That's a cruiser's dinghy. They are the ones wearing long sleeved shirts and immense, floppy hats in ninety-five degree weather. They wear polarized sunglasses, even while they sleep. The sunglasses take root to the side of their head."

"It is the eccentricity and independent spirit of these individuals that make the people of the Keys such a welcome place. If you can ever truly find a "locals" spot, like this, you should put on an old sailing shirt, shorts that are not khaki and order up a dozen oysters and a beer."

The group hooted their approval at Tad's dissertation. Ramon saluted Tad with his beer and said in his best David Niven voice, "Bravo, Chap! Just ducky!"

Sandy smiled, as she drank from her strawberry daiquiri. "Which group are you and Ramon in, Tad?"

Tad drained his margarita and signaled for another. "Actually, we fall in two different groups. You see, Ramon and I have only been here for a few years. So we are pretty much refugees. That would be accurate. But we hope to one day sail our own sailboat around the world. You know, circumnavigate. That's a few years down the road. In the mean time, we're just trying to build our business up, make some money and have some fun."

Tiffani said, "I know I'm having fun! Let's order. I'm famished!"

The group enjoyed excellent fare in the outdoor sea air of Key Largo. Jimbo pulled a big cigar out of his pocket and hollered at the waitress, who was not really deaf at all, "Hey Baby! You got a match?"

"Yeah," the waitress said, "…your face and my ass."

"Naw, not that kind. I need a light."

She tossed him a pack of matches on the way by.

The music was lively and nautical. There was a guy playing a guitar and taking requests. He nailed most of the songs and kept the crowd tapping and singing. The waitress, Angela, spent most of the night flirting with Ramon. Ramon shamelessly flirted with Angela, until the group left just shy of midnight. They walked back to the marina, with a little bit of a stagger in everyone's step.

Tad's last words were, "Be on the boat and ready to sail at eight o'clock." And they went off to their respective dens. Jimbo and Tiffani went to their Polynesian paradise. Ramon went to his bed. Sandy went to Tad's bed and Tad reluctantly headed to the couch. Ah, crap. This sucks.

Eight o'clock found everyone on board, with their gear stowed. Ramon and Tad had organized the supplies and checked to make sure there were no loose objects that might tumble to the floor if the boat heeled sharply in the wind. There was plenty of fuel already, so they took on no more. Tad gave the order, "Cast off the lines."

Ramon, Sandy and Tiffani untied the thick dock lines from the dock cleats. They neatly wound each line and stowed it in a locker. The big diesel slowly backed the *Who's Your Daddy* out of the slip. Tad turned the wheel hard to port, causing the aft end of the ship to swing to the port. "No Jimbo. Port is left. Starboard is right. We're swinging left, so that's to port."

Once the bow of the boat cleared the dock pilings, Tad turned the wheel hard to starboard and put the boat in forward gear. The front end swung around and the boat began to straighten itself in the channel. Once straight, Tad gave it some throttle and the boat picked up speed to about three knots. He held a steady three while exiting the channel.

Fifteen minutes later, the *Who's Your Daddy* was in twenty-two feet of water and less than a mile off the coast of Key Largo. This was more motoring that Tad wanted, and he called the group to the cockpit. He explained what they were going to do when they hoisted sails. Tad was a patient teacher, making sure everyone knew their job. He required each person to repeat their job. After he was satisfied, he swung the boat so that it pointed into the wind.

The commands were precise, as were the actions of the crew. First, the big main sail came out, slowly emerging to the humming of the electric winch that pulled it. Jimbo had opted for an in-mast furling rig, which was sweet. The big sail wound around a spindle in the middle of the mast. It just came out of the mast, as if by magic. Once the main was out, they prepared to set the head sail.

The *Who's Your Daddy* had a big genoa for a headsail. The genoa, or "gennie" was an enormous sail that attached to the bow. It rose the diagonal length from the front tip of the boat to the top of the mast. It was unfurled and furled by winches also. Jimbo's boat was custom fitted to allow one or two people sail it. Most boats the size of the *Who's Your Daddy* required three or four, in addition to the skipper.

The sails were popping in the wind, as the boat held its course in the wind. Jimbo hollered excitedly at Tad, "Those sails supposed to be popping all around like that?"

Tad said, "It's called luffing. When they are just blowing all around and they are not filled with air, we call it luffing. And no, at least not for long. Hold on."

Tad turned the wheel and the boat began to veer off to port. Suddenly, the sails filled with air, since they were no longer headed directly into the wind. The entire boat heeled over to port, causing everyone to hold on. The big Morris shot out of her own wake, responding to the wind like a greyhound out of the gate. Tad cut the engine, and let out a yell. "WhooooHooooo! This is living, folks. This is what it is all about." Ramon trimmed the lines so that the heel of the boat was not so dramatic.

Tad steered the boat, testing it at different points of sail. He liked what he saw. Tad had sailed many boats, but never one quite like this. He saw Ramon sitting on the high side of the boat, inspecting the trim of the sail.

"Hey, Ramon. Get over here. Take the helm a while. I need to check on a few things." There was nothing to check on. Tad wanted his friend to experience some of the joy of piloting this magnificent vessel.

Ramon steered for a while, while Tad poured over charts. Jimbo limped over to Tad and said, "What you doing with those maps?"

"Uh, actually, these are called charts. Maps are of dry land. Charts are like maps of water. I'm making sure we don't hit the reef out there. I'm guessing you would not like it if we sunk your new boat on a reef. You want to see how I am doing this?"

"Nah. You go right ahead. I'm gonna get a beer. Tiffani! Get your fanny down stairs and get me a beer."

Sandy walked over to Tad and silently watched him work. Tad was in his element. He worked intensely over the chart, plotting their present course and where they should go next. He had a handheld GPS unit giving him coordinates in one hand, and the chart book in the other.

"You really like this, don't you?"

Tad looked up, smiling. On the water, he was seldom intimidated by anyone. Sandy's magic didn't have the same hold on him that it did on the dock. "Ah, the green-eyed wench speaketh. Yes I do. Here, do you want to see?"

She sat down next to him and he explained it to her in detail. She listened to each word he said. Occasionally, she asked questions. She was a quick study. Tad thought, *"She smells good. God, does she smell good."* The trip was going well. They were going to make some money. Jimbo was plenty happy and this woman had a brain. Life was good.

When Tad took back over the helm, Ramon said, "Hey boy, you talk to her, then you smile, then you talk to her, then you smile. What's up with that? She wearing your sweater?"

Tad spoke very quietly. "Ramon, she smells good. Her hair smells good. Her shoulders smell good. Her clothes smell good. It's all good."

"Oh, so you been smelling her up? That's just freakie deekie. She's going to have to lock up her panties and bra?"

Tad stared straight ahead and responded, "She might." The two busted out laughing. Ramon fetched them each a Corona and they began to put some nautical miles behind them.

By lunch, they had clicked off twenty-five miles. "Hey Tad, look! Tiffani and Sandy are actually talking. You think Sandy is going to throw her overboard?"

Tad saw the two women, stretched out on the front deck, chatting away. They appeared to be getting along well, which came as a great relief to Tad. Tiffani was, in spite of being an airhead, the customer's girlfriend. Or was she? Tad reflected that he had never seen Jimbo show her any affection. No hugs, no kisses. He had not even held her hand. Was he the sort of guy that needed a hot young thing around for a trophy? Is it possible that he was kind and gentle to her in private, but maintained a façade of being a horse's ass in public?

Jimbo was sprawled out on a berth downstairs, napping and snoring loudly. Tad and Ramon had the cockpit to themselves. "Hey Ramon, it is just me, or does it seem that Jimbo doesn't pay much attention to Tiffani?"

Ramon smiled like the Chinese Shoulin priest who patiently addresses the stupid, thickheaded pupil. "Thaddeus, Thaddeus." He was shaking his head, sadly. "Jimbo is not a man. He is a collector. This boat is part of his collection. It is, in fact, his penis. That's right,

Thaddeus, you are piloting his penis. That makes you a penis pilot. How does it feel? Good firm feel to the helm."

This made Tad smile. "I don't know. Kinda wobbly."

"Exactly, Thaddeus! And Tiffani is also part of his collection. He does not love her. He probably doesn't even like her, but he likes what she represents – youth, sexuality, passion. Eventually, he will tire of her or she will just up and take off. Then he will get a newer model, probably the newest he can afford. He's a sad, lonely piece of canine excrement getting along the best he can. As any good plumber knows, some turds float and some sink. Jimbo is a floater. He is the kind of guy who always ends up on top. That's just him."

"I see you making goo-goo eyes at Tiffani, Ramon. Please don't screw this up. Let's please the customer and make some money. After that, you're on your own."

"But Thaddeus, can you dive down below and tell Mr. Barracuda to stop eating the little fish that live on the reef? It's not in his nature; plus he has to survive. Can we tell Mr. Shark to stop prowling the mangrove creeks, patrolling day and night? I think not. Yes, Thaddeus, I will temper my actions in accordance with traditions and expected practices regarding the relationship between skipper, crew and paying passengers."

"What does all that gobbledegook mean?"

"It means I'll leave her alone, though I would rather jump her bones, why tempt fate?"

"You've spent your whole life tempting fate. Look at all the crap we used to do"

Tiffany and Sandy came walking back to the cockpit. "What sort of crap did you used to do? How did you two meet?" Tiffany said.

Tad groaned. "It's a long story."

Chapter Eight

(Afghanistan; 2001) "Gentlemen, welcome to Afghanistan. You may have noticed the mountains to your north. They look a whole lot like the mountains to your south, east and west. There is one big difference. The mountains to your north have over two thousand Taliban and al Qaeda that have single determined objective – killing your sorry ass. As part of the Joint Special Operations Command, you will be performing missions that assist the theater commander in killing them first. I am Brigadier General Brian Lipshitz." (snickers from the audience) "You better listen up, assholes. Assembled here are members of each service, all working under a unified command. Rangers, Seals, Marine Force Recon, Special Forces and even a few air force weenies thrown in to give the boys in blue a woody." Someone farted. "I heard that, assholes! Listen up! You will receive an orientation briefing, then move off to your respective units and prepare to begin missions."

Tad sat in the folding steel chair, staring at the big map in the front of the tent. It had little pins all over it. Ramon leaned over and elbowed Tad. "Well Staff Sergeant Hunter. Did you enjoy my little opera of the ass? The smell of sphincter is in the air. Do you think the general appreciated the timbre and resonance of that little jewel?"

"Actually, Sergeant Garcia, I believe it was the highlight of the briefing. Kind of like the explanation mark ending the sentence. You sir, are a maestro of methane."

A sergeant major who resembled the grim reaper in uniform eyed them carefully. "Get your stupid asses out of my tent and get on over to your unit. NOW!"

Knowing that timing is everything, plus fearing the wrath of the sergeant major, they egressed in an expeditious manner. They wandered over to their tent. A sign hung over the door. Company A, 1/5 Special Forces. Under it was their unit slogan. Killing is our business, and business is good. They entered.

They spied their team leader, Captain Carston. Ramon spoke up, "Hey Captain! What's the deal?" Captain Carston was a jovial guy and a baseball fanatic, but he had a grim look that spoke volumes. He said, "Assemble the team. Huddle for the game plan in twenty minutes."

Ramon arched his eyebrows and looked at Tad. "Shit! An operations order already? We just got here!"

Twenty minutes later, twelve men sat in the ubiquitous army folding chairs. The map was taped to a cardboard cut from a MRE box. MREs are Meals – Ready to Eat. They are typically called MRB's, Meals – Ready to Barf. The box provided some rigidity to the map, as Captain Carston began.

"Men, it's time to step up to the plate. The Colonel has thrown us a curve ball, but we're going to choke up on the bat and make contact. Remember – you gotta be a hitter. The wheel play is on for day after tomorrow, and we're taking out the bench of the other team. Now, they'll be watching the big hitters and those on deck. They'll never see us infiltrate from the dugout. We're taking out their radar guns so they can't tell how fast our pitches are coming. Now, don't be alarmed, but there's sure to be bench clearing brawl before it's all over with. By the time the teams are piled up on the mound, we're all going to be back in the locker room, waiting for the next inning. We'll be batting a thousand, while they are stuck below the Mendoza line."

Total silence.

Finally, a sergeant from Detroit said, "What did he say? Did anyone understand what he said?"

The master sergeant who was the senior enlisted man on the team stepped up. "Um, Captain, mind if I summarize?"

The captain looked very pleased with himself. "Well not at all. I mean, it was clear as a bell, but go ahead."

The master sergeant cleared his throat and paused for silence. "What the captain is saying is this. The enemy is getting ready to invade and take back the country. Our job is to infiltrate, sneaky like, and take out their radar sites. Then we sneak out. If we do our job, then they can't see our planes and missiles. If we screw up, we die and so do a lot of other people who depend on us to kill the enemy radar. This is our particular site." He pointed at the map. "Any questions?"

Immediately he was flooded with questions. "What sort if intel do we have?" "How many enemy are there?" "How do we get there?" "How do we get back?" and on and on. The captain again approached the center of the group.

"Men, I know you all have questions. This time, we have some pretty good answers. We're going to have a couple of extra personnel with us to help out." The groans and streams of profanity spewed. The one thing a Special Forces A Team does not want is outside help.

"Now, now! Here they are now." Two men entered the tent. The first was a tall, thin, muscular soldier. The other wore a uniform, but not very well. He had a country club hairdo amidst the crew cuts and Mohawks.

Tad barked out, "Hey! Arnie! You're with us? Excellent! Hey everybody, this is Arnie! I know this guy. He's OK!" The crowd calmed immediately. Having a team member vouch for you was as good as gold. The other man furrowed his brow and made an expression of hurt feelings, "Thaddeus! Dear boy, do you not remember me? After all we endured together?"

Thad studied the man. He seemed oddly familiar. He nodded his head. "Yeah, I do. Murph. The consultant, right? The only thing we endured was bad liquor."

Murph beamed. "Bully for you! At least we have something in common. Let's get to work."

The captain cleared his throat. "Mr. Murphy is a field agent with a government intelligence agency. He has been assigned to our team to lend assistance."

Ramon spoke right up. "He's a spook. What kind of help can a spook offer to blowing up a radar site?"

Murph spoke up. "Sergeant Garcia – Cuban, right? Oh yes, I think so. Cubans do have a way of being suspicious of those of us in, how should I say, the low profile organizations. But your question is right on the money. How can I help?"

Murph continued. "The radar facility you will be destroying is near a training site. More particularly, a terrorist training site. If the team is able, we will make an incursion into this site to visit the cadre. I suspect that we will find a plethora of baddies there. Al Qaeda, PLO, Hamas and others. You see, I specialize in terrorists. I would dearly love to invite a few of them back here to chat. I'll bet we have much to talk about."

The captain continued. "That's right! So we might just try to steal a base, in addition to getting a hit. Hunter's friend is Sergeant First Class Arnold. He's played in this park before. Sergeant Arnold?"

Arnie walked up front and grabbed a chair. He turned it around and sat in it, propping his elbows up on the back of the chair. "I've been here. Already. I've been to this particular radar site. Let me tell you about it."

Arnie went on for over twenty minutes about the site. What the terrain looks like. The elevations. The best approaches. The best escape routes. The buildings. How to take them out. On and on. Finally, someone asked him, "How did you get to see this? The war hasn't kicked off, yet."

Arnie smiled. "Son, for special ops units, we are always, repeat, always at war. We've had a few personnel operating deep in enemy territory. Recon, snoop and poop, black bag type operations. We've gathered an enormous amount of intel. Now it's time to act."

Tad asked, "Arnie, did Murph go with you?"

Murph spoke up. "Well I couldn't let him go alone. He'd surely be lost in thirty minutes."

Everyone eyed Arnie, seeking confirmation. "Look, men. Murph was there. Every step of the way. He might look like a yacht club pansy who can't find his ass with both hands and a map, but he can pull his own weight."

And that was all it took. They planned for the next six hours. Each and every detail was covered. The next evening, at five minutes after midnight, fourteen men loaded up on a C-130 cargo plane. The pilot briefed them. "Gentlemen, welcome aboard the Ebola Gray. I'm Major Dirk Mallington, and the co-pilot is First Lieutenant Tyrone Johnson. We will be getting you to your debarkation point so you can HALO into your objective." HALO meant High Altitude, Low Opening parachute jump. It is a preferred method of arriving into an area.

"As we approach the area, I will lower the ramp. You will then take your instructions from the jumpmaster. Good luck, gentlemen, and thank you for flying the Ebola Gray."

They flew at an altitude of 24,000 feet. The group left the plane, each man wearing oxygen masks. The group settled into a wedge formation that carried them two miles past their objective. As they were flying toward their target, they watched a fiery streak of light leave the ground over twenty miles away. It wound its way up into the night sky, black as ink. Suddenly, there was a giant fireball. The Ebola Gray fell to the earth. Tad thought, *"So this is it. It's starting."*

The fourteen men popped their chutes and landed near a wadi. They buried their parachutes, and began to slip quietly toward the objective. As they topped a rise, Arnie gave everyone the sign to halt. They crept up and peered over the hill. There below them was a radar site, sure enough. Five dishes were outside a small, corrugated metal building. Three guards were milling around the building, but they did not seem to be aware anything was wrong. They would soon know different.

Off to the left, about four hundred yards away, there were three buildings inside a fence. Murph whispered, "That's the compound I was talking about." It was clear to Tad that they had to take out both. As soon as they hit the radar site, the people inside the training compound were sure to come streaming out. The men huddled together to make last minute changes to the plan. The priority was taking out the radar. To survive afterwards, they had to take out the training site.

Ramon, Tad, two demolitions experts and three others crept down the hill. The plan was simple. Tad and Ramon take out the three guards, and the demo guys would wire the radar site. The three others would storm the building, killing everyone inside. This had to happen with precision timing. They had to kill the communications; else an armored patrol would soon be on their heels. The remainder of the team would take the compound.

Tad and Ramon crept within fifty yards of the guards. Even in the night, the guards stood out like a sore thumb. Tad brought the weapon to his shoulder. He reviewed all that he had learned about shooting. Breathe, Relax, Aim, Squeeze. The weapon jumped twice, then twice again. Ramon had shot a three-round burst. The Taliban guards were on the ground in a clump.

Simultaneously, the demo guys sprang into action as well as the team that stormed the building. There was some automatic fire inside the building briefly, then it ceased. Three soldiers emerged from the building and ran to help the demo team. The satellite dishes and other transmitting equipment were wired. Everything was going exactly as planned.

Then it all fell apart.

Tad heard a big, "Ba-BOOM!" He turned to look at the compound, but the flash of light had blinded him temporarily. Automatic weapons fire rained down on the American soldiers from the top of a hill. Ramon turned and calmly said, "Ambush. They are in trouble."

The five soldiers who had just set the demo and cleared the shed next to the radar site hustled over to Tad and Ramon. "What'll we do, Sarge?" It took a second for Tad to realize they were talking to him! A calm, cool feeling came over him. A feeling of certainty. He surveyed the situation with a clarity that until this point had eluded him.

"Come with me. All of you." It was clear that the door to the compound had been booby trapped with explosives. There was also some sort of liquid fuel in the explosion, like diesel fuel. Probably a drum set next to the door on the inside.

Tad turned and ran back the way they came, away from the firefight. "Hey! Where the hell you going? They're over there!"

Tad turned and looked at the man who had said that. "You do what I say. We're going in from over here."

The man said, "Screw you. Look! They're pinned down! We gotta go help!" The sergeant started to move out of the line.

Tad said, "Hold it right there." The soldier stopped. Tad calmly walked over to him and drew his .45 pistol. Tad racked a round in the chamber and grabbed the man with his left hand. He jammed the pistol in his mouth. The soldier said, "AHHHH . . . QUUUIIIII . . . AHHHHHH!"

"That's right. I hear what you are saying. You are saying, 'I'm sorry Staff Sergeant Hunter for disobeying your lawful order. Let's do it your way.'" Tears drained from the man's eyes, as Tad released him. He crumpled down to his knees, coughing.

Tad had every man's total and complete attention. They headed off in a line, up the ridge and over it. They turned to the right and trotted in line, again. This time, toward the firefight. Tad had effectively maneuvered his squad behind the enemy. The Americans were trapped in the front of the compound. They were pinned down, with a hail of red hot steel raining down on them. Every few minutes, a WHOOSH would announce the arrival of a rocket-propelled grenade.

There were bodies on the ground in front of the compound. The slaughter was continuing, but not complete. Tad halted everyone and said, "OK, from here we go around this outcropping of rocks and up the hill. They will have some sort of rear security. Take it out hard and fast. Then it is a charge up the hill. Ramon, you set up on the outcropping and take them out, one shot at a time. Smith, you go . . ." He continued to give instructions to each man. "Everyone knows what to do?" Each man nodded solemnly. "OK. Let's go."

They burst around the rock outcropping at full speed. A silhouette stepped out to challenge them and fell in a short burst of rifle fire. The group continued up the slope. Ramon peeled off and took up a position. He began to pour on fire, one round at a time. He also concentrated on the basics; steady position, sight picture, breath control, trigger squeeze.

There appeared to be about a dozen turban-clad men on top. Ramon took out three before they could figure out where the sniping was coming from. They turned their attention away from the compound and began to shoot at where they last saw Ramon's muzzle flashes.

When Tad's group was about fifty yards away, they opened up. Four fell immediately. A couple of the bad guys tried to slip back on the compound side of the ridge. Immediately they were cut down. The American soldiers in the compound were no longer pinned down and they took advantage of the enemy with their backs to them.

The four remaining scruffy-looking soldiers threw down their weapons and fell on the ground, face first. They were screaming something incomprehensible, but everyone could easily understand it. "Don't shoot. We surrender" was a pretty close translation.

Tad barked out the orders, "Jones and Dawkins, get these four gomers down the hill. You two, search the dead ones. Everyone else, down the hill. We gotta help them. We have men down!"

They hustled down the hill. Murph was walking out to greet them, .45 Colt Commander pistol in hand. His expression was stone cold. "Well done, Thaddeus, who have you brought me?" He moved off to talk to the captured prisoners.

Just that moment, a series of explosions went off. The radar equipment disintegrated in a dusty cloud.

Tad and his men hustled over to the area where the bodies lie. He turned over the first one - Captain Carston. He had a six-inch long piece of steel sticking out of his forehead. Dead. The master sergeant who had translated for the Captain was also dead. There was so much blood on him, it was difficult to tell what killed him. Two others were dead. Tad heard groaning. He peeked over a small wall and Arnie looked up at him.

"Tad. Look, I'm leaking. If I were a superhero, I'd be called The Sieve. Help me out."

Tad hollered for some help. The other soldier in the compound miraculously did not get a scratch on him. He was the medic. "Doc! Get your ass over here. Man down."

Ramon walked up to Tad. He was holding the radio. "We got evac on the way. But we gotta get everyone up that hill and on the flat spot. They'll be here in thirty minutes."

Tad was amazed. "Thirty minutes? We need them here now!"

Someone cleared his throat. "Aheeem! Thaddeus, un momento?" Murph was on the edge of the compound, looking to the west.

Tad walked over to him. "Thaddeus, they knew we were coming. I don't know how, but they set us up. Right now, there is some sort of quick reaction force on the way. Probably a dozen vehicles with fifty or sixty men. Lots of firepower. Heavy machine guns. An ugly, ugly sight. What news do you have for our evacuation?"

Tad thought hard. "Well Murph, the choppers will be here in thirty minutes. That's the plan."

Murph nodded in agreement. "Good. That's excellent. They should find our dead bodies somewhere around here in thirty minutes. Let me clarify - the nasties will be here soon, verrrry soon."

"You know this?"

"It's a guess, but probably a good one."

"How long?"

"Fifteen minutes - tops."

Tad turned to the soldiers in the compound. "Alright everyone. Listen up, NOW! Vehicles with a platoon-sized element on the way. We have fifteen minutes to haul all the bodies up that hill and over to the flat spot just east of here. MOVE!"

Everyone grabbed something and took off. Tad turned to Murph, "Help me with Arnie."

Murph turned and eyed Tad and then scanned the perimeter. "I'm afraid you'll have to take care of him. I have four lads that I want to bring home for dinner." He turned and walked toward the four Taliban huddled nearby.

Tad let out a stream of profanities that would make a sailor blush, but headed to help Arnie. "Let's go, Big Boy. Time to get your ugly ass out of here."

They stumbled like drunken men, but managed to walk to the edge of the perimeter. Tad heard a shot ring out. He looked over and Murph was leading three men in front of him. One crumpled form lay still at his feet. Murph looked over and said, "How to win friends and scare the bejeezus out of those who don't want to go with you. You won't find this in a Dale Carnegie course." From the looks of the three remaining Afghanis, he would have no problem with them.

Ramon rushed over and helped Tad carry Arnie. The team reached the landing zone in twelve minutes. Tad had everyone form a perimeter. He saw lights coming down the sandy road, approaching the radar site. Murph surveyed the vehicles. "four, five . . . that's it. Five vehicles. Probably only fifty or so. No problem. What's the plan, Thaddeus?"

Tad was back in planning mode. "Ramon, you take the ridge. Let us know when they figure out where we are. That should be less than five minutes. Take three with you. They'll send recon up the hill. Wait until they are almost on you, and then take them out. You two, . . . " He barked out orders and everyone scattered. It was going to be close. Where were those damn choppers?

Precisely six minutes later, the ridge opened in gunfire. Then the heavy machine guns opened up from the compound on the top of the ridge. Green tracers arched out across the night. Murph walked up and said, "Well, the secret is certainly out. I'll be protecting our friends."

Tad whirled, angry. "What is it with you. We have four dead, one wounded badly. You're only worried about those miserable derelicts who were guarding the place. They're probably only privates or whatever they call them. They're not terrorists! Look at them! You think these are your terrorists?"

Murph never changed his poker-faced demeanor. "No Thaddeus, these are most certainly not the baddies we were after. But they were here. They know something. I want to, check that, I MUST get them back to question them. If not, then this whole trip was a waste. Four dead for nothing."

"What about the radar site. We zapped it."

"Sorry to be the bearer of bad news. You killed the dishes, not the equipment. They knew we were coming. The important equipment was moved before we arrived."

"How could you know this? How?"

"Thaddeus, when we get back, maybe we can sit down and chat. Maybe strum a guitar and sing Kumbaya. Right now, you have a battle to win. Now go on."

Ramon the others hustled down the hill. "They're not coming up the slope. They loaded up and they are taking off!"

Tad looked around slowly. "Nope. They're driving to a different place. They will attack us from there." He pointed. "This may work. We need time. You bought us some. Everyone to his position."

They settled down in their defensive positions. They knew that if the armored cars found their way to the group, there was little they could do. The heavy machine guns would chew them up.

Five minutes passed. The whir of truck engines was getting louder. Suddenly, Ramon said, "Hey! It's choppers! From the south!"

Tad thought, *"No way! They'll fly right over the armored cars. They'll be cut down."* He grabbed the radio, and tuned in to the pilot's frequency. "Night Hawk four, Night Hawk four, this is Bushmaster Six over." The pilot answered him almost immediately.

"Go ahead Bushmaster. Our approach time to LZ is two minutes, over."

"Night Hawk, there's trouble between us. Armored cars with heavy machine guns. Watch out."

"Bushmaster, thanks for the tip. That's a surprise, but we brought our own surprise. Keep your head down."

Suddenly, the sky lit up with fire. Tracers rained down on an unseen enemy a half a mile away. Rockets shot out from unseen helicopters.

"Little birds! They brought the little birds!" Ramon said. The Little Bird is a variant of a light observation helicopter. The AH-6C carries rocket launchers and 7.62 mm mini-guns. They were a formidable force in helping out troops on the ground.

The four blackhawks landed and the dead and wounded were quickly loaded. The three Taliban were almost eager to jump aboard. They didn't want anything to do with the carnage the Americans were dishing out. Surrender seemed a good option.

As the helicopters swung to the south, picking up speed, Tad could see five burning vehicles in the distance. He thought, *"It's good to be on the right team."*

Twenty-seven minutes later, the choppers landed at their base camp. An ambulance was waiting to take Arnie to the surgical hospital. The dead were transferred to a different truck and taken off. Tad wondered where they were taken.

The sergeant major who had spoken so gruffly to them in their orientation walked up to them. "You in charge of the returning group?"

"Yes, sergeant major. I guess so."

He nodded and said not at all unkindly. "Son, get accountability of your men. Make sure those that are left are OK. Meet me in the old man's tent in ten minutes for a debriefing."

"I'll be there."

Tad spent the next three hours explaining and answering questions. He was amazed at the rank in the room. One brigadier general, one full colonel, two lieutenant colonels and several sergeants major. They listened intently, asking intelligent questions at times.

Finally, they dismissed him. He stumbled back to his tent. Ramon told him that some officers and staff sergeants had debriefed the men. Tad didn't know, didn't care, didn't want to hear about it. He fell asleep and stayed that way for ten hours.

The next two weeks went by in slow motion. Because of all the casualties, Tad's team was officially out of action. That was, of course, until replacements arrived. Ramon came into the tent one day and said, "Hey, they want you over at the old man's tent."

"What's up?"

"Ah, I think we got a new captain. Let's don't keep the lad waiting"

Tad and Ramon walked across the dusty compound to the head shed. There were the usual number of officers and high-ranking noncommissioned officers there. They were all sitting in the briefing room, but there was no briefing going on. When Tad entered, someone hollered, "Group, At Ease!"

Everyone in the room jumped up to the position of attention. Brigadier General Lipshitz walked up front, followed by the sergeant major. The sergeant major boomed, "Staff Sergeant Thaddeus Hunter. Front and center."

Tad snapped into motion, wondering, *"Good grief. What now?"*

"For you actions on the morning of . . . " He began to read a long and descriptive citation of Tad's actions during the battle. ". . . you are awarded the Silver Star with a "V" device for valor." The general pinned the award on Tad. "Congratulations, son. We are all proud of you. That was a heroic thing you did."

Tad didn't feel much like a hero, but there you go. They called up Ramon and awarded him the bronze star for holding off the armored column, buying the group time. Three other group members received awards, including Arnie receiving his third Purple Heart. Ramon whispered, "I'm staying away from that guy. He's a bullet magnet."

The award ceremony convened, and the sergeant major said, "Hold up there Hunter. Your new team leader is here."

A man walked up to Tad and said, "Wake up boy. You think you're in Key West or something?"

Tad spun around and recognized the droopy mustache. "Chief! You're here? Wait a minute, you're the team leader now?" The Chief smiled and nodded.

"Well alright! That makes a lot of sense! Take a diver and send him to the mountains. God bless the Army!"

The Chief Warrant Officer, Tad, Ramon and the others spent the rest of the night talking and getting to know each other. In fact, they spent the next six months performing missions. Then they left the desert and returned to Fort Bragg, North Carolina.

Tad and Ramon spent long nights talking about sailing, navigating, boats and anything else that could take their minds off of the mountains. They devised a plan and made a pact. When they got out of the army, they would open a business. It sounded crazy, but they would go to the Keys, open a full service sailboat business and live like you are supposed to live.

Ramon got out first. Tad was set to get out two months later, but he wondered if Ramon was still interested. On Tad's final day, he heard a knock on his door. He opened the door, and the Chief was standing there. "Get up Scad. There's someone here to see you."

Ramon was standing in the hall. He was wearing cutoff bluejean shorts that looked like he had dragged them behind the car. He had on a t-shirt that said *"Sloppy Joes, Key West."* He was barefooted as a caveman.

Tad surveyed him for a few moments. "You look like Joe Shit the Ragman."

Ramon's bloodshot eyes narrowed. "Yeah? Key West can be a cruel mistress. She has grabbed me, tossed me around and wrung me out like a wet dish towel. She has beat me with the liquor stick for two months. Let's go. I think these animals here in this barracks are going to steal our women."

"Women?"

"Yeah. In the car. Outside. Veronica and Hortencia. They're sisters." Ramon rolled the "R's" in the girls' name - Verrrronica and Horrrrtencia."

"Veronica is mine. Hortencia is yours. But listen, don't say anything about her skin condition. She's sensitive."

Tad froze. "Her what?"

"Yeah, and that big hairy mole. She says she's getting rid of it soon. The same doctor who cleared up that drip is going to burn it off."

Tad remained frozen. "What is outside that door? Do I want to know?" Tad followed Ramon out. There were two smiling brunettes in the car, waving at the boys.

"Just kidding you Thaddeus. Hey, where's your sense of humor? Welcome back to the world."

Six days later they left the mainland of Florida on US1 headed south. They crossed into Key Largo together and renewed their pact. They were both out of the army and on to new adventures. But as Murph had said, "You are never really out of special operations, are you?"

Chapter Nine

The big Morris yacht continued to slice through the water. Sandy took a great interest in all aspects of sailing. Tad spent time explaining in detail how to pilot, trim the sails to achieve the best steerage, read charts and other sailing knowledge. It took Tad many years of sailing to reach the level of proficiency he possessed. Sandy was soaking up his years of experience like a sponge.

"Tad, tell me about yourself." And he did. He told her about growing up in California. The college years and the complete lack of motivation to get a real job. He told her about the fateful meeting with soldiers in Key West some years ago and how it led him into the army. He told her of how he got out and formed the business with Ramon.

A pod of dolphins escorted the group as they paralleled the shoreline, two miles out. The water was an aqua blue, crystal clear and absolutely beautiful. They had winds out of the southeast at twenty knots, putting them on a fabulous beam reach. The boat heeled over slightly, but not so much that they were uncomfortable.

"What sort of work do you and Ramon do in your business?" she asked.

"Actually we do just about anything that is needed for a boat. Sailboats, preferably. Let's look at who owns yachts. They probably have a business, or at least are a mid to upper level executive. Who has time to do all the maintenance on them? Say you went to a boat show and you saw this really cool radar system that you just have to have. You pay out the three grand, but now you have to install it. Again, who has the time? Or you need the sailboat hauled out of the water and the bottom painted. That's us. There are so many things that need to be done to boats just to keep them properly maintained. We do other things also. We have been getting more into yacht delivery. Both Ramon and I have our Coast Guard Captain's license with a fifty ton rating."

"And now you run charters?"

Tad surveyed the horizon, watching a trawler pass off their starboard beam. "I guess so. Actually, this sort of just fell in our laps. We were only planning on installing a bunch of electronics and deck hardware when Jimbo just up and asked us to take him sailing. He wants to learn to sail. He bought a seven hundred thousand dollar boat and doesn't even know how to sail. I'm supposed to be teaching him but he just lays down there in a berth and sleeps all day. Unbelievable, huh?" That earned a smiled from Sandy.

"Tad, where are we going to stop for the evening?"

"There's a key not too far from here that I like. It's called Plantation Key. We'll be there in less than an hour. You want to steer some more?" Sandy took the wheel while Tad stood behind her, talking quietly, giving her more instruction. The boat responded well to Sandy's steering. Tad closed his eyes and breathed deeply. He wasn't sure if it was the smell of the ocean, or the smell of her hair as the wind whipped it around. It was a magical moment, one Tad wanted to last forever.

Just then, Jimbo rushed up from the cabin. His face was white as a ghost. He ran to the side of the boat and blew chunks all out across the water. "Ahh shit! I think I'm dying....bluhhhh..."

The dolphins examined the chunks and took off. So much for a great mood.

• • •

Tad steered the boat up into the cut between the islands. He found the right place he was looking for, and dropped anchor. The big spade anchor dug into the muddy bottom. Tad put the boat in reverse and pulled the anchor tight, setting it securely. Once the boat was anchored, Tad heard a "WHHHRRRRRRRR" come from the cabin and smiled.

Tiffani came up from below holding two large plastic cups in her hand. "Boat drink, anyone?" Tad and Sandy each took one. It was an island drunk's dream drink. Fresh strawberries blended with ice and spiced rum with a pineapple wedge garnish. There was even the ubiquitous little umbrella.

Ramon, Tiffani and Jimbo came out into the deck salon, each holding a drink. Jimbo surveyed the surroundings. "Well, boy, this ain't bad. Not too bad at all. What are all them trees on those islands?"

"Those are called mangroves. Those mangroves formed all of these islands, or keys. The roots help hold the sediment as the tide comes in and out. There are hundreds of these tiny mangrove islands up and down the keys. For our purposes, they help protect us from the wind so we get to have a quiet anchorage without the boat rocking all around."

As they finished up their drinks, Ramon stepped out of the deck salon and on to the deck. He hooted loud and sprinted to the rear of the boat. His momentum carried him about ten feet through air before he hit the water with a big splash. "Hey everyone! Come on in!"

Jimbo looked out skeptically. "You all go on in. I'm going to stay up here and fiddle with this GPS unit."

Tad, Sandy and Tiffani spent the next thirty minutes splashing around. The water in the mangrove creeks was more cloudy than out in the ocean, but it was somewhat warmer. As the sun began to disappear over the mainland, they climbed out of the water. They stood around the deck, dripping water and toweling off. A smaller sailboat motored in towing a dinghy, obviously looking for an anchorage.

"Hello there! Mind if we share your anchorage?"

Tad called out, "Not at all."

The smaller boat motored around in water far too shallow for the Morris to sail in. Jimbo asked, "How do they get all the way up there? That water is mighty shallow."

Tad explained. "That is a MacGregor sailboat. It's twenty-five feet long. They have a swing keel. That means the keel retracts up into the boat. They can float that boat in a foot of water. It's a pretty neat idea. I used to have one just like it in California."

The smaller boat swung into the wind and dropped anchor. Soon they were anchored.

WHHHRRRRRRRR! Tiffani emerged again. Ramon bent his head in deference. "Oh lady of the blender. Thou comest at my moment of greatest need. I shall drink to your divine capability as a mixologist. As

I survey this chalise of nectar, I realize that I am a man without want."
Ramon turned the cup up and took a big swig. Two seconds later he
was cringing. "AHHH! Brain freeze!"

Everyone laughed. Jimbo was looking at the small boat. "Tad, why
don't you get on the radio and invite them over here for a drink?"
Tiffani raised her eyebrows at Jimbo's sudden display of humanity.

Tad picked up the VHF radio. "*Wild Hair, Wild Hair, this is Who's
Your Daddy, over.*"

There was a pause, then the radio squawked. "*Who's Your Daddy,
this is Wild Hair, over.*"

"*Wild Hair, we wanted to invite you over for a daiquiri. How about it?*"

"*Be right over.*"

The other boat was about two hundred yards away, anchored nearer
to shore. The couple climbed in their rubber inflatable dinghy and
motored over. They tied off at the stern of the Who's Your Daddy and
climbed aboard. The man carried a bottle of Captain Morgan's rum,
while the woman brought a paper bag. "Munchies!" the lady said.

Introductions were made all around. The couple, Carlton and
Lynn, was from Georgia. Tiffany kept the blender growling. The two
were headed down to Key West also. They were members of a sailing
group called the Conch Cruisers. A couple of times a year, the group
assembled in Florida and sailed in a flotilla. This year, they were meeting
in Key West and sailing to the Bahamas. This was their fourth time
making the Bahamas trip.

Jimbo was astounded. "You mean you sail all the way to the
Bahamas in that little boat?"

Carlton explained. "We pick our travel days carefully, so the weather
is not so bad. But yes, we've done it three times. It's a blast. I'd love to
do it on this boat. What a beautiful sailboat."

Jimbo beamed. "Let me show you around." And he did. As Jimbo
and the couple poked into every nook and cranny below, Tad explained.
"This is how it is. This is why sailing is so much fun. Put two sailboats
in one anchorage and soon everyone is throwing back beer and drinks,
having fun. It's the best way to meet the best people around. I love
cruising."

They all sat around the cockpit for a couple of hours. Ramon
brought a cooler of iced down Coronas. Tiffani put in a Buffett CD.

Jimmy philosophized for the crowd. *"...Give me oysters and beer for dinner every day of the year and I'll feel fine..."* Tad could not remember a better evening spend in a long time.

They drained cold beer, told sailing stories and watched the sun go down. The mood was very upbeat. Jimbo laughed and told off-color jokes. Ramon made goo-goo eyes at Tiffani, Carlton and Lynn regaled the group with stories and Tad and Sandy relaxed a little.

Sandy smiled at Tad, "Look at that sunset. Is it always like this?"

"No, not really. Sometimes it is better."

"I think I am going to put a house right over there and never leave."

Tad didn't think that was such a bad idea.

When the sun was good and down and the beer was good and gone, the boat guests climbed in their little dinghy and putted off to their boat. Jimbo stood, stretched and scratched his hairy belly, yawning loudly, "Hell's bells! C'mon Tiffani! Let's get on to bed. Early morning tomorrow, right Tad?"

Tad raised his Corona in a mock toast. "Up with the chickens."

Tiffani looked at Jimbo, "They have chickens here?"

Ramon piped up, "They're all in Key West. Chickens tomorrow."

Tiffani smiled, "Okay! Chickens tomorrow."

Jimbo said, "He's bullshittin' you, Honey. Use your head. There's no chickens here. Tell here, Ramon! She don't think too well sometimes."

Ramon smiled, "Lot's of chickens, Jimbo. Bone Island Chickens."

Tiffani and Jimbo disappeared below. Ramon looked at Tad, who was doing his best to send a telepathic message. *"You're getting sleepy. Sleeeeeepy. Go away now."*

Ramon, not to be one to miss a signal, faked a really bad yawn and begged leave of Tad and Sandy. He headed below and left the two in the cockpit. Ramon sent his own telepathic message, *"Go gettum Tiger."*

Tad pretended to adjust his seat, but really slid over in the cockpit, closing the thirty-six inch gap between Sandy and him by ten inches or so. Chalk one up for Mr. Sneaky. "So what are you planning to do once we get your sister back?"

"Well, I'll probably go back home. I have some things going on that I need to take care of. What about you?" Tad slid another few inches closer. Mr. Sneaky, meet Mr. Tricky. This girl doesn't stand a chance.

"What sort of things?"

"Just things."

"Things that involve a guy?"

Sandy smiled and stared at the beer she was nursing. "No, Tad. There is nobody in my life right now."

"That's good."

"You think?"

"Well, not like that's good in a bad way, but that's good in a good way. Does that make sense?"

"Tad, at this rate, it will be sometime past two in the morning before you finally slide over here next to me. Step it up."

Tad said, "I've got a better idea. Come on." He offered here his hand and led her to the back of the boat. They stood on the swim platform watching the moon shimmer on the water. He took off his t-shirt and threw it up on the deck. Sandy took off here t-shirt and threw it on top of his. They both removed their shorts, as well as their undergarments. He tried unsuccessfully to not stare at her standing there naked, but couldn't quite contain himself.

"Follow me." He quietly climbed down the swim ladder into the water and swam away from the boat. Sandy followed. They swam down the mangrove island a couple of hundred yards, far enough away to be out of earshot of the *Who's Your Daddy*.

The couple from the other sailboat was out in their cockpit with all the lights out. The man poured his wife another glass of wine and said, "Hey, isn't that two of those people from the other boat?"

"No. That's Aquaman and the Little Mermaid."

"Thanks, Dear. Good one. Really. Not." Carlton moved close to Lynn and hugged her. "Hey look, they're hugging, like us."

"No again, Cassanova. They're not hugging."

He looked again. "Guess you're right. That's not exactly hugging."

She looked at her husband. "Not exactly."

"Well," Carlton said, "If they are not going to be like us, maybe we should be like them."

"Now you're talking, you bull-hunk of a man."

The two tossed back the remainder of their wine and headed below.

The only sound in the anchorage was gentle splashing somewhere over near the island.

• • •

The sun announced its arrival the following day by peeking over the mangroves. Ramon climbed out of the cabin shortly past six-thirty. Tad and Sandy were asleep on the cockpit seats. Her shirt was on backwards.

Ramon grinned as he made his way to the mast. *You low-down, dirty dog. On behalf of manly men everywhere, I salute you,* he thought. Ramon surveyed the still, morning water. He looked intently, a man with a purpose. Suddenly he took off running for the back of the boat. "Aiiiiiyiiiiiiiyiiiiiiii!!!!!!" Greg Louganis would have been proud of the effort Ramon put out trying to execute a perfect one and a half flip with a half twist. What really occurred, just before he struck the water, resembled Evil Kenevil at Caesar's Palace. SPLASH!!!

Ramon surfaced, scaring a school of baitfish that rocketed out of the water and toward the safety of the mangroves. "Whoooo Boy! Get up! Get your sorry butt out of bed and let's get going! Dragons to slay! Mountains to climb!" He went under and surfaced about thirty feet away.

"Chickens! Oh my God! It's chickens! Right here in Chicken Bay. BRRRAAAAACK, BRRRRAAACKKK!" Ramon continued to make chicken noises and ramble on about nothing in particular.

Tad and Sandy, assaulted by Ramon's splashing and rambling, sat up and looked at each other. Tad said, "I wondered how you would look this morning."

"Well?"

"Look pretty good to me."

Sandy moved closer and talked quietly, "Listen, Tad, about last night. Let's sort of keep this thing under wraps and give it time to work out, okay?

"Yeah. No problem. Now go brush your teeth and we'll go swimming. I like swimming with you."

"For your sake, that water better be cold." She disappeared below and reemerged a few minutes later with Jimbo and Tiffani.

"I heard chickens! I'm sure I heard chickens, Jimbo! Did you?" Tiffani said.

"For crying out loud! There's no chickens here! You find a chicken and I'll kiss every ass in Arkansas."

Ramon surface right next to the boat, but so close to the hull that Jimbo and Tiffani couldn't see him. "BRRRAAAAACCKKK! Gonna be some happy boys in Arkansas today!" He sank again and headed underwater for points unknown.

Everyone, except Jimbo, broke out with laughter. Jimbo turned to Tad, "Is he always like this?"

"Only when he hasn't had his medication."

"Ah, shit. Okay, he's pretty funny. Hey Scarface! You got me on that!"

Ramon was treading water behind the stern. "Come on in, everyone. What you waiting on?"

Tad and Sandy dove in. Tiffani climbed down the stairs. Jimbo stood on the deck. "I don't think I feel like swimming."

Tad said, "Hey, Jimbo, you swim first thing in the morning so you don't smell like crap this afternoon from what all you did last night. Get it?"

"Yeah. I get it." Jimbo carefully stepped on the top step on the swim ladder. Then he went to the next one. Slowly. Eventually, he was standing on the bottom rung and he carefully pushed off.

"This feels pretty good!" he said.

Just then, Ramon jerked once and again. His face got deadly serious, and then turned to a look of terror. "OH MY GOD!! ITS GOT ME! DO SOMETHING!" He jerked once to the left and once to the right and disappeared underwater.

Everyone froze in place. The seconds seemed like an eternity.

Tiffani thought, *"Where did he go?"*

Jimbo thought, *"I'm getting the hell out of here!"*

Sandy thought, *"What got him?"*

Tad thought, *"Not again."*

Ramon came blasting through the surface, "AAAHHHHH! SHARKKKK! RUN FOR YOUR LIFE!!!!"

That did it for Jimbo. Doing his best St. Vitus Dance stroke, he frantically swam for the boat. His arms were cartwheeling and feet kicking in an asymmetrical frenzy of wasted effort. He slipped off the first rung, banging his hurt toe and screamed, "AAHHHHHHHH SHIT, SHIT, SHIT!!!"

Tiffani looked confused. "It's a school of them! We're surrounded!"

Sandy looked at Tad with one eyebrow raised, as Ramon continued to thrash around in the water, making grotesque contortions of his face, brought on by the crushing bites of the yet unseen shark. Tad considered swimming to Key West. Right then.

Ramon, "AHHH, IT'S GOT ME!"

Jimbo, "AHHH SHIT, MY TOE!"

Tiffani, "IT BIT HIS TOE. WE'RE SURROUNDED!"

About that time, the small sailboat sharing the anchorage, the Wild Hair, motored by. Carlton leaned out, "What's all the yelling?"

Ramon immediately ceased. "Nothing much, Carlton. How are you?"

Carlton looked confused. "No, I mean what's the yelling about?"

Ramon answered again. "We're doing great. Hope you have a good day too."

Carlton shifted his gaze to Jimbo, who was dangling from the ladder, staring down at something in the water with great trepidation in his eyes. "Hey Jimbo! Morning! See you and your boat in Cayo Hueso this evening?"

Jimbo tried to act calm and slide back down in the water. "Naaah! We're headed to Key West."

The couple looked at each other, suppressing a grin. "Well alright then. Fairwinds! We'll be near Tank Island!" And the Wild Hair sailed off, leaving the five of them in the water.

Jimbo, not a man to be made a chicken of (keys chicken or any other kind), pushed off the boat and swam out near the others.

"That was funny. Really frickin' funny. I can't remember when I saw something quite that funny. I should have known there was no sharks here. That's stupid, but I gotta admit it was pretty funny."

Ramon touched his fingertips to his forehead and gave a little twirling salute to the group, much like an actor on stage acknowledges his performance. "Glad to be of service. But I have some bad news. This place we're in has sharks. They are right here with us right now.

Greys, lemons, bonnetheads, let's hope not bulls. They can be really nasty."

Jimbo smiled. "You got me once. Not again. Momma wasn't born last night."

The group stared at him.

Ramon said, "I'll bet I didn't raise a fool either."

Jimbo said, "Huh?"

"Nevermind."

They all climbed back aboard and toweled off. Jimbo announced, "I'm so hungry I could eat the east end of a west bound mule! What's for breakfast?"

Tad winced mightily and said, "Fruit. Croussants. Jam. Coffee. We need coffee.

Ramon agreed. "For once you are correct, my Anglo amigo. I shall prepare us coffee like none have seen since we left the old country." He disappeared below singing *Black Magic Woman*.

After a quick breakfast and requisite coffee, they weighed anchor and motored slowly out of the channel.

Tad signaled Jimbo over. "Jimbo, you want to take the wheel a little?"

Jimbo smiled and clapped Tad on the back. "Not just yet. You're doing a fine job. I'll drive some later on."

"No problem. I know you want to learn to pilot and sail and I don't want you to feel like I'm not living up to our agreement."

"Son, you just keep on driving the boat. You're doing a fine job and I appreciate it." Jimbo walked off to explore all the stainless steel gadgets that seemed to be randomly bolted to his boat.

Sandy came up behind him and ran her nails up his back. "Hey captain, how about some lessons?"

"I'm the man for the job. After that, I'll teach you about the boat, also."

"Calm down, Popeye. Show me these instruments and how they work."

Tad thought he would leave that one alone.

"This is the depth finder. See here how it says …" Tad spent the next hour showing Sandy all the gauges, electronics and communications equipment. "There's a lot more down below we have to install, but these are your basic pieces of equipment.

"What's that one do?"

"That's GPS. Global Positioning System. It's really simple. Watch." Tad showed her how to jump from screen to screen, how to enter waypoints, how to find your latitude and longitude and generally how to make it tell you where your are and where you need to go.

Sandy asked, "So you use this to navigate mostly?"

Tad shook his head. "No. That's a really big misconception. See the coastline there? A good sailor can navigate visually using the chart. Anyone who relies primarily on GPS and cannot visually navigate using a chart and their own two eyes is probably going to get in trouble one day. GPS is good to check positioning, but it can become too much of a crutch. But that's not the case out on the seas. If you cannot see land, GPS becomes extremely handy."

"Is it really accurate?"

"Very accurate."

"Let me try to put a waypoint in." She studied the chart of Key West, and found the anchorage near Tank Island. She began pushing buttons, slowly and deliberately. Two minutes later she handed it to Tad. "Check me out, skipper."

Tad studied the chart, then the GPS. He smiled, "You're a natural. It's right. It's perfect. " *"You're perfect,"* he thought.

The next nine hours were spent sailing with a fifteen knot wind out of the south. The big Morris yacht cut through the water with little effort. Ramon and Tad swapped off steering and tending the sails. Tiffani and Sandy talked much of the day and Jimbo puttered around down below. He would occasionally come up and enjoy the salt air, but only for a few minutes.

The *Who's Your Daddy* was making seven knots a half mile off of a key when everyone heard a thunderous roaring sound. Two FA-18's Navy fighter jets came screaming off the island toward the boat, not more than three hundred feet off the water. The noise was deafening when they passed over.

VVVVRRRRRRROOOOOOOOOOOOOMMMMMMMM-MMMMMMM! Ramon raised both fists in the air and greeted the jets, "WhoooooooooooHoooooooooooo! You hear that noise? You know what that sound is? Anyone know? How 'bout you, Sandy? You know?"

"What is an airplane? I'll have famous poets for four hundred, Alex."

"Sharp tongue you have, lassie. NO! I'll tell you what that sound is. It's the sound of freedom." Ramon turned to the departing jets and yelled out, "Go gettum boys! WhoooooooHooooooo! Kill'em all and let God sort them out!"

Sandy turned to Tad and mouthed, "Is he for real?"

Tad nodded and mouthed, "Later."

The jets climbed straight up in the sky and banked hard to the right. Jimbo came stumbling out from below. "We under attack? What the hell was that?"

Tad turned and pointed. "That, my friend, is Naval Air Station Key West. Right there."

Jimbo squinted and looked at the mangroves. "No shit? Doesn't look like much to me. I thought Key West was a little more, uh, fun-looking. The only building I see is that tower."

Tad explained, "That's not Key West. That's Boca Chica, which is two keys east of Key West."

"But you said it's the Key West Navy Station. Make up your mind. Been out in the sun too much?"

"Okay, I see where it is confusing. Jimbo, the Naval Air Station is on the island of Boca Chica, but it is called Naval Air Station Key West."

"So there isn't any Navy on Key West? It's all up here?"

"No, there's Navy facilities and installations on Key West. Four of them, to be exact."

"Right. I guess those are called Naval Air Station Boca Chica, right? I look like a dumbass?"

Tad gave Ramon a withering look that stopped short any response.

Tad patiently explained. "They are all a part of Naval Air Station Key West. They just are spread out over Key West and Boca Chica. There's also a Coast Guard facility as well as an army dive school here."

"Okay, what's that island there. The one that separates Key West from Boca Chica? Chicken island?"

"Well, actually it is called Stock Island."

Ramon muttered, "Could be Chicken Island. They got chickens."

Tiffany smiled. She was getting into the chicken gag.

Jimbo squinted hard. "Hey, that big building over there. It says… Oceanside Marina, Key West. What the hell? I thought you said this was Stock Island?"

"It IS Stock Island. They just call it Key West to attract business."

"Is every frickin' island here both Key West and some other name? We got a real estate identity crisis going on here. Wait, that's it! This is Key West, right!"

Everyone moved to the starboard side. Ramon spoke up, "Ladies and gentlemen, welcome to the lovely island of Key West, the most recent part of the nation to secede from the union, earning them the title of Conch Republic. Ah, yes! Margaritaville! Home to Hemmingway, Jimmy Buffett, Tennessee Williams and many strange and wonderful humans. The getaway that got away. Cayo Hueso, where it's easier to find a smuggled Cuban than a smuggled Cuban cigar. Breathe in the southernmost air and let the essence of paradise permeate your body. Let us pause."

Ramon bowed his head. Everyone stared. Sandy looked at Tad, but he only shrugged.

Ramon suddenly jerked into action. "OK! Enough rubbernecking! Let's get that blender going! Tiffani! Sandy! Move! There are thirsty men out here!"

More shrugging from Tad. As the two girls moved downstairs, Tad caught little snippets of their conversation, "…throw their asses over…" "…saltpeter in a daiquiri?…"

A sailboat about the size of the *Who's Your Daddy* was angling in on them, coming in from the ocean. It was heeling over and traveling quite fast. Tad and Ramon looked at the sailboat that was closing in to about four hundred yards. The other sailboat would soon overtake them. Tad and Ramon looked at each other, then back at the sailboat and then each other again. Ramon nodded. The two men moved to their stations. Tad announced, "Everyone up on deck. Come on, now! Forget the blender. You're in for a treat."

When everyone was on deck, Tad said, "Now sit here on the port side of the boat and be calm. Let's go Ramon!" A mad clicking, grinding noise occurred and the head sail began to flatten. The *Who's Your Daddy* began to heel sharply to starboard. "Up on the rail. We need rail meat!" Tad shouted over the rushing wind.

More clicking as Ramon surveyed the sails, looking for some seemingly unseen indication of whether or not the sails were trimmed right. The *Who's Your Daddy* was screaming through the water. As the boat dove down a swell, the starboard side would immerse itself in water.

The other boat was doing much the same. Both boats were about even and a little over fifty yards away from each other. The other boat was named *Serendipity*. It was painted on the bow of the boat. Sandy called out, "Tad, what is happening? Why are we racing those people?"

Tad motioned for her to sit nearby.

"Because they're racing us!"

"But they'll stop if we stop, right?"

"I hope they don't stop! This is great!"

The two boats sliced through the water, each heeling way over. Ramon continued to give the sails his rapt attention. On the *Serendipity*, two guys were trimming sails while one was at the helm. The race continued, neck and neck for five more minutes.

"Tad, when are we going to stop this?"

"Sandy, I thought you liked sailing."

"I do, but this is scary. The boat is going to fall over."

"Nope. That will not happen. Up on the rail! Let's go."

Jimbo and Tiffani seemed to be enjoying the race.

Jimbo barked out, "What's the matter ladies? You wanna eat our dust? Hang on!"

Tiffani corrected him, "Jimbo, we're in the water. There's no dust."

"I know that Honey. It's just an expression."

The two boats surged on. Two power boats were following them off to the side, hooting and hollering their approval. One was clearly pulling for *Serendipity* and the other for the *Who's Your Daddy*.

The VHF radio cracked to life. "*Who's Your Daddy, this is Serendipity. To the Channel Marker?*"

"*Roger,*" Tad said.

And the race continued. The two big yachts traded positions, first Tad gaining a slight advantage and then the other boat. "Less than a mile to go! Jimbo, we're racing to that big buoy. See it?"

Jimbo squinted and said, "Yes I do! Pour it on, Tad. Beat these boys like a rented mule!"

Sandy said, "Why don't you all just pull out your penises and measure them. That would solve this thing more expeditiously, wouldn't it?"

Tad laughed. "No, it's not like that! OK, it's exactly like that, but this is the best kind of sailing. Life slow, sail fast. A great man said that. You may never sail like this on a yacht like this again, so enjoy the moment. Wait a minute, you're father's rich. So you might, but you never have before so act like you like it."

The buoy was about a quarter mile away. The two power boats had zoomed ahead to see who crossed the imaginary line. Tad hollered, "Ramon, we need some juice! Let's go!"

Ramon replied in a Scottish accent, "She can't take any more, Captain. She'll break apart!"

The two boats continued on; spray flying all over the deck, occupants on the high side of the boat. As the boats passed the buoy, the power boats sounded their horn. Ramon released some lines, and the boat stood up again. The *Serendipity* slowed down also. Tad looked over to the helm of the competitor at their skipper who looked back at him. They both nodded. They both looked back to the power boats, who were side by side. Both power boaters had coolers out and one was transferring handfuls of cold beer to the other cooler in the other boat.

One power boat took off to the shore, while the other motored in between the two sailing yachts.

Tad said, "Well?"

The guy steering the power boat was the recipient of handfuls of beer. "It was close!"

"Yeah, but who won?"

The guy looked confused. Then he smiled, "I won! Won a case of beer!"

The other skipper said, "Who'd you take?"

The powerboater said, "Not you, Buddy. I bet on the *Who's Your Daddy*."

"Sweet! Oh Baby! Come to Papa!" Jimbo bellowed to no one in particular. He pantomimed spiking the football. "Boom! That's my baby! Go cry to your Mama!"

Tad looked at the other skipper like, "Sorry about this guy."

The other skipper mouth, "*Owner?*"

Tad nodded. Enough said.

The skipper picked up the radio and said, "Captain Tony's. Nine O'Clock."

Tad said, "Roger."

Jimbo continued his celebration with the Icky Shuffle and a really bad moonwalk.

Sandy said, "Who is he?"

Tad said, "I don't know. Just some guy with a sailboat."

"No. I mean Captain Tony."

"Oh! There's this bar on Duval Street called Captain Tony's. Actually it's just off Duval Street, but you get the idea. We're going to meet him there at nine o'clock."

"What for?"

"What for? Well… to drink a beer with him, that's what for."

"I thought you didn't know him."

"I don't. But we did just race and that calls for festivities. Beside we are here in Key West after all."

"What about the other thing?"

Tad's eyes showed concern. "That's tomorrow. We'll worry about that then. Tonight, we have fun."

Chapter Ten

The *Who's Your Daddy* gently docked at the Key West Harbor. Tad announced, "Girls, there's showers in that building there. Ramon and I will secure the boat. Jimbo, you can get cleaned up or whatever else you want to do."

Jimbo surveyed the harbor. There were hundreds of boats of every kind. Sailboats from tiny to massive. There were multi-masted schooners, catamarans, ketches, sloops and some things that defied description. There were massive power boat yachts, fishing boats, pleasure boats and funny looking flats boats. There was one boat painted gray like a World War II era PT boat. "Hey Tad. Look at that piece of crap imitation PT boat."

Tad said, "It's the real thing. The only one in private ownership."

Jimbo grunted and walked away, down the dock.

With the girls gone to the shower room and Jimbo gone to do whatever he was going to do, Tad and Ramon paused and sat down in the cockpit seat.

Ramon asked, "What now?"

"We call Murph."

"Do it."

Tad pulled out his cell phone from a bag he had stowed below. He dialed the numbers and the phone rang three times. "Bob's Colostomy Supplies – Bob speaking."

"Murph"

"I said this was Bob."

"Cut the crap, Murph."

"It's Bob and I bag it, not cut it. OK, you got me, you scoundrel. Where are you?"

"In Key West. Where are you?"

"Nearby, Thaddeus. Nearby. I trust the package arrived?"

"Yes it did."

"And I trust you find the girl suitable?"

"She's OK."

"Just OK? Thaddeus, I am sorely disappointed in you. I think you will find her extraordinary if you give her a chance."

Tad smiled devilishly and thought, *"I gave her a chance, alright…!"*

"Where's the swap, Murph?"

"Tomorrow night. 331 Elizabeth Street. There's an old dilapidated house there. You sit on the porch. They will contact you there."

"How's Sandy supposed to make the identification?"

"She's not. Too dangerous. We've decided to take her out of the operation. From now on she's just cargo."

Tad's head reeled. "What the … What are you doing, Murph? This was supposed to be a simple swap! Now it's too dangerous! What's going on?" Ramon grabbed him by the arm to make him quit raising his voice to the cell phone. "Where are you? I want to talk to you, now!"

Click. The line went dead.

Ramon said, "You are one smooth operator. Just scared him into submission. I'll bet he's changing his diapers right now."

Tad continued to stare at the phone. *Riiinnnggg!*

"Yeah?"

"Be in front of the Flagler Museum in ten minutes. An old friend will pick you up." Click.

Tad said, "Let's go."

• • •

Tad and Ramon stood in front of the Flagler Museum. Henry Flagler was the entrepreneur who civilized the Keys. He built a railroad from the tip of Florida to the farthest point, Key West. He's pretty much the patriarch of everything south of Miami.

Tad looked at his watch. "Don't worry, Tad. Murph's not sloppy."

A dark, nondescript sedan pulled up. "Alright, ladies! Let's go." Both Tad and Ramon looked in and smiled. They got in.

"Baker. Should have known. You at the dive school again?"

Baker looked over and smiled as he almost, *almost* made the yellow light. "Uh, …no. OGA."

"OGA? No way. What's up with that?" Ramon queried. Ramon and Baker seemed to be cut from the same cloth. Both were unpredictable, crazy and never dull to be around.

"Murph made me an offer I couldn't refuse. It's not so bad."

They pulled up into a hotel parking lot. The Southernmost Hotel. The walked silently into room 103.

Murph stood, as did three others. "Gentlemen, welcome to beautiful Key West! How good it is to see you again Thaddeus and Ramon. I feel as though we are long lost family reuniting!"

Ramon said, "I feel as though the excrement is piling up to my knees. Who are these guys?"

Murph turned and eyed the three as though he had never seen them before. "Ah, yes! Meet Paul, George and Ringo. They are here to assist."

"In what?"

"The operation."

"Which is?"

"As we said before, a swap. But with minor variations."

Tad winced. This could mean lots of things – none of them good. "What variations?"

Murph said, "Sit down. Both of you."

They sat. Either Paul or George handed Tad and Ramon a sheet of paper. They had seen this before – Statements of Non-Disclosure. Tad and Ramon glanced at each other and at Murph. He smiled sweetly. "Let's get this out of the way."

They both signed the document that guaranteed that they kept their mouths shut or ended up in someplace where no one would ever be able to ask questions. Or dead.

They handed the documents back to George, or was it Paul?

Murph began to explain. "It started in Virginia with Johnny and his fiancée, Elizabeth. She was kidnapped. We became involved immediately. The baddies behind it are part of a bush league eco-terrorist group. At least that is what they want everyone to think. In reality, they are a splinter group of what used to be an active IRA. They have replaced all the college rejects that were in the eco-terrorist group with pros. Their sole purpose is to raise money by squeezing corporations who are more concerned about their image than ridding the world of scum like these.

"They're pros, Tad. They shot Johnny and took Elizabeth. You are to deliver the package to them. They will give you Elizabeth. You go home with the girl. Leave them to us. End of story."

Tad mulled over the story. "No way. There's more. You're hiding something. This is going to end badly. What is it?"

Murph continued, "We have to take out the leaders. It is simply an imperative. But we cannot take a chance on losing the girl, Thaddeus. For God's sake, the family has already lost one daughter to this group. No more. Just give them the package and take the girl. Walk away and enjoy your money. What is the problem?"

"What is in the package?"

"Who knows? A billion dollars. A trip to Tahiti. Who cares? Make the swap, Thaddeus."

"Why don't you want Sandy there? I thought her old man insisted."

"He changed his mind."

Tad and Ramon sat still. For a full minute, they sat quietly. Ramon finally broke the silence and turned to TAD, "I don't know what it is, but he's holding out. Something smells funny here. It's up to you."

Tad nodded at no one in particular. Murph breathed loudly and opened the bed room door. A young man walked out and over to Tad and Ramon. He didn't look very good. His color was pale and he didn't have use of his arm. He obviously was in a great deal of pain.

Tad and Ramon looked at him. Ramon spoke first. "Hello Johnny."

• • •

"Who did this to you?" Tad asked.

"I don't know. A man and a woman, plus some gomers helping them."

Tad closed his eyes and looked pained. Very pained. It was all clear now.

"Murph – you're such a bastard. You're going to kill them and Johnny's going to verify if it is them. You don't want Sandy to be there in case this thing goes south. If the girl gets hurt, it cannot get back to daddy that you screwed this up. Best of all, I'm right in the middle of it. Some swap." Tad looked up at Murph. "Tell me I'm not right."

Murph opened the mini-fridge. He took out a bottle of Perrier and opened it. He took a long swig. "You always were a pretty sharp lad. Yes, you are, young Thaddeus. Close, but not perfect. One – yes we are going to take a crack at getting the baddies. Two – yes, Johnny is going to make sure that we get the two in charge. Three – we will get the girl out safe. Do you read me? Safe. No mistakes. We get her out safe and eliminate the garbage of the world."

"Who are the leaders? Who are this man and woman?"

Ringo laughed. "Yeah. Right."

Murph shot him a glare that could melt steel. "I'll thank you to keep your comments to yourself. I determine who has a need to know. Got it?"

Ringo looked like a scolded child. "Yeah. Got it." He studied the tops of his shoes.

Murph continued. "Since you seem to feel somewhat uncomfortable about my plan, I'll go on. The two baddies – Michael O'Brien and Catherine Hayes. Rising stars in the wide world of terrorism. They aerated young Jonathan in Alexandria with several nine millimeter rounds. I think they will be here. I do not know what is significant about Key West, except the obvious. Cuba. So there you are. Either they get the booty and scurry away to beautiful Habana or we bury them. The people working with them are foot soldiers. They will be working strictly for the cash. No inside connections."

Tad interjected, "Which means they take it in the neck."

"If they wish. Or they could surrender peacefully. Throw out their guns and come walking out with their hands in the air. What do you think?"

"I think they would rather die than be captured by you and the Fab Four. But what about O'Brien and Hayes? How are you going to take them alive?"

Murph smiled.

Tad continued. "OK, so no one leaves here alive. What does this all accomplish?"

Murph took another sip of his Perrier. He closed his eyes and swished it in his mouth like a connoisseur. "In all fairness, I have told you far more than I should have. Let's just say that two of the most dangerous criminals in recent history will be a distant memory and Jonathan's fiancé will be home with him."

"So how do I do this without getting killed? Sit on a porch? What kind of plan was that?"

Murph finished his water and stared into the bottle like he expected to find a genie. "That was a ruse, Thaddeus. I didn't want anyone with electronic ears to overhear us. You will make the swap on Duval Street. Your instructions are to walk down Duval Street wearing a particular shirt. When you pass Catherine Street, you will be summoned into a bar. Someone will come up to you and ask you if you brought the doughnuts. Give him the bag with the package in it. He will walk away. Inside the bar where he confronted you will be a girl wearing a Washington Redskins shirt. That's Elizabeth. Get her and leave. Tell her the following line, "Dixon sent me to take you home. Can you remember that?"

Tad nodded. "Dixon sent me to take you home. Check. Who is Dixon?"

"A good man. Now focus, Thaddeus. You are to take her to your boat and set sail immediately. You will dock at the Naval Air Station's marina. We will meet you there and take the girl. Then it's happy trails."

"Where's Ramon in all this?"

"Since I know it would be fruitless to try to keep him away, he will be with you."

"With me? Wouldn't that be blowing my cover?"

"Not at all. Here is the t-shirt you will wear." Murph pulled out a bag and threw it to Tad. Tad unfolded the t-shirt and held it out. Across the front it said, I'M NOT GAY. THOSE ARE LIES TOLD BY THE MEN I HAVE SLEPT WITH.

Tad solemnly eyed it and said, "You have to be kidding."

Murph handed Ramon a t-shirt. It said, PENIS – IT'S NOT JUST FOR BREAKFAST ANY MORE. Ramon was chattering so fast in Spanish that Tad could only understand a few words. They were not friendly.

Murph continued, "So you see it is brilliant, gentlemen. You are posing as homosexual lovers visiting the fabulous Keys. You will both blend in perfectly and be able to navigate Duval Street without scrutiny. What more could you ask?"

Ringo and Paul began to snicker. George had his face buried in his hands, trying not to piss off Murph, quite unsuccessfully. Baker was making kissing motions and winking at Ramon. Tad said, "OK, welcome to Operation Frat Boy Hazing. Let's get on with it."

Murph gave them the package, the time and place. The next night. Ten o'clock. Be there.

Ramon and Tad walked back to the boat. Tad was war-gaming the plan back and forth. It was pretty smart on the part of the kidnappers. There were glitches – how would they know if the girl was really Elizabeth? How would they know if there really was a girl in the bar at all? Where were the two leaders in all of this? Surely they would not expose themselves. Too many holes in the plan.

When they got to the boat, Jimbo was standing on the dock talking to the owner of the sailboat in the next slip. Both had a blender pitcher of frozen margaritas in their hands. The entire pitcher. Like a massive mug. Both were half in the bag and having the time of their lives.

Jimbo slurred as he made introductions, "Tad! Come meet my new friend! This is Angus. Angus meet Theodore Altimore Hinkins."

Angus was half snockered himself and made introduction in a thick Scottish voice, "Theodore! Glad to meet ye, lad!"

Tad started to correct him, but decided there was no point. Jimbo continued, nearly shouting to Angus, who was nearly shouting back. "Angus, this boy can sail a boat! If I could sail like him and he had a feather up his ass, we'd both be tickled. You should have seen the way he kicked the shit out of this hunk of crap boat today!"

Angus seemed to pause, as if confused. "Now wait a minute! The boat he raced be my boat! Did ye not see me boat beat yours? We won fair and square! Me nephew was at the helm and he beat your worm-ridden galley by two lengths!"

Tad realized that while he and Ramon were gone, the boat they were racing had taken the slip next to theirs. The word *Serendipity* was emblazoned on the hull near the bow. Jimbo had been drinking for an hour with Angus and now only figured out he was his earlier nemesis.

"I didn't see you on board!" Jimbo charged.

Angus countered, "Ah, what do ye know, ye momma's boy? I was in the cabin, pukin' my guts out. BUT I WAS THERE! AND WE BEAT YOU, YOU DONKEY'S ASS."

"Beat us?" Jimbo roared! "We spanked you! Spanked ya, spanked ya…" Jimbo did the spank ya dance by bending over and spanking his own left buttock with his left hand while closing his eyes in mock enjoyment. The entire spank ya dance was done in a slow circle in a clockwise manner.

"…spank ya, span…"

Jimbo was almost about to complete his full rotation of the spank ya dance when Angus let loose with a shot to Jimbo's head with the glass blender pitcher. TWOCK! Jimbo dropped like a sack of concrete.

Jimbo lay on the dock in front of a horrified crowd, moaning softly and dribbling spit out of the corner of his mouth. Angus then began the Scottish version of the spank ya dance. "Spank ye! I spanked ye! I …" Angus rotated slowly, mocking Jimbo's dance. Tad did a double-take and reached down to help Jimbo, when Jimbo's eyes suddenly popped open.

It was like Glen Close in Fatal Attraction when you just knew she was drowned and dead in the bathtub and then, POP!… her eyes opened up and she was fully awake and ready for action. It was just like that.

Jimbo slammed his glass blender pitcher straight down on the top of Angus' foot, terminally interrupting the spank ye dance. Jimbo dropped also, but not quite like a sack of concrete. His drop was more like a flailing banshee corkscrewing to the earth. He let out a devilish howl and dropped, landing partially on the dock and partially on Jimbo, who watched in horror as he was about to be smushed by the ragin' Scotsman.

Actually, only one small part of Angus touched Jimbo, and that was his bony knee to Jimbo's groin, which caused the induction of another member to the screamin' banshees duet. The two drunken men rolled on the dock, howling in pain. Angus vomited on Jimbo, causing Jimbo to vomit on himself. Tiffani and Sandy turned their back and walked to the aft end of the yacht, concentrating on the vanishing point in the horizon. Anything to remove the last ten seconds of mental video stuck in RAM that haunted their minds. Tad backed away, certain that police, EMT's and God knew who else were on the way.

Ramon said, "Hey boys! Look out!" A blast of water hit the two infirmed men lying on the dock. Ramon had the presence of mind to grab a coiled water hose and go to work. "This'll do it. Yeah, that's right. Just lay there and we'll have you clean in no time."

He hosed off the two carefully, making sure no chunks were stuck in their hair, clothes or anywhere else. He had them stand up and hosed them some more. Twice Ramon hit Jimbo and Angus in the crotch with the stream of water, causing them to yelp and wince. One might think it was not by accident, and one would be right. When The Disgusting Scene was cleaned up, the two men retreated to their neutral boats, not speaking. Angus limped off to his boat, while Jimbo nursed a goose-egg knot above his ear of which Fred Flintstone would have been proud. Tiffani followed Jimbo down to either nurse him back to health or do him in for good – her expression could have communicated either intention.

Ramon walked over to the two glass pitchers on the dock and examined them carefully. He picked up the one that matched the blender on the *Who's Your Daddy*. He held it up and lectured to it, much like Hamlet and his skull. "Alas, you have proved yourself in battle, O chalice of malice. You have taken the mobility of thy enemy in battle. What cause have you to make beverages of merriment any more? None, I say to you. You will join me in honoring battles of yore. You, or should I say, *ye* have earned a place on the mantle of honor." Ramon tucked the glass pitcher under his right arm and gently carried it down below. Ramon emerged from the cabin, stepped off the boat and strolled down the dock. Sandy turned to Tad with a furrowed brow.

"OK, I give up. Is he certifiable? Clinically insane? What was that?"

Tad thought for a few seconds and spoke slowly, choosing his words carefully. "That? Well, it's like this. We go back a ways, as you know. In the past, we have had, how can I put it, *confrontations*, with… others. More than once Ramon has had to improvise in finding the right… uh… tool to use to solve the confrontation. When he or someone around him does find a significant… uh… improvised tool, he keeps it. He's got a shelf full of… tools in his room."

"By tools you mean weapons, right?"

"Right."

"Like what? Give me some examples."

"Examples. Well, there's two or three bottles. There's a sock. There's…"

"A sock?"

"Ah… with twenty dollars of quarters in it. There's a coconut. Could have been two, but the damn police in Tonga took the other one. There's a boat paddle, a can of Bean and Bacon soup (Ha, Ha!). Now that's a great story! We were…"

"Forget I asked. What's on tap for tonight?"

"Tonight we have fun. Experience life like only it can be experienced in Key West. Maybe Sloppy Joes. Without a doubt Captain Tony's. At midnight we end up on top of the Red Bull – butt naked."

"That's funny. It sounded like you said butt naked."

"I did. They have a nude bar that overlooks Duval Street. We won't go there, though. Just kidding." He was but he knew Ramon had a bad habit of ending up there.

"What about the job? The exchange? What is my role?"

"Your role? Hmmm. Well, the plan has changed a little. Your role has been minimized somewhat."

A dark look came over Sandy's face. "Minimized? You mind expanding on that word – minimized?"

Tad recognized a minefield when he was in one. He treaded on very carefully. "You see, it is felt that we can properly identify Elizabeth and to bring you would needlessly put you in harm's way."

"And who felt this way? You?"

Whoaa! Big frickin' heat-seaking, armor-piercing mine ahead! "No, no, no. Well, not exactly, but I am, of course, concerned about your safety."

"Sure you are. Who made the call?"

Tad squirmed. *Mr. Tricky has left the building.* "You know, he made the call."

"He?"

"Yes. He. HE he."

"Who is he? I mean the HE he?"

Tad lowered his voice to a whisper. "Murph. Him. He made the call."

Sandy seemed to contemplate this for a while. She said, "Murph."

"Right. You met him before you came down, right? He called me to let me know you were coming."

"Yes. Yes I did meet Murph. He's here and he doesn't want me to be near the swap. So that's it. Why do you think he's changed his mind?"

To navigate Sandy's minefield was one thing. To mess around with Murph was something altogether more dangerous. "I don't know. It's just the new plan. It's workable. You'll stay here with the boat."

"To make a fast getaway? You want me to keep the motor running?" she said dripping with sarcasm.

"Something like that. Look, we're bringing your sister back here and leaving immediately. That's what you wanted. What's the problem?"

Sandy thought for a while. "The problem is this – I am not here to identify Elizabeth. You could do that with a picture. I am here to make sure you all don't screw this up. My father wants a set of eyes on the ground to make sure this thing is done right."

Tad sat back in the cockpit seat and laughed and shook his head. "That's just perfect. Perfect! You've been reporting this to your father all along, haven't you? When you call on your cell phone, you've been giving status reports! And we're supposed to have operational security! That's just great. Who the hell is your father talking to? Who else knows about this?"

"I don't know."

"Right. Sure."

"Really, I do not know. I just call... him and report in. That's all."

Tad sighed. "This is not a game. When people like Murph get involved, it's for real. People die. They disappear. They leak blood and have bones break. I don't think you understand what's going on here."

"Maybe I don't. Tell me."

Tad measured his words. "As you have probably already figured out, Murph works for an Other Government Agency. OGA. You can use your imagination in figuring it out. He specializes in taking out really, really bad people. Terrorists. Scum of the Earth that needs to disappear. When Murph gets involved, it's serious."

"How do you know this? I thought you fixed boats for a living."

"In my past life, I was a soldier, as I said before. I just didn't say what kind of soldier. I was in a special operations unit. We did some hairy missions overseas. On the first mission, we went into Afghanistan to take out a radar site. There was a terrorist training facility next to it. Murph was there to check into that. The mission was compromised before we got there. Someone sold us out. We lost a few good men, but most of us got out."

"How were you sold out?"

"I'm not entirely sure, but I know this. We were all pissed off about it for a couple of weeks. Then one day, Murph comes back to our compound. Two days later, three of the supposedly "allied" officers, that is, those Afghanis who were there helping us, disappeared. Murph walked into our tent and dropped six ears on the table. He said, 'These are the lads. We're square.' Then he walked out."

Sandy thought intensely. "So what you're telling me is that these eco-terrorists, the...what is is...E.E.L. people are dangerous? I didn't take it that way at all. I thought they were kooks who hang out at coffee shops and write nasty letters to the university newspaper editorial section."

Tad exhaled, "It's complicated. Let's just say that you are safer here than there."

"So you are going to get Elizabeth and then what?"

"I'm coming back here with her."

"But what about Murph? Wait...he's not here to make any swap is he? He's here on his business, not our business. Damn it! What else are you holding back?"

"Look Sandy, there's different levels of business going on here. Let's stick to our business and leave Murph's business alone."

"What exactly is your business, if I might ask?" she asked frostily?

Tad picked up her hand and looked her directly in the eye, "A week ago my business was boats. Three days ago my business became Jimbo. Then your sister went to the top of the list. Now I have lots of business – getting Elizabeth, protecting you and pleasing Jimbo, in that order."

Sandy seemed to relax. "So you get her and come here. Fine. Did Murph give you the money to give them?"

Tad glanced at the cabin, "No, not at all! I've had it here all along. It's in my duffel bag. It's a CD, I think. No money. I suppose they take it and somehow transfer money. Who knows?"

Sandy went from zero to pissed in one point two seconds. "You've had it here and you didn't tell me? You idiot! I'm sitting here worried that you are going to screw up this whole thing and you don't even think to tell me this snippet of information?"

"What's to tell? It's not like it's a bag of money! It's just a CD ROM or something. So what? Now go down and check on Tiffani before I spank you, which you richly deserve. Git, woman. Go while your virtue is still safe. My self control is dimishing. Must... Not... Grab... Woman..."

Sandy stood and headed for the cabin. *Hey! Mr. Smooth – back in the house!* That poor girl never had a chance. Tad stood and searched for Ramon. He was two docks over. Tad could not hear him, but he was standing behind a cruising trawler, talking to a trio of college-aged girls. They seemed to hang on to his every word, giggling and smiling. Tad whistled, getting Ramon's attention. Ramon shot him a look that said, "So you caught me again, eh?" Ramon said something else and left the girls, who were visibly disappointed.

Ramon made it back to the *Who's Your Daddy* and stepped aboard. Tad queried, "Friends of yours?"

"It's terrible. These poor lasses are from some dreadful college in Massachusetts, Vermont, wherever, and their fathers sent them to Key West for a week. They are stuck here with no clue of what to do other than party, shop and chase boys. Why they had to resort to staying on that magnificent trawler over there. It's owned by Felicia's father, by the way."

"Felicia?"

"Yeah. She's standing next to Elke."

"Elke?"

"Yep. She's from Iceland. Her father sent her to America for college. She's friends with Babs, Felicia's cousin."

"Babs?"

"What are you, a parrot? They're just simple girls eking out a simple existence in New England and then, BAM, they're marooned in Key West for a week. It's a good thing I came along when I did."

Tad started to say, "*It is?*" but resisted. "Why is it a good thing?"

"Well, Thaddeus. Is it not apparent? I've invited them to Captain Tony's tonight."

Tad could feel his face flush. "Walk over here." They walked a few slips down. "I'm trying to do something with Sandy. It just might work out. And then you invite three nubile college girls to show up. This is good?"

Ramon beamed, "Nubile? You think they are nubile? Cool."

"Focus. If you're Sandy and you're sitting in Captain Tony's enjoying yourself and those three show up at your table, what do you think?"

Ramon nodded sagely. "Ahhh. I see. I would think... lesbian. The way I'm looking at those girls, who happen to be broke out with nubility, I must be a lesbian."

"Well, you would. You would probably think that if you are Sandy. But Sandy's Sandy and she's not going to be digging this. Hey, wait a minute. What about Tiffani? I thought you were after her, if of course she was not the girlfriend of the man who is paying our bills and supporting our lifestyle of avoiding occupational security."

Ramon pondered. "Tiffani. Hmmm. Once again, your logic prevails, Thaddeus. I cannot argue. It would be selfish of me to quash the hopes and dreams of dear Tiffani by showing up with other women who might appear to be competition. I'm a selfish ass. We shall go without the trio. I must inform Elke. Be right back."

Ramon trotted down the dock, hung a hard right and trotted to the second dock and trotted down to the trawler. The girls came out. "*Let's see,*" thought Tad, "*One with dark brown hair, one with light brown hair and... BINGO, a blonde. That's Elke!*"

"Penny for your thoughts." Tad jumped and turned around and saw Sandy who was looking at him looking at the girls who were looking at Ramon.

"Can you believe that Ramon? Comes all the way to Key West and runs up on his cousins. Long lost, thrice removed." Why Mr. Tricky, when did you return? Great to have you back.

"As long as his cousins stay over there, there won't be anything removed over here." She handed him a long neck beer. "What time are we leaving?"

"Assemble the troops. First dinner and then festivities."

"Tad, I'm not the concierge. You go get them yourselves. Besides, we have a little problem."

"What problem?"

"It's Jimbo."

Ramon came jogging back up. He was holding a plastic cup with Greek letters on it and filled with some sort of frozen concoction.

Tad continued, "He's a major problem, like hemorrhoids. What else is new?"

"He just dumped Tiffani. She's down there crying."

Tad and Ramon looked at each other.

Tad thought, *"Oh crap. This is going to screw up the charter. If the boss isn't happy, nobody's happy. What now?"*

Sandy thought, *"The dingleberry should have seen it coming. Stupid but sweet."*

Ramon thought, *"Yes! There is a God!"*

They all shuffled back to the boat.

Sandy asked Ramon, "How's your cousins?"

"Cousins? What cousins?"

• • •

So Jimbo was pissed like no man had been pissed before on the *Who's Your Daddy*. He was in fact so pissed that he refused to go with the others to eat and enjoy the night sounds of the southernmost island in the continental United States. He was not, however, so pissed that he couldn't open an expensive bottle of single malt scotch. And it came to pass.

Sandy consoled Tiffani with much compassion, *"He's goat vomit. He's a donkey turd. Get your ass up and come with us."* The breakup deeply affected Ramon, who wore an expression that said, *"Come, let me give you a hug. I feel your pain. I feel your sorrow. Let me hug you so that we both may feel better."* In passing, Sandy told Ramon, "You should have heartworm shots and a flea collar."

They all went to a restaurant that used to be a turtle processing facility. They sat on the deck, which stuck out over the water. The restaurant specialized in seafood, as one might expect. Ramon tormented the waitress, "Oh Agnes, how is the fresh conch? Were they harvested right out there?" Ramon pointed to the channel.

The waitress smacked her lips, sucked her teeth while she looked at Ramon. "It's Angie and the conchs are from Honduras. You can't catch conch here any more."

Ramon continued, "But of course. How about the oysters? They look good and nothing beats Key West oysters except Key West Chickens."

That made Tiffani smile a little. Oh, if it only made the waitress smile. "No sir. There are no oysters here. They're from Apalachicola."

"Heavens! Well let's fall back on the famous Keys Grouper! How's the grouper today?"

"The frickin' grouper is trucked in, mister." Angie was smacking her gum and glaring at Ramon who was greatly enjoying himself.

"You kiss your momma with that mouth? Do you have anything on the menu from Key West?"

"Shrimp. Big pink shrimp caught here. Really good."

Ramon stared intently, captivated with the offerings. He snapped the menu shut and announced, "Cheesburger. Medium Well. All the way – wait – hold those onions. Fries. Beer." Then in his best Elvis voice he said, "Thank you very much."

"What-EVER," Angie snapped.

Everyone else ordered. Shrimp. Fish. Tad ordered a dozen oysters on the half shell. The dining was excellent. As they were winding down the meal, Tad got everyone's attention. "Watch this."

They were sitting on a deck overlooking the water. He tossed a shrimp tail out on the water. Almost immediately, an enormous splash shattered the calm water and the shrimp tail was gone.

"What was that?" Sandy asked, genuinely perplexed and staring into the dark water.

"Tarpon. Big one. Probably over a hundred pounds," Tad said.

Ramon added, "Yeah and they can bite your leg clean off. Happens all the time."

Tiffani stared, wide-eyed, "Really?"

"Nah. I was just kidding. Tomorrow you can feed one. Right out of your hand. No joke."

Tiffany didn't look too sure, but grinned and played along. After a dessert of Key lime pie, everyone shuffled to the door and out into a beautiful night. The stars gleamed over the water as the group casually strolled down the waterfront. There was a wooden walkway, similar to a boardwalk, which seemed to go on for quite a ways.

They talked about the dinner. They talked about the boats. They talked about just about everything as they casually paced themselves down the waterfront. They had just passed a quasi-health food grocery store when Ramon said, "Hey everyone, wait right here. I'll be right back. Got a surprise."

He ducked into the dark around the side of the building and disappeared. The girls looked at Tad for an explanation, but he only shrugged. Sixty seconds later, Ramon came running toward the group. Running is not the right word, for he was dodging and weaving. He would dart to the left for a few steps and then dash to the right. He was running hard but making slow forward progress.

He hollered out, "Almost there…(pant, pant)…This is good… (wheeze, wheeze)…Here they are!"

Six small chickens broke out of the shadows on a dead run in any direction that Ramon was not blocking. They were small, rust colored birds who seemed on the verge of heart failure from being accosted by the crazy Cuban. Ramon continued herding the chickens until they were all on the wooden walkway. He stopped and bent down, panting like a man who just finished the marathon. "(pant, pant, wheeze)… THERE! I bring you…(pant, pant)…Key West Chickens!" He spread his arms wide like the benevolent lord who had just presented his vassals with sacred poultry.

Tiffani covered her face, and then broke out in a big squeal and ran to Ramon. "I knew you were telling the truth! You got these chickens – just for me! You're so sweet!" She threw her arms around him and hugged him hard, choking off critical oxygen that Ramon still needed from his chicken herding exhibition.

Sandy looked at Tad with one eyebrow raised. "Where's my chickens?"

"Chickens…uh, yeah. I'm working on it."

The six birds regained their composure and darted back into the shadows to do whatever Key West chickens do at night. The group, who was now clearly two couples, continued their walk. At some point they turned left and began to wind through streets.

Sandy said, "Is that where we are going? Where all the people are?"

Tad nodded, "Yep. That's it. That's Duval Street. It runs from the Gulf of Mexico to the Atlantic Ocean, which makes it the longest street in the United States."

Tiffani said, "Peachtree street back in Atlanta is really long, like over ten miles. So this street is longer than that? I thought the island wasn't that big."

Tad looked at Ramon like, "*You take this one.*"

Ramon cleared his voice, "It's not the longest in mileage. It's the longest because it runs from the ocean to the gulf. Kind of like a joke, get it?"

"No."

"Well that's OK because it's a stupid saying. Isn't that right, Thaddeus? Didn't you say something stupid? Wait, don't answer that. We leave your dignity intact. Longest street? Yeesh!"

Tiffani smiled because she didn't feel stupid and Ramon smiled back because he was so slick and Sandy smiled because Tiffani was so stupid and Tad smiled because he was visualizing hitting Ramon with a dead frozen chicken. Everyone smiled.

They stopped on Duval Street and looked both ways. People were crowding the sidewalks, going to and fro the bars, the stores and the restaurants. Sandy observed, "This looks a lot like Bourbon Street in New Orleans."

Tad nodded, "Something like that, but not quite so seedy. Same concept with an island feel. Shall we?"

And they began their walk. The night was clear and cool as they surveyed the t-shirt stores, the souvenir shops, fine clothing and jewelry stores and of course, the bars. Many fine restaurants dotted the landscape and the girls stopped to read each menu and comment on items that looked good.

Finally, Tad said, "Here's the place. Over here. Let's go in."

Sandy looked pensively at the big fish over the sign that read, *Captain Tony's*, "Here? This is where we are going?"

"Oh yes! This place is awesome. The oldest saloon in Florida. Ernest Hemmingway used to hang out here when he live here in Key West. This is a very cool place. Cold draft beer. Good drinks. All within the framework of Keys culture and positively saturated with a southernmost ambience. Lot's of memories here."

Ramon nodded, "He's right. It's out of our hands. In we go."

The four stepped up off the sidewalk and into the bar. Business cards covered the ceiling and support posts. A band was on stage banging out a Marshall Tucker melody, "*...Fire on the mountain, lightning in the air. Gold in them hills and it's waiting for me there...*" People were whooping it up, throwing back draft beers in little plastic cups with Captain Tony's picture on it.

Sandy said, "Remind me why we are here instead of somewhere communicable diseases are not an issue?"

Tad jumped right in, "This place is history! Living history! Hemmingway himself used to hang out here with his posse and drink with his friends and tell lies about the big fish they caught that day. Jimmy Buffett himself got his start on that very stage. Other significant things occurred right here!"

"Name three." Sandy Said.

Tad chose rather to ignore the request and move on, mostly because he couldn't. "Besides, there's a reason…There they are! Come on, over here."

He took Sandy's hand and led here to a corner table where three guys were sitting. Ramon and Tiffani followed. Tad stuck out his hand, "Hey skipper, I'm Tad. *Who's Your Daddy*. Glad to meet you."

The young man stood up and returned the handshake. "I'm Gavin. Call me Gav. This is William and Michael." Ramon and Tad shook hands, and introduced Tiffani and Sandy.

After Ramon scrounged up some chairs, they all crowded around the table. A pitcher of cold draft beer appeared and Ramon gave the waitress a ten dollar bill. "Gav, that's a beautiful boat you have!"

Gav had a slight Scottish accent. "Thanks. It belongs to Angus McFracken, of the Highland McFrackens. You've heard of them?"

Ramon's eyes opened wide, "No shit? The Highland McFrackens?"

Gav smiled slyly, "Oh, so you do know them?"

"Who doesn't? I thought you said McFricken, who I have never heard of, but then I realized that you said McFracken, which is totally different. Get out here! Old man Angus himself, here in Key West! Angus McFracken!"

Gav said again, "So you know of him, do you?"

Ramon drained his plastic cup of beer, "Nope. I was bullshittin'. Don't know any frickin' McFracken."

William and Michael exploded with laughter. Gav furrowed his brow, but began to chuckle himself. "Of course not. Well, now you do. I'm Gavin McFracken. These are my cousins William and Michael McFracken. We're frickin' McFrackens I guess."

William and Michael pounded on the table and hooted with laughter. Both boys were lucky to be a day over twenty-one and they were enjoying themselves immensely in a frat-boy-party sort of way. Gav and Tad immediately sank into a deep conversation, reliving every move of the race they had earlier that day. "…then I sheeted in until…" "…spilling wind but trying to…" Ramon had Tiffani's hand in his, staring at her palm and telling her fortune, "…this line here? It's your…uh…life line. And this one's your love line. That little crinkly one is…"

Sandy leaned over to Tad, who was discussing sail material and said, "I'm stepping out for some air. Be right back." Tad nodded and never missed a beat while Gav seemed captivated by the finer points of Kevlar sails.

She walked out the door and down the street, away from the smoky bar and loud band that was playing David Allen Coe, "…*I was drunk the day my Mom got out of prison…*"

The party continued in Captain Tony's until past eleven. Gav and Tad were hitting it off famously. Gav's cousins had rounded up two lost blondes who were in Key West for the night off a cruise ship. Ramon had Tiffani, the McFracken cousins and their impromptu dates and half the bar up doing some strange island dance while the band wailed away with a Buffett song, "…*You can hear it on the Coconut Telegraph, can't keep nothin' under their hat…*" The band played on and the beer flowed like cool, clear water rushing off of a mountain. Another Key West night out on the town – life was good, good, good.

At ten minutes to midnight, Tad realized that something wasn't right. He just couldn't put his finger on what it was but something was definitely not… "oh no!," he thought, "Sandy!" He walked out on the dance floor and tapped Ramon on the shoulder, which greatly disturbed his island rendition of the funky chicken as the band picked up steam, *"...play that funky music white boy. Play that funky music..."* "Sandy's gone. I don't know where she is."

Ramon continued flapping his wings, "How could you know, Ensign Hornblower? She left after you neglected her so." He did a flapping 360 degree turn, much to the delight of Tiffani and fifteen other funky chicken-ers."

"What do you mean? You saw here leave?"

Ramon embellished his funky chicken with a series of facial contortions, simulating the ecstasy of the dance. He was clearly the crowd favorite and king of the beer soaked-dance floor. "Yes, you clod. She said she was leaving. You said OK. And she did. Oh Good God! Look at that!"

Some rat bastard tourist from Akron was doing the dreaded one-legged funky chicken, much to the delight of the crowd. He wiggled on leg in the air while he deftly flapped and smiled for the audience. Madness! When he did the chicken-head-bobbing, Ramon knew that he had lost his following for good. The King is Dead – Long Live the King.

"Come on Tiffani. Let's get out of here," Ramon said as he pouted leading her back to the table. Tad announced that they had to leave, and away they all went.

As they were walking back to the dock, Tad said to Gav, "I don't know if you know this, but your uncle and my client beat the shit out of each other on the dock."

Gav furrowed his brow, "Really? What about?"

"Who knows? Well, it was the race – and the spank you dance. That pissed them both off. I just wanted to let you know that they are liable to still be mad and since we are docked in slips right next to each other..."

"Oh, I see. Well, we'll just have to try and reason with them, won't we?"

The group made its way down the dock and to the boats. The lights were out on both boats, but there was two people sitting on the dock leaning up against a plastic dock box. They cautiously approached and saw that Jimbo and Angus were sitting there, laughing and drunkenly slurring their words. They each had their glass blender pitchers, but each pitcher was about one third of the way full of a brown liquid. Scotch, of course.

They were hammered, shit-faced, three sheets in the wind, falling down, stone cold drunk. Jimbo had a red knot on his head that had come down some, but was beginning to bruise. Angus's right foot was swollen up like a Bilbo Baggins. Since Angus had puked on Jimbo's shirt, Jimbo decided to go shirtless rather that find a clean shirt to wear, which afforded anyone walking by a good look at his sweaty, hairy back.

They laughed at some joke that didn't make sense and clinked pitchers and took another drink. "To Granny's floors!" "No, that's Frannie's drawers" "Haw! Haw!" Angus leaned over and spit, this time off the dock instead of on Jimbo. Jimbo leaned over and put one finger on his right nostril and blew several boogers out of his left nostril into the water. It was an ugly, grisly thing much like a car wreck on the interstate where bodies were strewn everywhere – You know you shouldn't look but you just couldn't help yourself.

Gav piped up, "Good Gawd! These two should be in a sideshow!"

Tad agreed, "Let's get them to bed." Everyone agreed, but didn't want to touch them. Ramon was Johnny-on-the-spot again, "Look out!" The hose of sobriety spewed forth the stream of water that drenched both of the drunken men. They let forth a barrage of profanity that would make a pirate blush. After each were hosed off, the respective crews hauled their not-very-respectable boat owners off to dry off the get some shut eye.

Ramon took Tiffani off to the side and said, "Look, let's play it smart. I'll talk to Jimbo tomorrow. You crash out with Sandy tonight. Don't worry about it."

Tiffany took his hands and said, "I'm not worried." She stood up on her toes and lightly kissed Ramon on the lips. "Goodnight." She disappeared in the cabin.

Ramon walked over to Tad who was rolling up the hose. "Handy hose you got there. Where's your woman? Doing the funky chicken with another caballero?"

"Real funny you are. I don't know where she is."

"Why don't you ask her?" Sandy was approaching their slip, walking at a deliberate pace and carrying several shopping bags.

Tad tried unsuccessfully to intercept her, "Uh… sorry about that back at the bar…you know…"

Sandy's eyes never turned to face Tad, "No, I don't know."

"I just got caught up in talking sailing with Gav. He's a pretty good guy."

"I'm sure. Why don't you go bunk with him since he's so marvy. I didn't realize that I was such bad company!"

Like Brer Rabbit punching the Tar Baby, Tad continued the assault, "Not like that! It's not that you're bad company…" *Please Tar Baby, release me. I am stupid man and I cannot stop.*

"Oh REALLY?"

"What I mean is that you don't get to meet anyone as skillful of a sailor and as enthusiastic of a racer as Gav was. I just got caught up in it. I'm sorry. I missed you. I'm racked with grief."

"Don't be a wiseass. I enjoyed shopping anyway. It was better than sitting in that musty, smoky bar with those beer-swilling boat refugees."

Ramon was listening in from the cockpit, "Great! That's great! Did you get me something?"

"Yes, Ramon. A do-it-yourself vasectomy kit. Try not to get blood all over the boat. See you in the morning, Thaddeus." She disappeared down into the cabin.

Ramon walked back and sat down next to Ramon, who had mysteriously produced two cold Coronas. They clinked bottles and sat silently for a while.

Ramon finally broke the silence, "You know, Kemo Sabe, this has been a pretty strange trip."

"That it has."

"Tomorrow is the day. You ready?"

"Yes I am."

"Good."

And they watched the stars for another twenty minutes and turned in.

• • •

The morning greeted them with the usual marina sounds. Boat motors growled as they motored by. Fishermen were the first out of the marina, most leaving on the funny-looking flats boats that had a platform over the motor. Other boats came and went. The voices of people walking by on the dock drifted down into the *Who's Your Daddy* and woke up the occupants.

Ramon shook Tad, "Up! Get up!" Soon everyone was up, including Jimbo who looked like he had been ten rounds with Apollo Creed. His eyes were swollen and bloodshot ("Jeez, Jimbo, your eyes look like a Georgia roadmap!"). Jimbo thanked Ramon heartily for his smartass contribution to a magnificent hangover. The whole group stumbled out into the blinding Key West sunshine, and quickly realized that the sun wasn't really shining at seven fifteen. Even dim light was blinding.

The McFracken crew were all spilling out of the *Serendipity* at the same time. Angus was truly a horrific site with his swollen foot and hair in a state of panic. He resembled a Scottish Don King with cotton mouth. Angus limped over to the water hose and turned it on. He drank deeply – greedily. And then he had dry heaves, but everyone was used to it by now, except for Jimbo, who had a queasy stomach and threw up a little bit in his own mouth.

After the gut-chucking was complete, everyone slowly walked up the dock to find something to eat. They found a small restaurant that was advertised as a locals' joint, and went in. In a great moment of McFracken generosity, Angus offered to buy everyone breakfast. And they dined heartily. Everyone emerged from the restaurant, except for Jimbo and Ramon. They stayed inside and talked for a few minutes. They soon emerged also.

When they came out, they were on the street corner across from the Flagler Train Station Museum. The younger McFracken set off in search of the things young men search for. Angus and Jimbo headed down Caroline Street, ostensibly heading to a marine supply store to show each other who can spend the most for boat equipment they probably couldn't operate. Tad and Ramon were left with Sandy and Tiffani.

Ramon told Tad and Sandy he needed a moment. He guided Tiffani over to the side of the store. "I talked to Jimbo. Everything is fine. He knows that you and I are... interested in each other."

Tiffany looked immensely relieved, "That is so...wonderful. Thank you, Ramon. Thank you so much."

They returned to Tad and Sandy. Tad spoke up, "Ramon and I have to take care of some business today. You two want to pal around? Go shopping?"

Sandy said in a syrupy, condescending voice, "Like…do girl stuff? Just the two of us? That would be just ducky!"

Tiffani perked right up, "Yes! We can get our nails done! Look at mine. That boat has wrecked them. And pedicures! I saw a place on Duval Street!"

Sandy winced, realizing that Tiffani had missed the finer points of her sarcasm. "What the hell. See you later boys. Come back when you don't have time to stay so long."

The two girls strolled off, Tiffani chattering on about something. Ramon looked at Tad, "What business?"

"Dive school business."

The taxi dropped them off at the gate of Naval Air Station Key West. Since neither of them were still on active duty, neither of them had the requisite ID card to get on base. From the visitor's center they called the dive school phone number.

A staff sergeant answered the phone and listened to Tad describe who he was and what he wanted ("I need to talk to you guys about a matter.") The army dive instructor arrived at the gate five minutes later and cleared them into the post. As they waited in the orderly room for the chief instructor, Tad reminisced. "You know, it was guys from here that started my military career."

Ramon reflected, "If you screw up this thing tonight, you might end it all here too."

Just then, a muscular man wearing the rank of Chief Warrant Officer Three walked in, "This one will probably screw it up if up it can be screwed."

Tad stared at the man for a second and then recognized him, "Arnie! My God, it's been a while! You still here?"

"I've had other assignments, but now I run the dive school. How have you been? Heard you did a jam-up job in Afghanistan."

"So they say. You know Baker's here, don't you?"

Arnie winced and looked around to see who else was in the room. "He's not with us any more. He's OGA. In fact, he doesn't exist any more. He bought the farm in Afghanistan."

Tad looked confused, "No way! We just talked to him yesterday – wait. I get it."

Ramon said to no one in particular, "Welcome to the panel Mr. Einstein."

Arnie continued, "He is non-person. That's what keeps him alive in his business. You aren't doing him any favors by talking about him, so don't. Now or ever."

"Gotcha."

"Good. So to what do I owe the honor of this visit?"

"We need firearms. Nothing too fancy. Can you help us?"

Arnie paced the room, "Let's see – first you show up out of the clear blue. Second, you tell me you have visited Arnie. Third, you want guns. Where is he?"

"Who?"

"Murph. That's who. What has he drug you all in? Wait, don't answer that. I don't want to know. Shit!" Arnie continued to pace, deep in thought. Suddenly he stopped and stood frozen for a few seconds. He turned to them and said, "Wait. I'll be back." And he disappeared.

Fifteen minutes later he emerged with a hard-shell gun case as big as the average newspaper box. He set it down, but did not open it. He turned to Tad and Ramon and said, "I can and will help you to the greatest extent that I am able. You need to understand that when you deal with the customers that Murph and Arnie deal with, it's serious. Real serious. I cannot imagine what is going on here and I damn sure do not want to know. Here, check these out."

He opened the case and inside were six pistols of different sizes and shapes. "All are unregistered and untraceable. Your fingerprints are not, so have some care not to leave your calling card. Will these help? Take you pick."

Tad and Ramon quickly and expertly sampled each weapon, each settling on their choice. Tad picked a Kimber Custom Defense forty caliber semi-automatic. Ramon chose a smaller Ruger twenty-two caliber magnum semi-automatic. In fitted compartments next to each weapon were cylindrical objects. "Silencers. Cool," said Ramon. They screwed the silencers onto the barrels, checking the fit. Perfect. There was a box of ammunition for each weapon in the case. Tad and Ramon were set. They were checking the feel and balance of their weapon. Tad aimed at a poster on the wall behind Arnie's desk – *Kill a Commie for Mommy*. "Hey Arnie, that poster was there the day you hauled me in here years ago. Isn't it about time for a new one?"

Arnie studied the poster. "What can I say? I guess I'm just a romantic." He then got serious, "Now listen to me and listen good. These weapons do not exist. Since silencers are seriously illegal, they also do not exist. It must stay that way. Under no circumstances are these weapons to fall into the hands of any law enforcement officer, got it? The only reason I give them to you is because you two inepts are apparently mixed up in some serious shit. When you resolve your "problem," I expect you to sink these weapons in some very deep water. Should you not run into trouble and you find yourself thinking, 'Hey, this is a pretty cool gun. I think I'll keep it for varmint control,' THINK AGAIN. These weapons will disappear when you have concluded your business. Do-I-Make-Myself-Clear?"

Tad and Ramon both said, "Yes, Chief."

"Do you need any backup? Or better stated, do you trust the backup you already have?"

Tad answered this one, "I think we have it covered."

"Good."

Arnie closed up the case and disappeared in the back room. He came back with three longneck beers and distributed them.

"To fallen comrades."

Tad and Ramon clinked bottles and took a swig. "Sit down boys and tell me what you have been up to!" Arnie said.

They talked for half an hour or so, catching up on who did what and where old friends were. Finally, Tad said, "Hey Arnie, we have to go. Can you give us a ride to the gate?"

"To the gate? What, you have a car waiting out there?"

"No, we were going to catch a taxi back to the marina."

"Get outta here. I'll give you a ride. Let's go."

They stowed their weapons in a gym bag and walked outside. Arnie said, "My ride's around the back. Come on."

As they rounded the corner, Tad had a sense of déjà vu all over again that nearly caused him to lose his breakfast, much like he did years ago. The same old Jeep Wagoneer was sitting in the parking lot that had taken him on a wild ride before he joined the Army. Tad said, "Don't tell me you bought that from Baker."

"Yup! What a classic! Hop in, ladies."

They piled in, moving a large assortment of diving gear, tools, fishing tackle and reels, knives, auto parts, gun cleaning kits and leather dog chew bones to the side so they could sit. "Buckle up, ladies."

Tad expected a rocket sled on wheels experience, and tensed up, only to watch Arnie pull out and drive at a moderate speed down the main drag of NAS Key West. "Obviously you drive better than Baker does." Tad observed as they headed out the gate and toward town. He dropped them off several blocks from the marina on a side street that obviously had little use. "You boys walk from here. Can't be too careful. Might be the enemy is on a little recon of your boat."

Tad said, "It's not like that. There's no enemy, just some people we have to work something out."

"Don't fool yourself. You remember what I said about Murph and who he deals with. Also remember that Baker might have been your buddy in far away lands, but he works for Murph now. Murph's problems and solutions are his priority, not you or yours. Don't let your guard down."

They exited the Jeep and watched Arnie drive away, babying the old vehicle. Ramon looked at Tad and said, "What now?"

"We're supposed to be fixing Jimbo's boat sometime throughout this cruise. Let's go see what we can do with that radar he bought. Tonight will come soon enough."

They trudged off in the direction of the marina.

• • •

They worked throughout the day installing the radar system. Shortly after noon, Jimbo and Angus came walking down the dock, each pushing a cart. Jimbo hollered out, "Hey Tad! Ramon! Come give me a hand!"

They walked over to Jimbo and gazed upon a massive pile of boat equipment. Tad queried Jimbo, "What all have you bought?"

Jimbo tried to play it off like he was humble, but that diminished in a nanosecond. "Well, not much really. But DAMN! Take a look at this barometer! That's made in Taiwan, see? Says so right here!

Best barometers come from Taiwan. Now we'll always know when a hurricane is sneaking up on us. And check out the propane grill. This baby's awesome! We'll (in a poor Australian accent) *throw some shrimps on the Barbie, Mate!* Oh hell yes! And check out my sailing shoes, and…" On and on it went. As Tad and Ramon made trips to the cabin, stowing the gear, Ramon said, "two grand. He blew at least two grand."

"I say closer to three." They helped Angus stow all the gear he bought in his boat also. Gav and the cousins were not in.

When they had the cart empty, Tad said, "Whose carts are these? Do I need to return it to the store?"

"Nope," said Jimbo, "We bought them."

"OK, you know they make carts that fold up and can be stowed in boats – not like this one."

"Whatever. Hey Angus! You're Scottish and its five o'clock in Stockholm. I'll bet all you drunk bastards are hugging bars and chugging Guinness right now back home."

Angus turned to Ramon, "Hey boy! Go fetch me blender pitcher. I need to decorate his head with some more red knots."

Jimbo held his hands up in mock defense, "Remember what I said, Angus? Violence doesn't solve any problems. That's alcohol's job."

"Fer one thing, Stockholm is in Sweden, not Scotland. Second, Guinness is brewed in Ireland, not Scotland. Can you think of one single thing besides scotch whiskey that is from Scotland, ye inbred fool?"

Jimbo thought hard for a minute and said, "Mel Gibson! I saw him in that movie where he painted his face blue. There you go! Let's drink to Mel. Tad! Go downstairs and bring us up a few beers. Twelve ought to do it."

Angus shook his head in disgust, "Mel Gibson? Give me a break."

Jimbo and Angus approached drinking much like Andre the Giant approached a battle royal. A beer was something to be destroyed. Bam! Take that you twelve ounce longneck. What? Another one has the audacity to be present? Boom! Now it's gone. Any more takers? Oh really? Come here you little smartass Corona…

Tad and Ramon were getting antsy and couldn't get any work done listening to the dynamic duo of Intoxico and Inebrio carrying on. They were preparing to leave the boat, when a girl's voice called out, "Like hey! Ramon! Like we thought we'd come visit."

The four men turned and saw the girls approaching. Ramon said, "Ahh! It's Felicia and Babs. But the blonde with large…uh…eyes, what's her name?"

Tad turned and stared into Ramon's eyes, "You're such a liar. You know good and well here name is Elke. No one ever meets an Elke and then forgets her name."

"If you say so. Hey girls! What's up? Want to come aboard?"

Tad leaned over and hissed quietly, "Tiffani! You idiot, remember Tiffani!"

"Oh yeah. That's right. The old testosterone autopilot almost took over. OK, watch me work. Hey girls! Sorry but I can't come out and play. My…uh…wife will be back soon!"

The three girls froze immediately, obviously having a difficult time cogitating the information regarding Ramon's marital status and the relevance it had on their day.

Felicia spoke up, "Wife? You're married?"

Ramon smiled from ear to ear. "But of course! This is our fifth anniversary!"

Babs spoke up, "Where's she at?"

"She's shopping. She's with…Tad's wife! They'll be back so you run along."

The three girls had a quick girl huddle. After quietly conferring with each other, Elke spoke up, "You come over for a couple of hours. We have our wedding gift for you. Bring him too." She pointed to Tad.

Jimbo spoke up, "Wait a minute there, honey! Ever had a Jimbo sandwich? That's two of you around one of …wait…that's not right. Messed that one up. Hang on, um, yeah…let's have a costume party. I'll get nekkid, put on roller skates and go as a pull toy. What do you say, baby dolls? How about me and Angus here show you around the old marina."

The girls walked the first ten steps backwards, as if afraid to turn around. They remained tightly huddled as they slowly backed away from Jimbo's boat. Finally, without a word, they briskly turned and walked away.

Jimbo beamed. "What do you say boys? That went over well."

Ramon nodded, "Slicker than monkey snot, Jimbo."

"Thank you. Coming from you, that means something, Ramon. I mean that."

Tad iced down another twelve pack for Intoxico and Inebrio. He and Ramon left the dock and walked to the payphone near the dockmaster's office. "We need to call Murph," Tad said. Tad put in two quarters and dialed a number.

"Speak."

"This is Tad."

"And I am not."

"Everything still a go?"

"Of course. Why would it not?"

"No reason. I just wanted to check in."

"Listen, Thaddeus. I am not your mother, nor your father. You do not have to check in with me after you arrive home from school, understand? We discussed the plan yesterday. Do you understand your part?"

"Yes I do, but I just…"

"Do not tell me you enjoy conversing with me. My witty repartee does tend to provide illuminating conversation, but there is a time and a place. Do not tell me you are worried about doing this because I know you are not. I have seen you in action, Thaddeus. The only reason you are calling me is to ask questions you should not ask. Is this not true?"

Tad hesitated. There's no good that comes from lying to Murph. "Yes. It's true. I still don't like the plan."

"What you do not like is that you will be long gone if, and when, any action takes place. You get the girl and leave. Period. I handle the rest. I do not care to discuss all the details of the operation, but I will say this – the girl is our first priority. Nothing will go down until she is safely out of the way. You, Thaddeus, will get her and leave. L-E-A-V-E. This is not your fight to fight. Do not mess around with my operation. It is too important."

"Okay, okay. I'm just a little nervous, that's all."

"Sure you are. And I'm Luciano Pavoratti. I need to go now and warm up my voice. By the way, how is Arnie doing? Wait, don't answer that. Remember, Thaddeus, follow the plan." Click. The phone went dead.

Ramon asked, "Well? Anything new? He give up anything?"

Tad looked perplexed. "He knew we went to visit Arnie! How'd he know that?"

"Give me a break. He knows everything. He's practically impotent."

"That's omnipotent."

"That too. What about the plan? Any more info?"

"No. Same plan. We walk together wearing those t-shirts. Someone makes contact. We give him the package; he gives us the girl. We leave. The rest is up to Murph."

"Sounds good. Let's go, Sunshine."

"Sunshine?"

"I'm practicing to be your gay lover. Maybe we better stop for some condoms."

"Don't get carried away."

"You knock out your teeth and grow a beard and I'll marry you."

"You're disgusting."

"That's what you said last night, Sunshine."

"Let's go. You're beginning to scare me."

Tiffani and Sandy returned from shopping just after four o'clock. They each had bags of items from stores up and down Duval Street, which may have accounted for the fact that they were in an exceedingly good mood when they arrived at the boat.

Tad and Ramon were already back on the boat, and offered to stow away the goods. They looked for Jimbo, but he was nowhere to be found on the boat. They all assumed that he was drunk in some bar somewhere, which was the most logical deduction. Tad and Ramon suggested that they have an early dinner. The girls agreed and they headed out to one of the restaurants that was on the waterfront.

When the girls went to the bathroom, Tad leaned over and asked Ramon, "What about Jimbo? He's got to be on that boat when we leave tonight."

Ramon nodded, "He *needs* to be on the boat. If not, we leave him. You understand that, right?"

"Yes, but I don't like it. This is just perfect. We run off and steal the owner's boat? So then every coast guard boat and marine patrol within five hundred miles is searching for us."

"Beats the alternative."

"Which is?"

"Screwing up the plan. Pissing off Murph."

"Right you are. Grab the girl and get the heck out of here."

The dining was excellent. They ordered two plates of grouper, oysters, scallops and shrimp and shared the meal. Tad and Ramon liked to eat light before an operation. Old habits die hard.

They left the restaurant and began the walk back to the boat. Tiffani said to Ramon, "You're quiet tonight."

Ramon looked at her and smiled, "I am struck by your smile. It puts me in a trance, not allowing me to think of anything else. One look into your blue eyes melts away my will to do anything but be near you. Don't get me started on your booty."

Tiffany gushed, "That's the sweetest thing anyone has ever said to me!"

Sandy whispered to Tad, "That's what his cousins on that other boat said."

Tad agreed.

They arrived at the *Who's Your Daddy* to find it empty. Jimbo was still AWOL. Angus was sitting on the back of the *Serendipity*, fishing and drinking.

Tad asked Angus, "You seen Jimbo this afternoon?"

Angus shook his head and commented, "Nah! Not seen the lad since this mornin', though I hadn't been lookin' for him either!" He began to slowly reel in his rod until some monstrous lump the size of a football slowly came out of the water.

Ramon looked over the dock and said, "What in the world did you catch?"

Angus cursed and threw the lump thirty yards out and began to slowly reel it in again.

"Catch? I caught nothin'! Did ye see anythin' on the end of the line? Did ye see a big fish floppin' and kickin'? I think it is apparent that nothin' was on the line but the bait."

Ramon cautiously asked, "Bait? What are you using for bait?"

"Chicken."

"Chicken? You're fishing with a chicken?"

"Well not just any chicken! It's a rotisserie chicken! Lemon pepper!"

Tad and Ramon looked dumbfounded. They looked at Sandy who looked also dumbfounded who was looking at Tiffani who seemed pretty happy and content, except for a nail, which had a chip in it.

Ramon continued, "You are using a lemon pepper rotisserie chicken. Of course. How did you hear about this miracle bait? And what do you wish to catch?"

"Didn't ye see Jaws? Didn't ye see the part where the two men use their wives' ham and the shark ate it and almost pulled the dock down? Well I couldn't find a ham, but I did find these rotisserie chickens. They should work, don't you think?"

"You have more?"

"Well of course! You ever go fishin' with only one piece of bait? That's just plain stupid!" Angus pulled out several bags to display. "I got…let's see…here! Barbeque. And…uh…here we go…mojo. That's how Cubans barbeque their chicken. Ye should know, right lad? And finally, I have a Ranch flavored one. That's it."

Ramon commented, "Kentucky Fried Shark Bait. Finger Licking Good."

Angus was putting his bait back up. "What?"

"I said, 'Shark Bait – Looks Good!'"

"I thought the same thing."

They all crashed in the cockpit to enjoy the sunset and prep themselves for the night's activities. Tad addressed the group, which was actually addressing Tiffani since everyone else knew what the plan was except her, "It has come to our attention that we have to vacate this slip tonight. So Ramon and I have to go into town for a little business and then we'll be back around 10:20 or so. We'll probably be leaving soon thereafter."

Tiffany raised her hand to ask a question, but Tad didn't call on her because Sandy butted in and said, "What about Jimbo? Where is he? Surely we won't leave him!"

Tad dodged the question in a slippery manner, "It's all taken care of. He'll be here. *Dr. Lugubrious!*

Sandy continued, "But what if he isn't?"

"But he will be."

"How do you know?"

"I just know."

"You don't know."

"So you say."

"So I know"

"OK, how is it that you say that I don't know, but now you do know what I don't know? Huh? If you know what I don't know, then you should know what I also do know. I don't think you really know what I know."

Tiffani's hand was still in the air to answer the question, but now she was waving it around furiously to be called on.

Sandy was about to jump back into the fray when Tad put his hand up, "Stop! I call on Tiffani."

Sandy stopped in mid-sentence, but she looked really pissed about it.

Tiffani said, "Let's just leave him. That'll teach him."

Tad breathed out a long sigh. "Okay everyone. News flash. This is Jimbo's boat. We are not going to leave him because he will be here before we leave. Period. No more discussion."

Tiffani looked placated and Sandy looked grumpy and Ramon looked contemplative. *"Great,"* though Tad, *"The crew from Hell."*

At nine-thirty, Tad and Ramon emerged from the cockpit. Both had on shorts and t-shirts. They also had on light windbreakers zipped up. Ramon carried a small gym bag, as did Tad. Tad was also carrying a brown paper bag with rope handles from a mall in Miami.

Sandy commented, "Going shopping?"

Tad considered his answer, "In a manner of speaking."

Sandy left it like that.

Both gym bags had a towel in the bottom, cushioning the firearms they carried. Inside the brown shopping bag was the package that Tad was to give the man, whoever he was, in exchange for Elizabeth Forbish.

They gave final instructions to the girls to stay PUT and they would be back soon. Jimbo still had not made it back. They walked several blocks over and turned onto Duval Street. Nine forty-two. It was approaching the designated time. They both unzipped their jackets, showing off their two new t-shirts.

Tad said, "Let's go. And move slowly, like we aren't in a hurry."

Ramon said, "Aren't you forgetting something?"

"Like what?"

"Listen, Bitch, if you're planning on being my significant other, you need to show a little affection. A girl gets lonely, you know."

"Oh! Yeah…we're…uh…yeah. Okay. How about we just walk sort of close together?"

"Now that's what I thought you would say. YOU'RE ASHAMED OF ME!"

"Cut it out. Well how are we supposed to walk?"

"Holding hands, stupid. Here – hold my hand."

Tad tentatively held Ramon's hand. It felt weird, holding another man's hand.

Ramon said, "Now there. Good. Now you have to loosen up and act like I'm Sandy. Just think of me as being Sandy."

"Sandy doesn't have a hairy ass."

"You ungrateful strumpet. Play the part. Let's practice."

They strolled up and down the street, pausing to look and point in windows. Ramon was obviously the best actor, as he had always had a flair for the dramatic.

A middle aged caterer from Topeka with a close haircut walked by and smiled and winked at the couple. Tourists passed by without a glance.

Tad said, "No one is looking at us. This just might work."

"Of course it will work. This is Key West, remember? You have any idea how many gay couples there are here?"

"One more couple now. Let's get going. Wait a minute. We have a problem."

"What?"

"I can't hold your hand with my right hand. That's my shooting hand."

Ramon thought and offered a recommendation, "True. And I am not primarily left handed, but I can shoot with reasonable proficiency left handed. No problem. After all, I am ambiguous. Bilateral also."

And off they went, what ostensibly looked to be just another pair of gay men shopping and enjoying Key West wearing t-shirts proclaiming their gayness.

As they crossed Catherine Street, Tad checked his watch. Nine fifty-eight. "It's time. Heads up."

"What side of the road do we walk on? This side or the other side?"

"I don't know. Crap! I didn't ask! Just keep on walking."

They strolled slowly past shops, stopping to admire things in the windows. They talked to street vendors and walked slowly past bars. Really slowly. Nothing happened. After walking eight blocks past Catherine Street, Tad said, "Maybe we should cross over Duval Street and walk back down." Ramon concurred.

They kept up their act, playing the part. Tad and Ramon were constantly scanning the street, the stores, the crowd, everywhere and everything. The threat always comes from the most unexpected places.

They were just two short blocks from arriving back at their starting point when they walked past an open air pizzeria. A squat, balding man walked out to Tad and looked at his shirt. He had a big scar from the corner of his mouth to his left ear – or where his left ear should have been because it was missing. His attire didn't seem too remarkable, but he had a distinctive look in his eyes that marked him as a predator – dumb as dirt but predator nonetheless. Showtime.

The man looked hard at Tad, not smiling. His eyes slowly turned to Ramon and back to Tad. It was a Mexican standoff for twenty seconds. He seemed unsure of what to do, so Ramon tried to break the ice.

"Can I help you, girlfriend?"

Tourists streamed by the men, since they were standing on the sidewalk. Baldie continued to stare and blink. You could see the wheels turning slowly in his head.

Finally he said, "You got the package?"

Tad said, "Yes."

He nodded, scanning left and right. "There's only supposed to be one of you. Why is there two? This is not the way it is supposed to work." Clearly Kojak was formulating his own Plan B since Plan A didn't seem to be working out like he planned.

Tad said, "No matter. Here it is. What about my…friend?"

He looked exasperated, "That's what I'm talking about! You're not supposed to bring your friend! How the hell we gonna do this now?"

Tad looked at Ramon. This was just too odd to make sense of it all. Tad said, "No, not *him*. He's just my…mate. Right, Ramon?"

"Yes dear." Ramon made kissy poo sounds in Tad's ear, which messed up Tad's concentration. The burst of surreal visual and verbal information seemed to confuse Yul Brenner even more.

Tad rephrased the question, "Where's the girl? You know, the one I am supposed to…pick up?"

Ramon hugged Tad, putting his head on Tad's back shoulder. He whispered, "One target at the entrance of the bar across the street. Hang on." Ramon tiptoed around Tad, fussing with his shirt and hair. He leaned in to hug him again. "Another two about a half block up."

Baldie spoke up, "What's he sayin'? You up to something? Give me the bag, now!"

Tad said, "Oh, darlin', he's just being himself! Walk yourself over here and take this bag!"

The bald man walked the eight feet that separated them and reached for the bag.

Tad held the bag down by his side, causing Baldie to reach for it. When he did, Tad pressed up against Baldie's side with his gym bag. The feel of a gun barrel is unmistakable, even when it is in a gym bag. "Now listen up, pinhead. Can you hear me?" Tad questioned.

"Shit! Yes. You're going to screw this up. Two fags were not part of the plan."

"We're not gay, you imbecile. I want to know where the girl is."

"But you could be! I thought you were fags! You sure you're not really queer?"

Tad leaned over and said quietly, "No you idiot! Let's just make the swap. And besides, what do you have against homosexual Americans?" Ramon was pretending to stick his tongue in Tad's ear, but only Baldie could see him.

Baldy said, "Hah! There! Did you see him? I knew you were fags!"

Tad looked at Ramon who shrugged his shoulders, "No clue what he's talking about."

Tad said, "Focus. The girl. Where's she at?"

"She's in the bar."

"Which bar?"

"That one. Across the street."

They turned slowly and looked into Irish Kevin's, a popular Irish bar. The place was full of people and the music bellowed out.

Tad turned to Baldie, "Let's go. Walk right in front of us. When I see her, you get the package."

"But that's not the plan!" he protested. When Tad poked him in the ear with the gun, it helped him make the right decision. They all three turned to walk to the street when a figure came running out of the crowd screaming, "AAIIYYYEEEE! Ramon! It's me, Elke and ..." BOOM! She ran into Ramon, trying to hug him but only succeeded in tackling him and sending both of them sprawling to the ground. Mean Joe Green would have been proud of the hit she put on him. When he hit the ground, there was two coughing sounds, TWACK, TWACK. Two holes appeared in Ramon's gym bag and the neon lights over their heads advertising the pizzeria and the bar upstairs shattered in a thousand pieces.

Tad and Baldie ducked, but two other drunk girls, obviously companions of the girl who was lying on top of Ramon came rushing out squealing, "Elke! Elke! OMIGOD! It's Ramon!" Babs handed Baldie her frozen rum runner as she hobbled on her high heels to help Elke.

The crowd was not near as drunk as the three girls and began to flee at the sound of the glass hitting the sidewalk. Just then there were other coughs nearby – TWACK! TWACK! Baldie's right ear exploded in a puff of pink.

"My ear! You shot my good ear off you queer bastard!"

Tad said, "I didn't shoot your ear... and I'm not gay! It's your interpersonal communications – that's the problem!"

Baldy was holding his hand over his ear, looking around for the best escape route. Blood was streaming through his fingers. "Well if you didn't do it, who did?" In his other hand was Bab's frozen rum runner. He looked down at the drink and then switched it to his right hand and pressed the cup to his bleeding ear. The coldness of the frozen rum runner was painful. "Arggg! That should stop the bleeding. I'm out of here."

Tad hissed, "NO! Where's the girl?"

Baldy turned and faced Tad. "I told you, she's in that bar. Now, I'm leaving. Give me the…" He never finished the sentence. A hole appeared in Baldy's forehead and the rear of his skull exploded pieces parts in a conical stream all over the condiments counter at the pizzeria. Brain mixed with grated parmesan and skull parts on the napkin dispenser.

Ramon had finally got the drunk girl off of him and ran to where Baldy was laying on the sidewalk. Tad turned to Ramon and said, "Get Elizabeth – now!"

As they turned to sprint across the street, gunfire erupted in the bar across the street. It sounded like a war zone as shot after shot rang out. While Tad and Ramon could not see the shooters, they did see the flashes from the shots. Shots from inside the bar. Shots from rooftops. They were frozen on the curb, trying in vain to scan the crowd of tourists were fleeing. Trying to see the girl in the Washington Redskins t-shirt.

When most of the crowd had left running and screaming, Tad said, "Let's go. In the bar. Be careful."

They stepped on the edge of the curb preparing to cross the street, which was in chaos. Then a voice bellowed out right behind them, causing both of them to jump, "Tad! Ramon! Thank God! The girls! Let's get them and get out of here!"

Jimbo was standing there, flailing and pointing at the girls who had retreated to the pizzeria for safety - (Gross! This table's got stuff on it!). He stared at Tad, trying to focus his drunk eyes and then looked at Ramon. Then he stared at their t-shirts, struggling to read them with his inebriated eyes.

"Good God! You really are queers! Tiffani said you weren't but I told her the first time I saw you two! Nothing to be ashamed of. Some of my best friends are gay."

Ramon said, "Really? Who?"

"Well none really, but I was trying to be polite. Hell, there's the police coming. Let's get out of here before they think we all had something to do with this."

Tad took one last look into Irish Kevin's and looked at Ramon. Ramon nodded. They went and got Felicia, Elke and Babs. "Let's go girls."

Elke laughed, "Did you see the fireworks? Hey! Someone had a feta cheese pizza." She picked up the light gray chunk from the table and popped it in her mouth. "Not too bad."

Tad winced and Ramon nodded sagely, "It cannot get any worse than this."

Tad said, "Want be the one to call Murph?"

Ramon said, "I was wrong. You call him. But, sheesh, she ate *Baldie's brains.*"

They all left the area, sticking to darker streets. The wailing of sirens and flashing of blue lights adding to the ambiance of the normal party atmosphere of Duval Street. They could see police cars, ambulances and other vehicles roll up to the area of the shootout. Jimbo was actually being a great help getting the drunk girls to move quickly.

He explained, "I went over to their boat to apologize for acting like a horse's ass this afternoon. I offered to take them out to dinner and drinks – nothing serious, you know. Just have a little fun. We stumbled on to you and Ramon back there. Good thing you weren't hurt! What do you think happened?"

Ramon explained, "Gang fight."

"Jesus! I knew it! Frickin' gangs – can't go anywhere without that sort of stuff. Probably those damn Jamaicans. I've heard about them. You can't go anywhere without…Girls! What are you doing? Elke? Oh Jeez!"

Elke teetered off to the side of the road and leaned on a banyan tree. She was inhaling sharply and making the telltale low moaning sounds of a drunk preparing to vomit. And vomit she did. After thirty seconds of splashing sounds followed by dry heaving, she wobbled back over to the group.

Jimbo coached her, "Atta girl! Get it all out! Works like a champ for me."

"I'm shooo shhorry," she slurred. Chunks dangled from her blonde hair and her mouth and face looked like she had been bobbing for oatmeal. "I need a tisshhew…"

Ramon ripped off his shirt and handed it to Babs. "Here, you give it to her."

Babs looked questioningly at the shirt, "You really want to give this up, Liberace?"

"Funny. Clean her up. Let's go."

Babs and Felicia did the best they could with Ramon's shirt and the group continued on, just a block short of the marina. Tad stopped at the edge of the street, staying in the shadows.

"You girls go on to your boat. We'll see you in the morning."

They staggered on, weebling and wobbling toward their trawler. Ramon said, "I don't think I will ever look an Elke the same after that heinous demonstration of regurgitation."

Tad agreed. Jimbo said, "What, that? No big deal. Swish a little beer in her mouth and she's good to go."

"Right, Jimbo," Tad agreed, cringing at the thought. "Why don't you go down to the boat? Ramon and I will be along soon."

"Suit yourself. If I was you two, I'd be over at the three amigas boat making hay while the sun shines. Get my drift?"

He walked on toward the marina, still a little wobbly himself.

Tad pulled out his cell phone and punch in ten numbers. The phone rang twice, and then a voice said, "That was nice, Thaddeus. Very nice. Is it possible that you may have improvised on our plan just a wee bit?"

"Murph, I do not know where those girls came from. It was a coincidence."

"Not the girls, Thaddeus. I'm talking about you taking out the follically challenged man in front of the pizza restaurant."

"We didn't take him out. One of your guys did."

"No they didn't, Thaddeus. Hmmm…Let me think."

"Did any of your guys get hurt?"

"Yes they did."

"Who? Is Baker alright?"

"He's alive. Which I cannot say for Paul, George and Ringo."

"No way. They're dead? As in not living? It's a sad day for rock and roll."

"That's the only way dead can be. Baker took a bullet in his shoulder. He'll survive but he will be out of commission for quite some time."

"Johnny?"

"Not at the scene. He will be fine."

"Elizabeth? Did you get her?"

"Thaddeus, she was not there. She was never there."

"What about the opposition?"

"Four dead. The principles were not captured or neutralized. Did you still have the package?"

Tad looked down at the brown shopping bag, "I have it."

"Good. Keep it safe."

"What is the next move, Murph?"

"I do not know. For you and Ramon, maybe nothing. I need some time to evaluate the situation."

"You need time for the bad guys to contact Old Man Forbish is what you are saying."

"Something like that. Thaddeus, I need to ask you something and I need to know the truth – Who could have compromised this mission? This is the radar site all over again. I need you to think."

Tad thought and hesitated, "I may have told Arnie that we were involved in a mission, but I didn't tell him any details."

"Yes, yes. I have already talked to him. Go on."

"Of course you have," thought Tad. "There's Forbish's daughter. She knows we were making the swap, but I didn't tell her any details. I made her stay at the boat."

"I know about her. I have personally cleared her. Anything else?"

"No. Not from my end. What makes you so sure there's a leak?"

"It's what I do, Thaddeus. Let me think and I'll call you back within two hours."

"And then what?"

"The next thing."

• • •

Tad and Ramon walked slowly back to the marina. They walked across Catherine Street and across the parking lot next to the Flagler Train Station Museum. As they were making their way to the docks, a car came screeching around the corner and stopped about one hundred feet away. Tad and Ramon scooted for cover behind a row of mopeds, expecting the worst. The back door opened and a body flopped out onto the pavement. The car burned rubber leaving the parking lot and all became eerily quiet. Tad and Ramon slowly approached the body, which began to stir.

"…mmm…hellllp…"

Tad recognized the voice, the body and the hair. "Sandy!" He rushed over to her and cradled her in his lap, trying not to move her too much.

"What happened? Can you hear me?"

Her left eye was bruised and swelling shut. Her lip was cut and bleeding down her chin onto her shirt. She opened her eyes and whispered, "Oh Tad. I'm sorry, I'm sorry…"

Tad visually inspected her for any signs of injury. Satisfied that she did not have broken bones or any apparent major injuries, he picked her up and carried her the quarter mile to the *Who's Your Daddy*.

He laid her gently down on the cockpit cushions and called for Tiffani. "Get the first aid kit and a bottle of water."

Tiffani saw her injured friend and quietly went below. She returned with the items and handed them to Tad.

"I tried to stop her, Tad. I really did."

Tad nodded, not looking at Tiffani. He was sure if he did look at Tiffani that she would see the anger in his eyes and assume it was directed at her. Tad knew the anger was apparent on his face. It was just his way. Somebody had to pay for this.

Ramon came along and took Tiffani to the front of the boat, consoling her. Jimbo was on the Serendipity, drinking White Russians with Angus, helping him fish for sharks with his rotisserie chickens. They appeared to be down to only one remaining chicken-bait laying next to the seven-foot long hammerhead on the dock – "…The damn thing nearly ripped me arms out of the sockets!"

Sandy began to stir. She opened her eyes again, and tried to sit up. Tad stopped her.

"Just lay there for a minute. Good. Have a sip of water." Sandy took a sip and then another. The cobwebs cleared from her brain and her green eyes began to sharpen into focus – at least the one that was not swollen over.

"I'm sorry, Tad. I'm sorry that I messed everything up. I just wanted to make sure my sister was going to be alright."

"Don't say that. You didn't mess anything up. It just happened. Who did this to you?"

She took another sip of water and then, with great effort, sat up. She put her face in her hands and sobbed quietly. Tad handed her a towel that was drying on the rail.

"I don't know. I followed you and Ramon to Duval Street. I lost you, but found you later when you were talking to that mean-looking man. When the shooting started, I didn't know what to do. I ran down the street, looking for a place to hide. I was in an alleyway when I saw Elizabeth being hustled down the street by two men. They were evil-looking, Tad! I hollered for Elizabeth and she recognized me. I ran toward them and then the world went black. I woke up with this lump on my head and three guys putting me in a car. They drove me to a dark street and parked behind a building. They hit me…over and over (sob)."

The anger was welling up in Tad. He wanted to strike out, but he remained composed.

"What else did they do?"

"They kept asking me, 'Where's the package?' and 'Who's got the package?' At first I told them I didn't know, but I…I…Tad, I told them you have the package."

Tad snapped to attention, scanning all around the marina. He whistled for Ramon, causing him to also snap to attention, sensing something wrong. Ramon hustled back to the cockpit.

"We may have visitors. Soon. We've got to get out of here, now."

Ramon spoke no words, but trotted up the boat to get Tiffani. Tad stepped over to the next boat, calling out for Jimbo, who was with Angus in back of the boat, fishing.

"Jimbo, come on over."

"Not now, boy. Can't you see me and Angus are fishing."

"Uh…yeah. Hey, really, it's important. It's about those Jamaicans. I need to talk to you."

"No shit? The fricken' Jamaicans? I'm on the way. Hold this rod, Angus."

Angus grumbled and took the rod. Jimbo made his way off the *Serendipity* and onto the *Who's Your Daddy* with all the grace and agility of a gout-ridden Sasquatch.

"What's all this about those Jamaicans, Tad?"

Tad was hastily prepping the boat for departure as he made up the story, "The Jamaicans beat up Sandy and they are looking for you. We gotta go, now."

"Looking for ME? I knew it! Good thing I made it out of there alive tonight. Let's get the hell out of here."

In ten minutes, the *Who's Your Daddy* was backing out of the slip and motoring out to the Key West channel. Ramon walked over to the helm and said, "Careful, Chico. It's tricky out here at night."

Tad scanned the dark water, aiming the boat at an imaginary reference point based on the lighted bouys to his port and starboard.

"Don't I know it."

Tad dialed his cell phone. Murph answered.

"Murph, something has come up…" Tad explained everything Sandy had said.

Tad listened intently and repeated certain things, "…package is intact…no significant harm…headed for Naval Air Station Key West to anchor…be there several days awaiting instructions…gotcha."

Sandy took a long swig of water and got Tad and Ramon's attention.

"No, wait! You didn't let me finish, Tad. After I told them you had the package, they gave me a message to give to you." She paused.

More sharply than he meant to, he said, "Hang on, Murph. Well? What is it?"

She exhaled slowly. "Bimini. They said go to Bimini. Be there in three days with the package to make the swap. Be there or Elizabeth dies."

Tad froze in place, making a thousand tiny calculations and decisions in his head before he spoke.

"Murph, change of plans. When is the last time you have been to the Bahamas?…"

Chapter Eleven

Tad pointed the big Morris yacht out to sea. He motored at near-full throttle, keeping the yacht moving at approximately seven knots. Ramon, Sandy and Tiffani sat in the cockpit, scanning the horizon but not talking much. Jimbo was down in the cabin, snoring like a lumberjack sawing redwoods.

After motoring for an hour, Tad and Ramon pointed the boat into the wind and set the sails – first the main and then the headsail. As the boat fell out of irons and into the wind, it heeled about five degrees to port and settled in on a comfortable reach. Tad turned off the engines and steered while Ramon trimmed the sails to their maximum efficiency.

After sailing on an easterly heading for another hour, Tad turned on the autopilot and quietly called everyone to the helm for a meeting.

"It's like this – we are sailing to Bimini. That's an island in the Bahamas. It's about fifty-five miles due east of Miami. The problem is we are one hundred miles southwest of Miami. We have to sail up and around the Keys to get to Bimini. The good news is that we can use the Gulf Stream to our benefit. Not to insult anyone's intelligence, but the Gulf Stream is sort of like a river in an ocean. It flows north between Florida and the Bahamas at a rate of around three knots. That means if we can sail at seven knots in a flow that is already going three knots, then we should me moving quite fast. The bad news is that it can get rough out there sometimes."

"Should a storm pop up, and it probably will, we have several safety rules that will not be disregarded. First, in a storm, if you are on deck, you have a pfd. That means a personal flotation device. A life vest. There are some really good inflatable ones back in that cabin with all the equipment that Jimbo bought at the boat show. Second, if you are on deck during a storm, you must have a lanyard on strapping you into the boat. We don't need anyone washed over. Third, the rule is: One hand for yourself, one hand on the boat. When you are moving around a pitching boat, ALWAYS be holding on to a stay, shroud or some part of the boat. Never stand around with your hands in your pockets or you will surely be knocked down and even thrown over."

"If you see anyone fall over, there are steps that you must take. First, throw them the doughnut. This is it." He held up a donut-shaped life preserver that had *Who's Your Daddy* painted on it. Second, yell out as loud as you can, "Man Overboard!" Finally, keep your eyes on the person. Do not look away. If you do, they may be lost forever. Got it?"

Everyone nodded.

"We will sail nonstop from here to Bimini. We'll keep watch in shifts. Sandy and I will take the first watch. Ramon and Tiffani will take the next one. Every four hours at night we swap. Every six hours in the day. I figure we can be there in around thirty-six hours or so."

Sandy asked, "Why the rush? We have three days."

Tad stared at the horizon as he checked their path. "Preparation, my dear. Preparation is the key."

Tiffani cleared her throat, "Uh…guys, I get the feeling that something is going on here and I am the only one who is not in on it. We're not really running from a Germanic gang, are we?"

"No, Tiffani, we are not," Tad said, "…and it's Jamaicans, not Germans. But that's not important now. What is important now is that you are in it as deep as anyone else. You have a right to know. Ramon, since you and Tiffani are officially off shift right now, why don't you explain to her what is going on while you get ready to catch some shuteye?"

"Right-o, monsignor. Come on, Tiffani. Let's go down and get some rest."

Tiffani said, "But I'm wide awake."

"Sleep is a mighty weapon, my little blue-eyed love muffin. Let's go." And down they went, through the companionway.

Sandy and Tad were left in the cockpit alone. The night stars twinkled and the cool wind pushed the big Morris along at a brisk pace. Off in the distance a small city of lights moved slowly across the horizon.

Tad pointed it out, "Cruise ship. Big one."

Over the next four hours, there were many ships spotted. Cruise ships, massive freighters, some ships that were simply lights moving in the distance, too far off to clearly identify their type.

Sandy stood close to Tad, who manned the helm rather than using the autopilot. "Hey Skipper, mind if I steer?" He looked at her face, smiling back at him. Her eye was bruised and puffy, but the swelling had diminished somewhat. Her lip was cracked and puffy also. Tad felt a flush of emotions over the power and resilience of a woman who could be brutalized as she was and still have a fighting spirit.

"The helm is yours."

She deftly steered the boat, slicing into a wave as the bow rose and then surfing down the backside of the swell. Tad felt a twinge of pride watching her steer the boat, knowing he had taught her what little she knew about sailing. She was sailing the boat like a pro.

She said, "You know, you kind of get a feel for the way the boat moves up and down the swells, don't you?"

"That's right. Head a few points to starboard. We need to get into the heart of the stream."

Two hours later Ramon and Tiffani came up from within the bowels of the yacht, yawning and stretching. Ramon made a trip around the deck, examining lines, fittings and the dark horizon.

"Hey Chico, I got the helm. You two get some sleep. See you in six," Ramon said.

"All yours. I'm beat. Did you tell Tiffani?" Tad asked, as he glanced at her.

"You betcha. Alabama Liberation Front. Asshole gang members who have been using Key West as their headquarters to organize a resistance force to liberate the great state."

"You're kidding, right?"

Ramon smiled, "Of course I'm kidding – or am I?"

Tad was beyond caring. He and Sandy trudged down the stairs. Tad was getting ready to duck into his berth, when she passed him and headed toward her berth. This caught Tad off guard.

"Need a place to bunk?" he said?

She turned and smiled. "Not tonight. Just get some sleep. We'll pick this up tomorrow." She turned and disappeared behind a door.

"Now that's just great. Tomorrow. Oh well." Tad settled into his berth and was asleep before his head hit the pillow.

• • •

Thirty-six hours of hard sailing did wonders for everyone aboard. Tad and Ramon were each in their own private sailing heaven. Sandy was quickly becoming accomplished at sailing a yacht. Tiffani was working on a killer tan, which seemed to be an unexpected bonus to both her and Ramon, who made sure she was properly lubricated with SPF something-or-another. He didn't really care. As far as Jimbo went, the pitching of the boat did wonders to help clear out any pesky food or drink in his stomach. He steadily retched his way up the Gulf Stream like a world-class athlete training for the pukeathalon. Where Jimbo goeth, vomit followeth not far behind.

The Who's Your Daddy sliced through the waves, making excellent progress. During mid-morning Tad was showing Sandy the finer points of using the global positioning system when Ramon sounded off, "HooWhee! Land ho and I'm not talking about my first girlfriend!"

There was a tiny sliver of brown that rose above the swells. Tad squinted into the morning sun and said, "Gun Key. Excellent. We're almost there. Bimini is just about ten miles north of here. The boat closed on the landform swiftly. The sails were full of wind that pushed the big Morris Yacht at a steady seven knots.

Sandy asked, "Is that island Bimini?"

Tad replied, "Yes...well no, not exactly. Bimini is two islands, North Bimini and South Bimini. See that cut there? Right where those boats are coming out? That's the channel that separates the two islands. Watch how the boats do not come straight out to the deep water. You have to parallel the beach for a half mile and then come out. If you come straight out, you will run into a big sandbar and ruin your day."

"Aye, aye, skipper. I'll keep that in mind."

Tad turned the boat into the wind while Ramon instructed Jimbo, who was a lovely shade of light green, how to furl the sails. Tad cranked up the diesel engine and *Who's Your Daddy* cruised into the Bimini Channel under a beautiful morning sun in ten feet of crystal clear water.

Tiffani was leaning over the lifelines and squealed, "Omigod! Omigod! Look at that fish! Is it a shark?"

Ramon looked over. "Nope. That's a tarpon...big one! 'Bout a hundred and fifty pounds." The big fish seemed quite unimpressed by the boat that effectively moved right over the top of it.

Jimbo added his two cents. "Holy Crap! Now that's a fish I'd like to catch. Be one hell of a meal."

Tad said, "You don't eat them. You just catch them, take a picture and release them."

Jimbo smiled and said flatly, "Release them, huh? Where's the fun in that?"

Tad was talking to the dockmaster at the Bimini Blue Water Marina on the marine VHF radio. He turned to the crew, "They have a slip available at the Blue Water. That's where we will stay."

Tad maneuvered the big boat toward one of several docks. Deckhands were waving and indicating where he should dock the boat. With Tad at the helm and Ramon scurrying around securing dock lines, the *Who's Your Daddy* was soon secure.

Ramon scanned the waterfront looking for some unknown threat. He didn't see anything that appeared to be threatening.

Ramon came back to the cockpit and said, "So here we are, Bubba. What now?"

Tad scanned the same waterfront. He looked over the old marinas, old boats, the bars and run down buildings. He scanned the people walking along the streets and congregating at various buildings. One person stepped out from behind the government building and stared briefly at Tad. Perhaps a bit too long. He had on a long-billed fishing cap with the flap that covered the neck. His ultra-lightweight jacket was right out of the Cabela's catalog. He looked remarkably like some prick who had way too much money to spend on fishing around the tiny island. The man nodded to Tad and disappeared.

Tad looked at Jimbo and said, "It's Murph. He would be what's next."

Tad chatted briefly with the dockmaster as Jimbo approached the dock office.

"Hey Tad!" he roared. "Who do I have to sleep with to get a drink around this place?"

The dockmaster gave a Tad a sympathetic look that said, *"One more asshole in paradise, eh?"*

Tad looked up and said, "Uh, wait a minute! I have to go clear customs and immigration first! You need to stay on the boat!"

"Ah ha! There it is! Come to papa." Jimbo ambled off toward the rundown looking bar he saw off to the left, far more concerned with the perils of sobriety than customs and immigrations.

Tad called over Ramon, "Go with Jimbo. Take the girls. Make sure he doesn't get into any trouble…and keep a low profile for God's sakes!"

Ramon waved for the girls and herded them along toward the building that Jimbo had entered.

Tad went back to the boat and got the passports and boat documentation.

Tad took a deep breath and started walking along the street, dodging potholes full of milky-looking water. He stopped at the Bimini Straw Market and picked up a t-shirt that had a smiley face with dred locks. He picked up a necklace that he thought Sandy would like.

A portly, black lady who was in the shade of the booth said, "That's a lovely necklace for your lady, mon. Beautiful Bahamian jewelry for your beautiful woman."

Tad said, "The sticker says made in Sumatra."

"Yes."

"Sumatra? Bahamian jewelry?"

"Yes, Mon. Sumatra is an island near Nassau."

"Sumatra is an island near China."

"Depends on how you look at it. Like I said, island jewelry. Ten dollars please."

Tad dug around his pockets and pulled out a ten.

"Here, keep the change."

"There's no change, Mon."

"Depends on how you look at it." Tad ambled off, pocketing the necklace. He continued to browse the market when a little boy came up to him and smiled.

Tad surveyed the youth, not more then eight years old. In his best Bob Marley voice he said, "Can I help you little Mon?"

The boy giggled and said, "You talk funny. Your father sent me to tell you to come meet him at the Dolphin House." He pointed at a location that was on the other side of the Compleat Anger Hotel, a legendary inn that was made famous by Ernest Hemmingway. At least it used to be. It was now a burned out shell. The Angler had recently burned down, taking with it the owner. A piece if every islander's hearts died in that fire. The hotel had been a part of the island culture for longer than anyone who was currently alive could remember.

"That's what he said? My…father said that? Anything else?"

The little boy smiled even bigger and said, "He said to tell you to give me five dollars or you are a…how you say… rat bastard."

Tad rummaged around in his pocket and gave the kid a fiver. "Get lost. And don't say bastard."

The little boy took off as if he was guarding the queen's jewels.

Tad walked past the foundation of the Angler and looked through the arched walkway. He felt a terrible sadness as he remembered the many wonderful nights in the establishment. Tad thought, "Even if they build it back, it won't be the same."

The bar was as bars should be. Dark wood stained with ten thousand spilled whiskeys. Floors worn from the heels of fishermen, sailors and others who had made their way to the tiny island of North Bimini. The Compleat Angler had once served as an eastern fishing headquarters to Ernest Hemmingway and his posse, who spent weeks in search of trophy marlin and tuna. Many times Tad had gazed around the room, taking in all the Papa Hemmingway memorabilia, noting that the place probably had not changed much in the decades since the fabled writer had held court here. Lots of people, bold, adventurous as well as dark and nefarious had graced the place.

And now Tad was here to meet a shadowy figure who would lead him and Ramon further into the dark side from where they once emerged. Tad walked another block and turned left toward the Dolphin House. The Inn was constructed by another island legend. The Bimini native had grown up and moved off to the States for an education. He brought back Ivy League credentials and returned to his small island to give back to the community.

He also built an inn that could be considered nothing short of a work of art. Few people knew about the Dolphin House. Tad did.

Tad recognized the man sitting in the back yard under a Kalik Beer umbrella. Tad approached him and said, "Buy you a drink?"

The man gazed around the yard, slowly pivoting his polarized sunglasses left and right, taking in the sights.

"Goodness sakes, Murphy, we're the only ones around."

"Are we? And using first names now? Just like that? No operational security?"

Tad's face reddened, knowing he had received a much-deserved rebuke.

"Sorry. What's the plan? What next?"

Murphy studied the straw in his sparkling water. "Did you throw the firearms overboard like Arnie instructed?"

"No. How did you know…nevermind. I thought we might need them."

"Ahhhh. A glimmer of hope you show. A shred of intelligence. Good.

"No need for sarcasm, Murph. Though smugness does suit you well. How did you get over here?"

"We chartered that seaplane you see out there by the government docks. It is at our disposal."

"Our? Who all is our?

"The team. I suppose you need to meet the team."

"I thought they were all…gone. Who now?"

"Let us go upstairs."

The two men wound their way up a steep staircase and turned right, stopping at room number one.

Murphy knocked twice, then once, then twice again.

"Wow," Tad muttered, "just like Rocky and Bullwinkle."

"Did you say something?"

"Nope. Just clearing my throat."

The door swung open quickly and a serious-looking black man holding a big-bore pistol greeted them with a look of indecision – who to shoot first?

"Murphy." The gun lowered. "What was that knock all about? We didn't say anything about a special knock."

"Rocky and Bullwinkle. Ask this young man here. He knows all about it."

Murphy entered the room, with Tad behind him.

The man with the gun introduced himself to Tad, "Dixon. Phillip Dixon. Pleased to meet you."

Tad greeted Dixon with a handshake.

From the other side of the room, a voice chirped out, "Just like a man! No manners a'tall. Come here, young fellow!"

Dixon said in a low tone, "I wouldn't get too close."

Tad walked over, his eyes adjusting to the darkened room to discover an elderly lady dressed in shorts, a "Legalize It" t-shirt and an enormous straw hat.

"My name is Edna Stribling and you don't listen to him! He's just pissed that he didn't get to sit next to me on the flight here."

Tad looked at Edna, then looked at Murph, and then looked back at Edna. "Uh…pleased to meet you…Edna. Murph, can we have a word alone? Outside?"

Murphy assisted Edna to her feet and escorted her to the outside porch that overlooked the harbor. "Edna, why don't you rest outside and let us talk for a few minutes?"

Edna replied in a sweet voice, "Why thank you, Murphy! I appreciate you using the fact that I do not have a penis to ostracize me from what might be the most exciting moment in my last ten years of existence. I'll just be out here on the porch, watching the world pass me by. Maybe I'll die out here. You would like that, wouldn't you?"

"Sure…wait, I mean no. I would not like that. But if you expire, better in the Bahamas, rather than in Northern Virginia." Murphy countered.

"Well since you put it that way…and also like I have a damn choice."

Murph shut the door leading to the porch and blinked, trying to regain his vision.

"Hold on gentlemen, let my eyes get adjusted."

Dixon flipped on the light switch. "How's that? Light on command? Or is this not dramatic enough?"

Tad's brain was reeling, trying to process all the facts, but he was having no luck. Murph seemed to sense his frustration.

"Thaddeus, Dixon works for Bradford Forbish, the father of Elizabeth and Sandy. He has proven himself to be most capable and is fully vested in this… project."

"So he's going to kill the kidnappers? You and him and Aunt Bee?"

Dixon sprang into the conversation, "Whoa! No one said anything about killing anyone! My job is to get Elizabeth Forbish back safe and sound. I don't even want to *talk* about killing anyone."

Murphy studied Tad like he might study a pimple. "That was very elegant, Thaddeus. Even for you, I must admit you once again torpedo my plans. I want you to take out the dictionary behind you and look up the word, 'discretion.'"

Tad looked behind him, but did not see a dictionary.

"A figure of speech, Thaddeus! Oh, …nevermind! Dixon, no one is being killed tonight, so rest your conscience. We have to establish contact with the subjects. From there, we make the switch. Plain and simple."

Dixon looked skeptical. "Look, that girl is my primary and ONLY priority. If she is harmed in any way…"

Murphy waved his hand in front of his annoyed face, swatting an imaginary insect, "At this point, killing them is not an option. We tried in Key West and it all blew up. We still do not know what happened. The two principals, Michael O'Brien and Catherine Hayes – we are not entirely sure they were there or not. There was so much shooting that happened so fast, we did not get to spring our trap. So now, our best option is to make the trade and trace the money. We are going to get Elizabeth back alive, I promise."

Murph continued, "So now, they either are here or will be here. They will contact Thaddeus and give instructions. Thaddeus will then call me with this radio…" Murphy handed Tad a radio the size of a cell phone, "…and wait for instructions. In the meantime, Dixon, I would appreciate it if you could take care of Darling Edna."

Dixon scowled, "That's great. You want me to babysit Granny Clampett while you go after O'Brien and company. Doesn't compute. Sorry."

"Why…" Tad mused out loud, "…is Edna here? What is her purpose? Why is she so special? Can someone help me out?"

"Why, Thaddeus," Murphy said, "…finally a good question. She is special indeed. Edna is a very distinguished lady. In fact, she has completed a task that no person alive on this earth has ever done. She saw Michael O'Brien and Catherine Hayes. She knows what they look like."

"She saw them?"

"She saw them shoot Johnny. So now you know her role."

Tad nodded, his calculating brain in overdrive formulating plans, exploring possibilities.

Murphy turned to Dixon, "Why don't you take Edna to get something to eat and then let her rest. I anticipate tomorrow will be eventful."

Dixon nodded and left the room.

Tad asked, "Murph, we're really going to just let them take the package and leave?"

"Oh no. We're going to kill them all."

• • •

Tad wandered down the street to the bar where Ramon, Jimbo and the girls were. Jimbo was regaling the girls with off-color jokes – "…a quarter pounder with cheese. Hah! Get it?…Hey! There's Tad! How about a drink? This one is called a Sex on the Beach with a Conch stuck up your Ass. That's what the bartender calls it. Don't know what he means by that. Let me get you one."

Tad snuck a look at the bartender, who was laughing with a couple of locals, staring and pointing at Jimbo. "No, Jimbo, that will not be necessary. Thanks anyway. Sandy, how are you feeling?"

Sandy's eye was no longer swollen, but it was very black and would likely be that way for a while. To her credit, she was taking it like a trooper.

"I'm fine. What now?"

Tad said, "You know what I think we all need right now?"

Jimbo blasted out, "Scotch and a blow job?"

Ramon was nodding in agreement to that one.

Tad said, "No. We need to go to the boat and wait."

Tiffani said, "Super! What are we waiting on?"

Ramon interjected, "The next great idea, kitten! The next great idea. Now let us all return to the boat."

The group ambled their way back to the *Who's Your Daddy*. The sailboat rocked slightly in the wind. As Ramon was assisting Tiffani and Sandy stepping on board, Jimbo piped up, "This is bullshit. That's what it is, Tad. Just bullshit."

"What, Jimbo, is the problem?"

"Where we are. Why didn't we put the boat in at that marina over there? The Big Game Club?"

Tad paused, not knowing where this conversation was going. "Well...because I have used this marina many times in the past. I know the people. It is a little cheaper here. Those sorts of reasons."

Jimbo did not look placated. "I know good and damn well the people who are broke out with money and have big, nice boats park them at the Bimini Big Game Club Marina. How come we are here? You make me look like I can't afford it. It's embarrasin.'"

"Here among the white trash?"

"Yes! ...I mean no, it's not like that. Hell, I don't know what I mean. The point is that I'm the owner and you're supposed to ask me where I want the boat. I, meaning ME. Maybe I would have wanted to boat here or over there at the Big Game Club or maybe in a field of buffalo shit but you didn't ask. Sheesh." Jimbo burped and spit into the water.

Tad was floored by Jimbo's assault. His face was getting red and he could feel himself getting angry when Ramon came to his aid.

"Hey Jimbo, Tad and I, we talked about this. You see this is the very dock where Papa Hemmingway parked his boat, Pilar, right here. See the slip we are in? That's the one. THE SAME EXACT SLIP! You are a man of adventure, right? Now you have THE HEMMINGWAY SLIP. Now those boats over at the Big Game Club are big, nice boats. Very nice. But their people are now wondering, 'Why is that big, nice sailboat parked over there? Why is he not here with us?' And their dockmaster will tell them all, 'Because that man has parked his boat in Papa Hemmingway's slip.' At which point all the owners of those boats will be getting on the collective asses of their skippers wanting to know, 'Why didn't you park this boat there? Over there in Hemmingway's slip?' So when you show up at their bar, they will know they are in the presence of a man who emanates the same essence of adventure as the Old Man himself. Go on over, Jimbo. Show them who you are."

Jimbo was nodding in agreement as Ramon laid it on thick. He said, "I do got some essence don't I!"

"Hell yes!" Ramon agreed.

"Sorry, boys! I was just puttin' you on! I knew the whole time you were taking care of me and the girls. I just had an idea. I think I'm going over to the Big Game Club and take a look around. Might just have a drink with those clowns over there."

With those parting words, Jimbo made his way down the three hundred yard stretch of road that separated the two marinas.

"Thanks," Tad said, "I was getting pretty flamed there."

"Hey, no problem. That's what I am here for."

"You ended you sentence in a preposition."

"That's what I am here for, Dipshit.

"Better. We're really in Hemmingway's slip?"

"Who knows. A little deception is a beautiful thing."

"There seems to be a lot of that on this island today."

The crew of the Who's Your Daddy sat around the boat, watching a gorgeous sunset. The wind had died down and the colors of the sun danced in the ripple. Tad had already told Ramon and Sandy of his meeting with Murphy, Dixon and Edna. They had said little to Tiffani, who seemed content to sit in the cockpit and sip Diet Coke and throw bread to fish.

Tad had explained to Sandy and Ramon, while they were in the cabin, away from Tiffani, that when the message was delivered, they would probably have to go quickly. Tad emphasized, "Sandy, under no circumstances, that means NO circumstances, do you leave this boat. You are only going to get Elizabeth killed. Murphy and Dixon are on the shore. Ramon and I are here. We are only going to make the swap and get the hell out of here. Understand?"

Sandy nodded here approval.

"No, I mean it! You look me in the eye and tell me you won't get involved. Seven people died in Key West. You are lucky you did not get shot yourself. The only reason they did not kill you is they needed a messenger. Now tell me you will stay here."

A look of anger flashed in Sandy's eyes, "OK! I said I will not interfere! I'm sorry all that happened, but that was not my fault. I'll be here."

Tad studied her and said, "OK. Let's go up"

Tiffani was feeding a group of gulls who were methodically crapping all over the boat. She did not seem to notice. Ramon said, "Hey Chica! Go easy on the bread. Someone has to clean up this mess."

"Omigod! I am so sorry! I did not even notice…I'll clean it up."

"No, no. I'll take care of it. You just relax."

As Ramon hosed off the cockpit, Tad was checking the standing rigging all along the deck. The dockmaster walked up to the boat and said, "Hey Mon! You got a letter here!"

Tad stepped off the boat and looked at the envelope in the dockmaster's hand. "Who brought it?"

The dockmaster handed it over to Tad, "A child, Mon. He said it was for the rat bastard."

"Great. That's me. Thank you."

Tad walked over to Ramon and opened the envelope. There was a piece of paper inside. Tad withdrew it and turned it over. It said, "END OF THE WORLD. 9:30. SCREW UP AND E. DIES. BRING THE PACKAGE."

Tad said, "I think I need to go into the cabin and use the radio."

Ramon and Sandy followed while Tiffani painted her toenails.

"(static)… (click) L.L. Bean, L.L. Bean, this is tadpole, over."

"(static)… (click) You are so funny. I cannot stop laughing. You do not have to use code names. These are secure radios. No one but us can listen in."

"(static)… (click) Roger that. The eagle has landed."

"(static)… (click) …what? The eagle…I told you this is a secure radio. Please attempt to use the King's English."

Ramon snickered to Tad, "Why are you doing this to Murph?" They both suppressed laughter.

"(static)… (click) The bird is in the hand. The conch is in the shell. The lion sleeps tonight. I know you are but what am I?"

"(static)… (click) Good. I think I am following you, though God knows how or why. What information do you have?"

"(static)… (click) We are to meet at the End of the World Bar at 9:30 and bring the package. That is all the instructions I have."

"(static)…(click) Good. Do just that. …and bring your weapons."

"(static)… (click) What is the plan, Mr. Bean?"

"(static)… (click) Make the switch. Walk away. Protect Ms. E. We will take care of the rest."

"(static)… (click) Roger. Out."

Tad stared at the radio, deep in thought. "Something is missing or out of place."

"No joke," Ramon offered, "There is a lot missing. Has been lately. What you thinking of?"

"He said 'We' will take care of the rest. Who is 'we'? Dixon is not involved in the neutralizing of the bad guys. Edna certainly can't help, other than identifying the two principle targets."

"You mean O'Brien and Hayes?" Sandy asked. "How can she do that?"

"Oh, I forgot to tell you. She saw them shoot Johnny and kidnap Elizabeth. Dixon didn't tell you?"

"I guess not. No matter though. I am sure Murph has everything taken care of."

"Knowing Murph," Tad said, "he certainly will."

Tad and Ramon careful disassembled and cleaned their handguns. They put a light coat of oil on the cool metal and reassembled the weapons. They also oiled the cartridges and magazines. Salt air is rough on weapons. They put on shorts, t-shirts and light jackets to cover up the guns.

At 9:15, they stepped off the big Morris and on to the dock. Tad had given final instructions to Sandy and Ramon. "Once we make the switch, we come straight back here. Murph and Dixon will come get her and take her straight to the seaplane. They are out of here. We hunker down for the night and get out of here tomorrow morning. Everyone OK with the plan?"

Heads nodded somberly and the two men began the walk into the fray one more time.

Tad carried a backpack this time, rather than a shopping bag. Inside the backpack was the Fedex package that he had carried for their first failed rendezvous in Key West. They moved casually, both constantly scanning the area. There were many people out on the pleasant evening. Locals walked around and chatted with each other in that island accent that brought back memories of the colonial British days. Fishermen walked down the streets, moving from one bar to the next, puffing on Cuban cigars. Kids were still out playing and throwing rocks at the skinny dogs. Nothing looked out of place. Everything looked absolutely normal for a night in Alicetown, Bimini. This bothered Tad immensely.

The End of the World Bar was also called the Sand Bar, after the sand floor. Tad and Ramon had spent many nights here, hoisting Kalik beers and enjoying the sailing life. They knew it well, every nook and cranny. They could both visualize the layout of the building, the fact it overlooked the water. Overlooked? It practically hung out over the water. They pictured the women's underwear hanging all over the wall, donations from many a female who had ordered one too many drinks on someone else's tab.

It all looked too difficult. Too small a building. No way that backup could fit in the bar. Tad wondered what Murph's plan was. No doubt it would become apparent in time, but at who's expense?

They paused in the doorway, peering in and evaluating the occupants. By 9:30, the bar was full of loud patrons. The fog of cigar smoke and laughter and loud boasting contrasted with the focus and attention both Tad and Ramon gave to their task. A band blared on, "…Don't worry 'bout a ting. Every little ting gonna be alright." The spirit of Bob Marley was alive and well in island music.

In slow motion, Tad and Ramon stepped into the bar, both unconsciously checking their weapons, feeling the outline of the pistols for security. They moved to a corner table and set the backpack down on the table. A tall, thin Bahamian girl came over to them and took their drink order. "Two Kaliks, please."

They sat and sipped on the beers, taking in the crowd, assessing each person.

"No gomers here." Ramon offered.

A young boy walked in and stopped in front of the table in front of Tad. He was smiling big and had a note. "I knew it would be you, rat bastard. Here is a note for you."

Tad took the note. "Go home. Now. Do not stop. You hear me?"

A swat on the head by Ramon convinced the child to move out quickly. Tad opened the note. WALK OUTSIDE. A CAR WILL DRIVE UP. GET IN. Tad showed Ramon the note and then folded it and put it in his pocket. Both men got up without talking. Tad grabbed the backpack and they headed for the door.

The cool, fresh night air was a welcome relief from the smoky bar atmosphere. They looked to their left and there was a pickup truck making its way slowly toward the bar entrance. It looked like an old Nissan truck, held together by wire, electrical tape and old fashioned determination. The truck slowed and stopped in front of the two. There were three men in the back, two black and one white. The driver and passenger were impossible to see due to the darkness and dirty windows.

"Get in, Mon," one of the black guys in the truck bed said with pleasant accent that was betrayed by his stern disposition and a shotgun in his hands.

Ramon and Tad hopped in the back of the truck, eyeing the three men. The white man obviously was the leader. He studied both Ramon and Tad, and then said, "The bag, please." His Irish accent gave him away immediately to Tad and Ramon. O'Brien.

Tad handed him the bag. "Where's Elizabeth Forbish?"

"Near. You'll get her soon."

The truck began to drive off. Each time the small truck hit a pothole, the bed would bottom out and hit the concrete road and make a loud "crumph!" sound. They drove past the Blue Water Marina. Tad strained to see if he could see Sandy or Tiffani on the boat. He saw neither.

They rolled just past the Big Game Club where Jimbo was no doubt drinking himself into a stupor. As they passed the club, Tad asked the white man, "Where are we going?"

"To see the other parts of this island. Very beautiful, the other end."

This was bad news to Tad and Ramon. They both knew the other end was pretty much deserted.

The man continued, "...and to go somewhere Mr. Murphy cannot interfere again."

Tad was incredulous. "You know Murphy." It was more a statement that a question.

"Of course I do, Tad. We know everything about you."

"You are O'Brien."

"Aye. I admit it. I confess."

"And these are your henchman. Like a bad movie, right?"

"This is Paul and Silas. Brothers. They have volunteered to help us make this transaction."

Paul smiled. He was holding the shotgun pointed at Tad's stomach. Silas made no sign that he heard anything.

"So now we're like a family. We all know each other"

"Except," Ramon added, "You have guns pointed at us."

"Well, laddie..." O'Brien said, "...a dysfunctional family, but family nonetheless."

The mood was grim as they rolled past the Big Game Club into a stretch of darkness. O'Brien surprised them all as he grabbed the backpack and threw it into the bushes on the edge of the wall that surrounded the venerable Big Game Club. "That ought to do it." He said.

"O'Brien, you just threw out..." Tad never finished his sentence.

Out of the dark from the left, a small car came speeding out of a side street. It was the sound that first alerted the group, since the lights were off. The whine of the engine and crunch of the gravel caused everyone to look to the oncoming car.

If anyone in the truck had time to see, they would have seen a very determined-looking white man gripping the wheel tightly, a fit-looking black man yelling at the driver and a little old lady buckled in the back seat, smiling like she was on Mr. Toad's Wild Ride.

All the trucks passengers strained in that last microsecond to see what was about to impact them. Everyone except Ramon, who reached out and snatched the shotgun out of Paul's hands.

The little speeding car t-boned the truck with a loud sound of crumpled metal and yelps of surprise from all the passengers. The truck slid off the road and into a coconut palm tree. The truck stopped immediately, but the forward momentum of the passengers caused them to continue their motion over of the right side of the truck bed and into space.

Newton's laws of physics took over as Paul and Silas became bodies in motion. Paul, however, took a very short flight as he went face first into the coconut tree, crushing his face and dropping limply onto the ground.

Tad and Ramon were thrown around in the truck, but not thrown out. O'Brien leapt out of the truck, sprinting toward the bag he had thrown out. The driver of the vehicle apparently was not injured too badly, as he opened fire on the driver and passenger of the car that had just rammed them. Bullet holes appeared across the windshield of the car, but the driver and passenger had opened the door and rolled out. Murphy and Dixon popped up firing, both of them scoring fatal hits on the driver of the truck.

Ramon and Tad bailed out of the pickup, in pursuit of Silas and O'Brien. Tad was chasing Silas, shotgun in hand. Tad fired one shot into the back of the legs of the man running away and he crumpled and surrendered immediately. "Don't shoot me, Mon! Please! I got a family, Mon!" Tad stood near him and then looked around for Ramon.

Silas saw his opportunity and whipped out his ancient Model 1911 .45 pistol and fired off two quick shots at Tad. Tad heard the first one whine by his ear. He then felt something slam into his side, spinning him around.

As he was rolling, trying to regain his feet, he heard five quick shots ring out. He got to his knees and saw Murph standing over Silas, who was now not moving at all. Ramon was thrashing around in the water with O'Brien. Both Tad, who was now holding his side and Murph made their way to the edge of the water. Dixon was already there, staring at the spectacle taking place in the water. He had a young girl with him who had a horrified look on her face. Despite the blood trickling down her forehead where she had hit the windshield, Tad knew she had to be Elizabeth Forbish.

The turned his attention to the two men in the water.

Blood exploded in a bright red spray as the brown, barnacle-covered shell smacked loudly into the man's head. THWOCK! The man's eyes rolled back into his head and a big gash just above his temple revealed his skull, glistening with a patina of blood. None of the people watching were paying much attention to the dying man with a big hole in his head. Their attention was focused on the other man standing next to the dead guy.

That would be the guy with the shell.

Snapping out of his stupor, Tad stumbled down into the gin-clear shallow water, the bottom visible even at night. "Ramon, I think you beat him to death with… that shell. That's a new one, even for you."

"Not just any shell…," he continued, "…a Queen Conch shell. Definitely not just any shell. The shell most associated with the Florida Keys and this Shangri La called the Bahamas. It stirs the imagination and fires the passions. It'll also hold a door open, but that's another story. Can you hear me, O'Brien? Are you listening? Conch – rhymes with conk – like what I just did to your head."

O'Brien heard nothing. His head was six inches under water and no bubbles were emanating from within. No input from O'Brien.

"Shell, I proclaim that you are a killer. You have killed Mr. O'Brien, who needed to be killed and hence is such and done is the deed. You and I have become one. We are brothers of the molluskial dark arts."

Murphy looked at Tad impatiently. Tad replied, "You know how he is. The spirit moves him."

Murphy grumbled, "Something better move us all."

A red stain spread around the vicinity of O'Brien's cabeza muerta throughout the water.

Murphy cleared his throat and said, "Ramon, you know the difference between killers and murderers? Killers are the ones that have not been caught yet. And we have not yet been caught. Murderers have been convicted. We have not and I would prefer to keep it that way. Now, please pull your head out of your fourth point of contact or we going to be stuck in a Bahamian jail with Jamaican drug runners using us for blowup dolls. We have to go, Ramon. Tad, you and Ramon get to the boat and we will get to the sea plane."

"Ah, yes," Ramon said, "There's that. Time to leave," he said slowly, "…but the shell comes with us. It's all about synergy. Working together. Man and nature. Mano y Shello."

Tad exhaled in a measured breath nodded, "Goes on the mantle. Let's go home, Conch Killer."

"Conch Killer? I like it!" Ramon said. His face brightened as he washed the blood off the edge of the shell. "Time to go."

It was then that they watched the big Morris Yacht motoring swiftly out of the channel and headed toward the Gulf Stream.

Their way home was leaving without them. Great. What now?

• • •

"Murph, that's our boat leaving. You have to stop it."

"How, Thaddeus, do you propose I do that?"

Ramon had walked over to the bushes where the late O'Brien had tossed the backpack. "It's gone. The backpack is here, but the contents are gone. Someone was waiting for it and took it."

Dixon asked, "Who? Who got it?"

Murph rasped at them, "Does it matter? We have to leave – now! Let's get Edna and get out of here."

They sprinted up to the car to get Edna. Murphy opened the back door and looked inside. He froze in place and then moved aside. Dixon looked in and cursed quietly. There was a bullet hole in the middle of Edna's forehead. She had a smile on her face. She had been granted her last adventure.

Murph said, "To the plane. Dixon, get Elizabeth and get to the plane.

Tad inquired, "What about us?"

Murph reached in his pocket and pulled out a roll of bills. "You two have finished your assignment. Thaddeus, that red spot on your shirt indicates a wound. I am assuming it is a flesh wound, since you are still perpendicular to the earth. I wouldn't have an island doctor look at it. Get Ramon to patch it up. Find your way home tomorrow. Dixon will make sure you get the rest later."

"No way. It is not over! We're going with you."

"Not enough room in the sea plane, Thaddeus. Call me when you get back." Murph made the "call me" sign by putting his thumb to his ear and pinky finger to his mouth and giving the "wiggle."

With that Tad and Ramon watched Murphy, Dixon and the young woman they had been searching for melt in the darkness. Dixon was carrying Edna. Ramon made his own finger sign that didn't look anything at all like Murphy's. It wiggled also.

Tad and Ramon drifted back up the street. "What we gonna do now?" Ramon mused?

Tad thought for a few minutes. "We have to find Jimbo. If he discovers that the boat is gone and starts to raise hell, everyone is going to put two and two together very soon. We find him and keep him quiet until we can get off of this island."

They drifted into the bar of the Big Game Club, looking much like a hundred different boat hands that come in on the big fishing boats from Miami, Ft. Lauderdale and West Palm Beach. They looked around but did not see Jimbo. They walked out on the docks, scanning the boats.

On the last dock in a slip was the small sailboat, *Wild Hair*. Tad and Ramon both looked at each other and smiled. They walked over to the *Wild Hair* and hailed them, "Hello *Wild Hair*, anyone aboard?" There was no answer.

"What now, Einstein?" Ramon asked.

"Well, we just have to borrow it."

"Hey, Bubba, boatnapping is a serious crime. I don't know if my karma can take it."

"Can your butthole take thirty years in a Bahamian jail?"

"Let's get going."

Tad wrote a note on the back of his business card. TOOK BOAT. SORRY. LIFE AND DEATH. MONEY FOR THE INCONVENIENCE AND DISCRETION. SORRY. COME GET IT IN TWO DAYS. Tad then counted out twenty hundred dollar bills from the wad that Murph had given him. He stuck the note and money in the empty backpack and headed to the dockmaster's office.

There were three locals who worked at the Big Game Club sitting around, drinking Kaliks and swapping lies.

"What's up Mon? What can we do for you?"

"Where is the dockmaster?"

"I am John, the assistant dockmaster, Mon. How can I help? The Dockmaster is not here"

"The owners of that MacGregor, Carlton and Lynn, left this on our boat. Can you get it to them in the morning, bright and early?"

"I tink so, Mon. Shall I take it now?"

Tad said hurriedly, "No, no. Early in the morning. This is for your trouble." Tad handed him a twenty.

"Yes sir! I will deliver it myself! Have a good evening." John tipped his bottle of beer to Tad.

When Tad made it back to the boat, Ramon had it ready to cast off. "It's full of gas, boyo," Ramon said. "They already filled up. Let's get out of here."

Tad and Ramon cast off from the dock and retrieved the docklines. They stowed them below and tried to move out as quietly as they could. The outgoing tide and overcast sky allowed them to slip out of the Bimini harbor undetected.

They motored down the shoreline until they arrived at the range markers and turned the boat west, toward Florida. The chase was on.

Ramon asked, "They got an hour head start, at least. It is almost eleven o'clock. How fast you think we gonna go?"

Tad said, "Probably four or five knots at the most. We'll be fighting the stream the whole way.

"Tad, some questions, please. Who is driving the *Who's Your Daddy?* Who are we chasing? What do you think they did with the girls? What is Murph's game? What the hell happened back there? Stuff like that. You may comment now."

"The Hayes woman is the only one left, I think. She has to be on Jimbo's boat. Speaking of which, tomorrow morning when he wakes up from wherever he passes out tonight, he will pitch a fit and the Bimini Police will probably get involved. So we don't have long. I think the Hayes woman will go to some obscure place for her to get off the boat and get out of the country. I feel sure she has some sort of plan, though God only know what it is. I don't know what she will do to Sandy and Tiffani. Sandy has some value, since she is Forbish's daughter. Tiffani does not. Maybe they will be smart enough to keep their mouth shut and not piss her off."

"How did they know to take our boat?"

"I can only assume they have had us under surveillance since we arrived. They knew you and I were gone from the boat. Probably knew that Jimbo was out drinking. It's the easiest way off the island. They can probably make eight or nine knots crossing if they head northwest. That will put them somewhere around Palm Beach by early tomorrow."

"And where are we going?"

"Home. We're going to Key Largo. Conch Island Marina. Home. There we can reload so to speak. Get the resources we need and contact Murphy."

"He ain't gonna help us."

"He'll help. We're pretty much all he has left on this operation now that is constant and reliable. I'll talk to him."

"There's too much missing here. This O'Brien has constantly been one step ahead the whole time – that is until Murph's traffic accident ended his streak. I just don't like the way it all smells."

"Worry about getting all we can out of this boat."

They had a moderate easterly wind that was helping push them east, toward Florida. They used a whisker pole to push the clew of the headsail as far out as possible, collecting all the wind they could. They let the boom swing out also, and tied a line to prevent it from swinging back on the cockpit and knocking someone senseless.

The Yamaha 9.9 hp motor churned away, helping the wind push the twenty-five foot boat reach and maintain hull speed of six knots. The ride was rough and bumpy, as they were actually sailing against the Gulf Stream. The Gulf Stream is like a massive river that flows north between Florida and the Bahamas. The Stream has waves, eddies and swells just like any other part of the ocean, except it flows north. Mariners who sail south against the current usually have an exciting ride.

"Hey Chico, this is like a roller coaster ride. This boat going to handle it?"

"I think so, Ramon. This boat only weighs about three thousand pounds. The *Who's Your Daddy* weighed ten times what this weighs. Go up and check the standing rigging. We can't be dismasted out here."

Ramon checked all the stays and shrouds. Satisfied, he returned to the cockpit and disappeared into the cabin. Minutes later, Jimmy Buffett wafted from speakers in the bulkhead and inside the cabin.

"...*Oh the stories we could tell if it all blows up and goes to hell...*"

"He's right, Chico."

"Who, Jimmy Buffett? He usually is."

"No. Murph. He said you never really get out. You're liking this, aren't you? It's back in your blood. The chase. The hunt and the kill."

Tad didn't answer immediately. He checked the compass and the GPS. It didn't matter; Tad could have sailed this boat back home blindfolded.

"I guess so. Though we *did not ask* to be put in this thing we're in, now that we're in, I want to finish it."

"You don't even know what this Catherine Hayes looks like."

"I will know here when I see her. Count on it."

"I believe you, Chico. I believe you."

At the little sailboat plodded along, flying fish took off in panicked flights, skimming over the water. Airplanes made their takeoff and approaches from Miami. The clouds began to clear, offering a stunning view of millions of stars. The view of the heavens from the ocean is unlike anywhere else.

Six hours later, the horizon began to show evidence of a coming day. The sun rose right on the stern and seas began to quiet down a bit. The two men coaxed the sailboat on at all the speed they could muster. The wind gave out earlier and they were under bare poles. Even so, the boat continued to make six knots.

By seven, they could see the towers on Key Largo. Soon the horizon grew dark with the outline of mangrove-lined shores.

"There she is! Home sweet home! Let's guess on what awaits us – I'll go first. OK, four police cars, three FBI vans, two customs and immigrations agents and one nasty, foul-mouth blonde bitch from Two Egg, Florida. What you think?"

"You probably hit it right on the head. We'll know when we round the breakwater."

The *Wild Hair* slowly made its way around the mangrove-lined strip of land that protected the harbor. What they saw astonished both of them. Even Ramon was searching for words.

In the end slip of Conch Island Marina was the *Who's Your Daddy*.

• • •

Finally Ramon broke the silence. "OK, Chico. What now?" Ramon began to check and re-check their handguns. *"Damn,"* Tad thought. *"I have to get rid of these things. Arnie is going to kill me."*

Tad said, "We have the advantage. The Hayes woman does not know this boat. You stay down and I'll bring us up next to them. A quick assault on the boat is as good as anything. Fix a dock line around the lifeline stanchion and I'll bring it in right on their beam. Ramon, don't – I repeat – don't shoot the girls."

"I'm with you, Chico."

The small sailboat quietly moved up to the larger Morris Yacht. As the rubrail gently kissed the side of the large boat, Tad quickly wrapped a line around a cleat on the deck of the large boat. Both men sprang onto the deck and moved quickly to the cockpit. Anyone inside would now know they had visitors. No more surprises.

Ramon swung his head down into the cabin and jerked back quickly, expecting a fusillade of gun shots. None came.

Tad swung his weapon into the companionway, searching for targets. There! In the navigation station! A target...wait!

Ramon called out, "What you see, Bubba?"

Tad said, "It's Jimbo. He's shot up."

Both men vaulted down into the cockpit and cleared the remaining areas of the boat. They walked over to Jimbo, who was bleeding from many gunshot wounds.

"He dead, Chico?"

Jimbo's eyes fluttered and he stirred slightly. He tried to form words, but they were difficult to hear. Tad told Ramon to go tell George to call 911. Ramon took off in a sprint. Tad retrieved some dish towels and tried to stem the bleeding from the more copious wounds.

"Jimbo, can you hear me?"

Jimbo's eyes opened and took a few seconds to focus on Tad. He tried a couple of times unsuccessfully to form words and then succeeded. "Yeah. (a few seconds) ...call Murph...."

Tad tried to process the request. How the hell did Jimbo know about Murphy? Tad asked, "How do you know Murphy?"

"...idiot...set up...whole time...call Murphy..."

Tad continued to hold the towels in place. "What else, Jimbo."

"...my...name...is...Walter...work...with...Murphy. Catherine...Hayes...she...was...with...us. We're...so stupid...find... her...she's...sailing...out...another...marina near."

And Jimbo (or Walter, depending on who you ask) drew his last breath. He slumped over in the chair.

Tad's mind was reeling. Jimbo with Murphy? Could it be true? Why not? It was coming clear now. It was the perfect cover. Jimbo never showed any interest at all learning to pilot the *Who's Your Daddy*, though he hired Tad to teach him. What about Sandy and Tiffani?

Tad sprung from the boat and raced up toward the marina office. He opened the door to the office and confronted George and Ramon calling 911.

"George, did you see that sailboat dock?"

"Tad! There you are. What's this about someone in there shot?"

"Hang up, now. Did you see it when it came in?"

"Of course. I thought it was you. Where the hell you two been? And what kind of trouble you in?"

"This is important, George. Who got off? Who left the boat? Did you see it?"

"Yes I did, Mr. Screw-the-world-because- I'm-in-a-big-hurry. I certainly did. They arrived about two hours ago. You think I'm so old I'm blind? Sheesshh!"

A pregnant pause that weighed a ton enveloped the trio.

Finally, Tad could stand it no more. "Who? And what did they look like?"

"Ah, it was those two girls you took out with you. Real lookers. I expected you to get off but, hell, it was just those two girls."

Just two girls.

• • •

Tad again reeled from the information. He chastised himself, "Think, Tad, think!"

"OK, Ramon, who is it? Tiffani or Sandy? Which one."

"You got me. Tiffani is too dumb and Sandy is Forbish's daughter. Neither one makes any sense."

"Walter had us fooled. Maybe Tiffani could also."

"Who's Walter?" Ramon asked.

"Oh, that's Jimbo's real name."

"How do you know that?" George asked?

"Because he told me!"

"You said he is dead! How could he have told you if he is dead?"

"George! Jesus! He told me and then he died."

"Helluva way to go. That's what I say. By the way, just call me George, not George Jesus." Said George.

Ramon nodded, "Amen, Old Man."

"Who you callin' and old man? In my day I could..."

Tad grabbed Ramon and dragged Ramon out of the office. "Call you later! Don't mess with the dead guy."

The two trotted across the parking lot toward Tad's apartment. The door was ajar about six inches. They stormed the door, guns drawn.

There was movement in the corner. Pfft! Pfft! Two quick shots from Ramon's silenced pistol caused a slight explosion in the corner.

"Great. You shot the television."

"Well, shit! That thing scared me."

"Yeah, well you're replacing it."

"I can fix it. My old man's got tools."

"Fast Times at Ridgemont High. Sean Penn. Classic."

"On the couch, Chico."

The second surprise of the day was staring at them.

Tiffani was on the couch, bound and gagged. She appeared to be in good health. Ramon quickly untied her as Tad cleared the house.

When Ramon removed her bonds, she jumped up and hugged him, tears coming from her eyes. "Omigod! She shot him! She said you two were dead! She said the Jamaicans or someone shot you! She and Jimbo got in a big fight and she shot him!"

"Take it easy. You're OK now." Ramon said as he comforted her.

Tad walked in and said, "Why did she let Tiffani live? Why not kill her like Jimbo?"

Tiffani straightened herself out and sat upright, obviously straining hard mentally to recall something.

"Mmmm, let's see. OK, that's right! I'm supposed to tell whoever found me something. The game changes now. She has been identified. And I am supposed to witness bears. That's it!"

Tad and Ramon stared at each other. "Witness be… Bear witness! She is supposed to bear witness. Sandy…I mean Hayes knows her identity is no longer a secret and will soon be public. She wants the publicity for her cause! Tiffani is supposed to be the one to give her the recognition she wants."

Ramon agreed. "Sounds logical. But where is she?"

Tad thought back to Jimbo/Walter's last words. "'She's going to sail away…from a nearby marina.' I taught her to sail and she's leaving. The *Who's Your Daddy* would be too easy to trace. There has to be another boat nearby. In a nearby marina."

Ramon thought out loud, "There's the Mandalay and Largo Marina. Which one?"

"You take Largo Marina. I'll take the Mandalay. Take my truck. I'll take George's car."

Both men sprinted down the steps. Ramon cranked up Tad's truck, which groaned and squeaked in protest. Tad ran and jumped in George's El Dorado. The keys were on top of the visor, just like they always were. "Thank God for poor security" Tad told no one in particular.

The Cadillac sprang into life as the big V-8 rumbled and the tires threw chunks of coral everywhere. Tad fishtailed out of the parking lot and gunned the land yacht to the entrance of the Mandalay. He slammed on the brakes and threw it in park, shutting it off as he cautiously surveyed the place.

The tiny marina was surrounded by a restaurant and store. There were just a few slips, but Tad knew she would be here. He didn't know how; he just knew.

He had the pistol tucked in his pants, with his t-shirt over it. He slowly made his way around the marina, surveying the boats. There were tiny drops of blood visible from the wound on his side.

Up on the deck of the restaurant, lunch patrons were enjoying mahi-mahi and hot wings and pitchers of cold draft beer. No one paid scant attention to Tad as he walked by, looking at the boats.

Tad paused at the stern of a Beneteau, looking for signs that this was the right boat. Nothing here. In the fifth slip was an old thirty-six foot sloop that had seen its better day. Tad had just reached the slip when a person came out of the companion way.

Sandy.

They both stared at each other, a Mexican standoff. Tad reached for his pistol, but Sandy/Catherine pulled hers much quicker. *"Shit...,"* thought Tad, *"...a girl outdrew me. This is so embarrassing."*

The customers on the deck could only see Tad standing on the dock; Sandy was partially obscured because she was not entirely out of the cabin in the cockpit.

"Put your hands down, Tad and get on board." She said not in an unfriendly tone.

Tad stood frozen.

"Tad, don't be an idiot. Get on the boat. I don't want to shoot you, but I will."

"Sandy, Catherine, why are you doing this? Who are you, really?"

"I like being Sandy. That works fine for me. Get on the boat, please."

Tad tentatively took a step on the stern of the boat and stepped down in the cockpit. Sandy came out and sat across from him. Her hand was covered by a beach towel, which concealed a large bore pistol. Only the end of the silencer stuck out from the towel, leaving Tad with no illusions of his disadvantage in the exchange.

"Why? All those people dead. For money? You do this for money?"

Sandy shook her head as if she was lecturing a small child. "No, it's not just for money. Our dream of liberating Ireland lives still. But with the aftermath of September 11, our group has been demonized. Our contributors have dried up. We need to…jump start our efforts again. That takes money."

"You're not Irish. At least you don't sound Irish."

"No, Tad, I am not. But O'Brien was. He was my mentor. He had the vision and drive necessary to conduct the campaign. I will carry on his works. By the way, did Murphy get him?"

"No. A shell got him. What about Forbish's daughter, the real Sandy?"

"She's fine. She was released from a safe house in Virginia two hours ago. Tad, it's not about the money. Please understand, it's about the oppression our brethren in Ireland have had to endure. It's about a political climate that refuses to grant sovereignty to millions of Irish people who languish under Britain's thumb! Can't you see that? We're not terrorists in the sense that we are flying planes into buildings and blowing up cars, killing civilians. We have always gone after legitimate targets – policemen, soldiers, politicians who further the oppressive British empire."

Tad gazed into the cold, wild eyes of Sandy, knowing now manipulating and calculating she was. She a Believer with a capital "B." She would kill anything and anyone in her way. It all made sense now. Tad had kept her briefed on all their activities. He had explained what all Murphy's plans were. Murphy's team didn't have a leak. Tad was the leak!

Tad had told her of all the plans, all the moves, everything. He had confided in her – trusted her. He may have been falling in love with her. She had used him throughout it all.

He no longer wanted to kill her. He just wanted her to go. How could he have been so stupid?

"I'm reaching into my pants for a pistol. Don't shoot me."

Slowly Tad took out the pistol and handed it to her.

"Tad, come with me. Join me. I have a rendezvous boat that will meet me in three days on the Great Bahama Bank."

"I'm not going. I wish you would not have told me that. Murph will be calling soon."

"You have to come with me, Tad. You cannot leave. Not now."

Tad was angry, "Why did you tell me?!! Why didn't you just leave?"

"Because…because I need you! I need you with me! Not as an… accomplice, as a friend! The two of us always! We have something, Tad, something beautiful."

Tad stared at her, aghast. He shook his head. "I'm going now. Besides, I don't think England cares what Northern Ireland does anyway. You're living in the seventies." He stepped up on the seat, preparing to step off the boat. His side was hurting more and he grabbed on to a pole that was sticking out of the transom for support.

Sandy pulled the gun out in plain view, sighting it in between Tad's shoulder blades. "No! Get off this boat and I'll kill you!"

A woman sitting at the tiki bar glanced over and saw Sandy pointing a gun at Tad. She shrieked, "AIIIIEEEE! She's going to shoot him. Holy Shit-the-Bed-Batman, she's got a gun! We're all gonna die!"

The patrons couldn't have reacted worse if a bushel of scorpions fell on their table. They ran screaming, turning over chairs and spilling drinks to get out of the way.

Tad continued to hold on to the pole for support. With his back turned, facing away from Sandy, "I guess you'll have to shoot me. Just remember one thing."

Sandy kept her aim on his chest. "What's that?"

Tad yanked the pole out of the transom mount and swung it hard. It smacked hard in Sandy's head. Actually, the hooked pointed end buried itself in the woman's left eye. She fell to the floor, twitching, with the giant hook embedded in her cranium. Blood was squirting out in little rivulets.

Sandy was dead on the cockpit floor of the getaway boat.

Tad surveyed the damage. *"Dang. I thought that was a spinnaker pole, not a gaff. This is not going to look good on my resume. Oh well, Adios, Honey."*

Tad said to the corpse who was formerly known as Sandy/Catherine, "I was going to say something else, but now I guess I'll say that you should not forget that I don't know the difference between a gaff and a spinnaker pole."

Tad recovered his pistol and walked over to the bar and talked to the bartender he knew. The sirens were already growing louder in the distance. "Hey, Duane. When the police get here, give me about five minutes before you remember who I am and where I live, OK?"

The bartender nodded somberly and Tad took off. The big El Dorado cruised toward Conch Island Marina, passing Key Largo Police cars on the way out.

When Tad got to the marina, Ramon was just pulling in. "Those police cars for you, Chico?"

"Yeah. It's all over now. Let's go call Murph."

A voice came from out of the office. "That will not be necessary, Thaddeus. Please give me a quick rundown. I just arrived."

Tad gave him the two-minute version. Murphy said, "Mr. Gianis, may I please use your phone?"

George handed him the phone, "Yes you may! Tad, it's about time you brought someone in here with some class. What's your name again?"

"Dover. My first name is Ben. Call me Ben, please."

"Glad to meetcha Ben. Where'd you meet this guy, Tad?"

"George, you just don't want to know."

Murphy talked for a few minutes in quiet tones. Then he hung up the phone and turned to Ramon and Tad.

"I have to go. George, can you please give us some privacy? Thank you."

George left, mumbling, no longer sure that Mr. Dover was a classy guy or not. Murphy turned to Tad and Ramon, "A clean-up crew will be at the site and here also in twenty minutes. The Key Largo police will be here soon. You both will likely be arrested for murder and all sorts of customs and immigrations violations, but we will take care of that. Give me all of your firearms now, please. I will be in touch."

With that, he left.

Ramon said, "Police are coming? Man, I'm getting my conch shell and beer pitcher off of those boats. They aren't going to get them."

"You go do that, Ramon. Take them up to the apartment. Put them above the mantle, right next to the coconuts. They will be there in thirty years when we return. And by the way, bring a big jar of Vasoline on down. We will need it soon."

Chapter Twelve

(Northern Virginia) Phillip Dixon navigated his Jaguar up the drive of the Knottywood estate. He stopped to talk to Sonny and Beau, the guards at the gate.

"Morning Mr. Dixon."

"Good morning, Sonny. How are you, Beau? Has everything been copasetic over the last week?"

Both said in unison, "Yes, sir."

"Good. I need to go talk to the old man."

"I don't think he knows you're coming. At least, no one told us."

"That's OK. He'll know in a few minutes."

"Your passenger – he's with you, Mr. Dixon?"

"Well, since he is sitting in the passenger seat of a two-seat vehicle – yes – he is with me."

Dixon drove up the drive, parking in front of the house. He stood and took in the view. Beautiful house, beautiful grounds. "I'm going to miss this place."

As he walked up the steps, the front door opened. James, the Pilipino butler, greeted Dixon, "Good morning, Sir."

Dixon chatted briefly with James, always inquiring about his wife and family.

James escorted Dixon to the Marlin Perkins room. "I will tell Mr. Forbish you are here. Would you like some coffee?"

"No thank you, James. I will wait."

Five minutes later, Forbish entered through a side door. "Dixon! I didn't call for you. What are you doing here?"

"You're welcome."

"Wh..What? Oh, yes, old boy. Thanks for getting both of my daughters home. It's good to have the family back together."

"Elizabeth is here? Can I say hello?"

"…well, actually she has gone back to school."

"How about Sandy?"

"Shopping in New York…with her mother."

"Is there anyone at all here besides you, Forbish?"

"Ah, no."

"Not surprising. Sit down and write a check, please."

"What for?"

"The cost of getting your daughters back. One to Conch Island Yacht Service for fifty thousand dollars."

"I thought it was twenty-five thousand," Forbish said.

"Each. Twenty-five thousand each. It's a bargain, believe me."

Forbish furrowed his brow and scribbled out a check and handed it over to Dixon.

"Now for the next thing. Please sign this document donating your sailboat to the same company."

"I don't have a sailboat!"

"Well, I had to purchase one to use in getting your daughter back safe and sound. I did mention that she is safe and sound, didn't I"

Forbish's eyes brightened "You bought me a sailboat? Cool! What does it look like?"

Dixon winced. "It has sails. The normal stuff. No big deal. Look, it was part of the undercover operation. Now we have to get rid of it. People died on the boat. You want it traced back to you?"

"Shit no! Someone died? Good God Almighty Damn! Here, I'll sign it…where?"

Dixon pointed, "Here. Now sign this one."

"OK. I give. What's this one?"

"You had a kid get shot up trying to guard your daughter. This gives him a lump sum payment of two hundred thousand plus an annuity of seventy-five thousand for life."

"For life? Just for getting shot? Hell, I'll get shot for this!"

Dixon moved his jacket to the side to expose his firearm.

"Now don't get like that. Here, I'll sign. Hate giving my money to shitbirds."

"He's probably going to be your son-in-law one day. Maybe you ought to learn to like him. He's a brave kid."

Forbish waved, "Whatever. What's next? Am I signing my nads to scientific research?"

"Nope. Not unless it is microbiological research. Here, this next check establishes a trust for health care for James' family."

"Who's James."

Dixon closed his eyes and exhaled. "Your butler."

"No shit? He sick?"

"His wife has… just sign."

Dixon did.

"This document establishes a trust for the children of a man who died in this operation. His children will all go to college. Don't ask, just sign."

Forbish hesitated, then thought better and signed.

"This is the last one. This one makes Beau Tibedeaux the head of your security here and at our corporate office. Salary, benefits, etcetera."

"But you're my head of security."

"Sign it, Forbish."

Forbish scribbled his name and repeated weakly, "But you are my head of security."

"Not any more. I quit. I have a new job."

Forbish seemed near tears. "N-n-new job? Working for who?"

"Goodbye, Forbish. Thanks for the memories."

Dixon took all the documents and escorted himself out the front door. He got in the Jaguar and drove out to the front gate. He stopped by the guard shack and rolled the window down. Beau, the older of the two guards, walked to talk to him.

"Can I help you, Mr. Dixon?"

"Beau, call me Phillip, please."

Beau smiled, "OK, Phillip, can I help you?"

"I just quit, Beau. I guess I won't be around here any more."

"That a fact? Congrats, I think."

"Yeah. Hey, I think Mr. Forbish wants to talk to the new head of security. You think Sonny can watch the gate while you walk up to the big house?"

"I can do that, Mr...Phillip."

"Thanks. I knew you could."

The Jag pulled out of the driveway and left onto the road. Dixon's passenger said, "So Phillip, are you now ready to go to work?"

"Sure, Murph. What's next?"

• • •

(Alexandria, Virginia) – The couple walked into Don Vito's. The young man was moving slowly, holding onto his girl, limping slightly.

No one at the counter had noticed the couple. They walked quietly to the counter and the young man spoke up, "Waddya got to do go get some service here?"

The big, hairy Italian turned to give a snappy retort and froze in place, "Ya...Johnny! Hey Mama, it's Johnny and Elizabeth! Come here you two." He grabbed them both in a monstrous bear hug.

The little Italian lady shuffled around the counter and hugged both Johnny and Elizabeth.

"Oh, we were so worried! We knew you would come back. What's that on your finger, Elizabeth?"

The half carat solitaire gleamed on her left ring finger.

Elizabeth smiled broadly, "Johnny proposed to me! We're getting married next April!"

Vinnie and his mother roared their approval, "Married! Wonderful!"

Vinnie's mother whisked Elizabeth away to the back of the restaurant, chattering away about all the details of the wedding that had yet to be planned. Vinnie hugged Johnny again, causing him to wince in pain.

"Jesus, Vinnie! I'm all shot up! Watch it."

Vinnie held him at arms length, "Shot up? You're lucky I don't shoot you. Tell Cousin Vinnie about it. Hey, Shep, take over at the counter while I have a sit down with Johnny."

The emaciated looking worker behind the counter grunted his affirmation to Vinnie. Johnny and Vinnie sat at one table in the back while Elizabeth and Vinnie's mother sat at another and chatted for an hour.

"Johnny, this guy came in here. He was talkin' all sorts of things. He said you was in trouble. Said to act like you was dead. It's not my business or nothin', but what kind of business you in these days? Jesus! You scared me to death! And Momma! Hoo boy! And then this guy named Murphy came by. He said all sorts of things. You might be running with the wrong bunch, Johnny."

"You don't have to worry any more. It's all over. I'm still bodyguard for Elizabeth, but in the capacity of boyfriend and fiancé, not as an employee. Dixon came to talk to me. They are taking good care of me. I'm going to finish college. It's all paid for. We are making a pretty good start. Dixon even helped me set up a small stock portfolio. Like a starter kit or something."

Vinnie nodded his approval, "That's real good. Jonathan Ancio Perecci, a college graduate. You'll definitely be the first. Mama is going to be happy."

"There's this other thing. I didn't know about this, but here it is, anyway. Vinnie, there was this old lady that lived around here. Her name was Edna Stribling."

Vinnie, nodded, "Yeah? Wait a minute, you said 'was.' What's her name now?"

"Her name is now the *late* Edna Stribling. She died helping us straighten out this…thing."

More nodding from Vinnie.

"Vinnie, she left us her house. Everything in it. She don't have no family or nothing. She just left it all to Elizabeth and me. She saw the whole thing go down. Before she left to go help with the…uh…thing, she changed her will and left everything to us. I don't even know the lady, Vinnie. I don't know how to feel about all this."

Vinnie continued nodding, "Where's the place? Around here, you said?"

"Yeah. It's a brownstone two blocks up. Dixon say's it's worth half a mil."

Vinnie whistled. That he could understand. "She left you that?"

"Yeah. All the furniture also. Everything. There's like…art and antiques and stuff. And there's some money also, but I don't know how much. Dixon is supposed to get a lawyer to straighten it all out."

"No shit? That's great, Johnny! You and Elizabeth right here, nearby. What you gonna do wit' all the extra room? Bet it's bigger than your apartment."

"You better believe it. Three bedrooms. One bedroom for us, a guest bedroom and a nursery for the twins. Little Tony and, uh… Little Vinnie"

"TWINS! You got twins? …I mean having twins! Oh, shit! Little Vinnie? Really Mama's going to shit!" Vinnie seemed to be hyperventilating.

"Just kidding, Vinnie. Got ya good. Elizabeth is not prego. Not yet. Give us a few years."

Vinnie looked like a heart attack victim finding his last nitroglycerine pill. "Oh, God! Don't do that, Johnny! Twins. Yeah! That was good, now come here, ya freakin' delinquent!"

Johnny struggled in a giant hairy headlock. Elizabeth and her future aunt in law (maybe twice removed) chatted in the back. Lovers strolled down the beautiful Alexandria sidewalks, hand in hand. All was right in the world in Northern Virginia.

• • •

(Panama City, Florida – two days later) By two o'clock most of the lunch crowd had sifted out of Hunt's Oyster Bar. There was a strange mixture of tourists who had found their way down to the old Saint Andrews marina area, sorting through the antique shops and art galleries. The area was once a working marina, filled with fishing boats, shrimp boats, party boats and scores of rough, weathered seagoing men.

After the commercial boats moved across the bay and the charter boats left for Destin and Ft. Walton Beach, the marina and adjacent neighborhoods fell in abandonment. Now, there was revitalization in progress that invited many types of boats and people. Most notable, liveaboard sailboats and pleasure craft now filled dock space where slips sat empty for years.

But oyster bars were the constant in the Saint Andrews area that outlasted all the change. The oysters from nearby Apalachicola Bay were world famous and served up raw by the dozen raw here in Saint Andrews for many decades.

And nobody served them up any better and faster than Hunt's.

The two sisters had worked in Hunt's for a year now. The oldest, Eileen, was eighteen and was set to graduate from Bay County High School in the spring. Her younger sister, Tracy, would graduate the following spring. Both were honor students, though you would never know by their rough mannerism. Growing up around people who made their life on the ocean gave them a tough exterior. Both waited tables in their spare time, slinging oysters to the eclectic crowd who frequented the restaurant.

Eileen's stepmother was home, sleeping off a drunk she pitched last night. Her father was on the road again. His sales job kept him on the road for sometimes two or three weeks. Eileen and Tracy spent long hours planning their escape. Escape from this life that they hated. Escape from drunken stepmom and missing dad and oysters and beet-red tourists that leered and made rude comments.

She walked over to table fourteen. There were two men there, on white and one black. They didn't look like the watermen or locals who frequented the place. They didn't fit the mold of tourists either. They just didn't *fit*.

"What can I get you two?"

The white man smiled. *"Pretty smile,"* Eileen thought.

"Are you are Eileen Dinkins? That's your sister over there?" the man said.

Eileen frowned, "Yes. How'd you know that?"

"And your father is Walter Dinkins?"

"When he's home. He in trouble? I don't know nothing about where he is."

"I know where he is. Is there somewhere your sister and you can talk to us in private? It is important."

Eileen studied the man carefully. "What did you say your name is?"

"My name is William Braddock. This is my partner, Arnold Benedict."

Eileen said, "Let's go out back. Good thing it ain't busy. Hairy Mac would never give us a break yet."

"Hairy Mac?"

"Yeah. He runs this place. Hey, Tracy! Come on out back a minute."

There were two old picnic tables outside the back door. The place was obviously a break area for the workers. Eileen began the conversation, "Your names ain't really Braddock and Benedict, are they?"

"No, Eileen. They're not."

"Dad ain't coming home, is he?"

Murphy hesitated, "No, he isn't."

Tears well in both the girls' eyes. Eileen said, "I never did believe he sold vacuum cleaners and all the other stuff he said he sold. You going to tell us what he really did?"

"No, I'm afraid I can't do that. I can tell you that what he did was important. And honorable. And he loved you very much. He talked about you all the time, how much he missed being away from you. He was constantly bragging on you."

The younger girl said, "He did? Did he really?"

"Absolutely. My associate needs to talk to you."

Dixon stepped forward and brought out an envelope. "Girls, inside this envelope is the name of a local attorney. You need to call him. He will give you instructions on what you are to do."

"What do you mean, *to do*? Doing what? We do what we always do. We go to school. We shuck oysters. We take care of that wicked, mean-ass, drunk stepbitch daddy married. Ya know, it's like a day at the farm, know what I mean? A regular fairy tale life"

"You each have a trust fund set up in your name. It will pay for any college, university or trade school you want to attend. Additionally, it will give you a monthly stipend until you graduate. The trust will also pay for a down payment on a house, the full purchase price of a car and a modest investment portfolio. All of this only after you graduate."

The girls looked at each other. "I don't think we can get in no college. Our grades are good, but people like us just don't exactly get into colleges."

Murphy interjected, "If you could go to any college or university, which one would you choose?"

Eileen thought. "Well…I would like to go to Florida State. That looks like a lot of fun."

Murphy said, "Trust me. You will get in. I will make sure of it. You call that attorney today."

"What about me?" said Tracy. "I'd like to get in Frenchie's Nail and Cosmetology College! That's a pretty tough thing! They don't take just anyone!"

Murphy winced, as if having a severe stomach cramp, "Frenchie's it is, Tracy. I guarantee it. But first you need to take care of family matters. The attorney's fees are already paid. He will arrange for the... final services. Your stepmother will be taken care of, so she should be easier to live with. Understand?"

Murphy continued, "And understand this, girls. If ever, EVER you should need anything; if ever you should get in a jam, no matter what type of jam, you call this attorney. He will contact me and I will be here."

The girls nodded tearfully. Murphy and Dixon left.

• • •

(Five days later – Monroe County Detention Center) – At precisely six-thirty in the morning, John Moses Washington, the jailhouse guard slowly made his way down the isle, ostensible counting the inmates. Everyone knew he was either far too lazy or simply incapable of keeping those kind of numbers in his head. He stood six feet, six inches and weighed in at two hundred, eighty-three pounds. He was the pride of the Key Largo High School's linebacker corps ten years ago. After a short stint playing junior college football in Louisiana, he made his way back to the Keys. He was never the pride of any academic program. Still, he pretended to count, all the while his shoes clicked, clicked, clicked down the isle. He stopped in front of cell number twenty-two.

"You two get yo' stuff together. You getting' out."

"Ah, John Moses. Top of the morning to you, laddie. How can we be bonded out? We haven't been to arraignment?"

The guard looked puzzled. "I don' know. You wanna stay here or you wanna go? Don' make no difference to me."

"What do you think, Tad? Stay? Or Go? You know there are advantages to both choices. For one thing, the food here is really..."

"We'll go. Thank you, John."

John watched them with amusement as they both stood up and stretched. The jailhouse mattresses usually did not lend to a good night sleep. "Don' forget yo' stuff."

Ramon looked around, as if to perform a visual sweep for all his belongings.

"I think we got it all, Bubba."

The key turned and the two men slowly shuffled up the isle to another door.

John led them down a long hall that appeared to be administrative offices. This was not the way most prisoners were taken out of the jail. He opened a door to a room that had a sign outside that said, "Conference."

Ramon pointed, "We'll confer in here."

John Moses walked in the room first. A huge figure rose and approached the jailer. They went through an elaborate series of handshakes and then hugged.

Ramon noted to Tad, "This is the way athletes who want to look like they are hugging hug, but not gay-hugging. See?"

Tad looked at Ramon, "Gay-hugging?"

"Sure! You keep shaking hands with your right hand and put your left hand around your friend's shoulder and kind of pat it real hard. No soft patting. That would be gay-patting."

"Ramon," Tad said, "They're going to break you in half and tear you into little bits. ...and you deserve it."

"How's it going, Big John?" the big Hawaiian man said to the jailer.

"It's all good, Tank. How's your mama?"

"Mama's fine. You should come by. Visit sometime."

The second half of the Key Largo's finest outside linebacker crew greeted John Moses. Benjamin Taneikaika, known as Tank to his friends, was there to pick up Tad and Ramon.

"Come on, you degenerates." Tank said, "Let's get out of here before Big John changes his mind. And Ramon, come here. I want to gay-hug you."

Ramon looked pensively at the grossly oversized biceps covered with tattoos and said to Tad, "Those Hawaiians got good hearing."

"You're on your own. I'm going home."

Tank said, "Not yet. We have to stop off somewhere first."

The three walked outside the jail. The bright sun rising over the horizon caused Tad and Ramon to squint.

"Is that George's El Dorado?" Tad asked.

"Yes it is. You think we could all get on my Harley?" Tank asked.

They all got in, Tank doing the driving. They drove in silence for a few minutes, no one talking. Tad appreciated the silence. The county jail was perpetually loud. There was always someone yelling, making noise. The quiet sound of the car zipping down U.S. 1 was a welcome respite from the last five days.

Ramon obviously did not need peace and quiet.

"Hey Tank, where we going? And by the way, how many Hawaiians can you put on a barstool?"

Tank never took his eyes off the road. "Four if you turn it upside down, you ridiculous homophobe. That's supposed to be a gay joke. Are you by any chance stuck in the closet? All these repressed tendencies coming out now?"

Ramon parried back, "Hey, I don't know any Hawaiian jokes. Hold on, I might be able to come up with a dentist joke."

"Don't bother. I have another year. Here we are."

Tank pulled into the parking lot of a decrepit motel. Like the King Kamehameha, it had been around a long time. However, no one had taken the time to sink any money into renovations. Just the kind of place to have trysts, drug deals and covert meetings. Tank swung the land yacht into the gravel drive, crunching the coral pieces as he navigated the big car through an obstacle course of trash cans, parked cars and banana trees. He was looking around and said, "There it is. Unit 8C."

Ramon said, "You mean room 8C? Why you call it a unit? Something we need to know?"

Tank ignored him and parked right in front of the door.

"You to go on in. There's someone in there waiting for you."

Tad asked, "Who's in there, Tank?"

Tank shook his head and quietly said, "I don't know, man. This is all bad business. You need to go in there. That's all I know and all I can say. I'll wait here."

Tad nodded and they both got out and walked to the door. Tad knocked and the door opened. Both walked in.

Murphy and Dixon sat in the dim interior of the ancient hotel room. The television was on the history channel; Rommel was kicking

Montgomery's butt all the way across North Africa. Dixon and Murphy were in distinct disagreement on how best to stop Rommel.

"Come in, Tad. You can settle something. Do you think Montgomery should have focused on cutting off the supply line of the Afrika Corps? Or do you favor a more balanced attack on the combat power? Tell us, please."

Tad thought for a minute and said, "It doesn't matter. Montgomery didn't have the killer instinct to take on Rommel. Only Patton did."

Both Murphy and Dixon nodded vigorously. "Right you are! Let's get down to business. There is much business to settle. Please have a seat. You too, Ramon."

He continued, "You did your jobs well, just as we agreed. Although there were some…minor variations, everything seemed to turn out fine. Do you agree?"

"No. Johnny got shot. Jimbo died. I killed Sandy. We both got thrown in jail – by the way, are the charges dropped? We stole a boat from good people in Bimini. That old lady you called…Edna? She's dead. I don't even want to know what happened to her. I'm broke. I smell like a turd from being in jail for a week. Everything pretty much sucks."

Murphy looked philosophical. "Let's turn off the television for a while, please Dixon? Thank you. OK, let's examine each of your points. One, Johnny got shot, but that was beyond anyone's control. He is doing quite well, he will recover nicely, he has his job back and he is getting married. How is that for a happy ending?"

Ramon brightened, "Johnny's getting married? Alright! To who?"

"To whom…," Murphy said, "…and it is to Elizabeth, you dolt. Jimbo did die. That is true. I am sorry, but I could not tell you about him. His cover had to be authentic. He was a credit to the agency. His legacy will be remembered. His family will be well compensated, I can assure you."

Tad well knew the risked associated with the business. He nodded his agreement.

Murphy continued, "Edna Stribling was a remarkable woman. She was the only one we had who could identify O'Brien and Hayes. She actually saw them shoot Johnny in Alexandria. We needed her, or so we thought. It is a tragedy that she died like that, but she was not exactly a woman would be left on the sidelines. She lived life on her own terms. That is how she died. As for Catherine Hayes, or Sandy, or whatever her real name was, she was plain and simple a terrorist and a killer. You are not the first to fall for beautiful woman who turned out to be bad. She was, Tad, bad to the bone as the saying goes. I am genuinely sorry you had to go through that, but she would have killed many more. I think you know that."

"I do. It still sucks." Tad said.

"The sailboat has been returned to the couple from whom you… appropriated it. They were actually quite nice about it. They flew out the next day and George gave them back their boat. They stayed a few days at your friend's motel next door. They never reported a thing. All is well there."

"Good. I hate to drag innocent civilians in to this mess."

"Oh my, so you are conceding that you are not really a civilian? Ready to return to the life?"

Tad said hastily, "Nope. Not now. Not ever."

"Never say never, Tad. We recovered Arnie's weapons from your house. They have been disposed of. I notified Arnie. That was a tad sloppy, but it is one loose end tied up. Finally, the charges have not been dropped. Sorry."

Tad and Ramon said in unison, "WHAT?"

"They have not been dropped because it never happened. No arrest. No booking. Absolutely no record of anything at all. If I were you, and thank goodness I am not, I would steer clear of the Monroe County Sheriff for a while. He did not want to cooperate, but …um…certain parties who made certain phone calls convinced him to be a sport. He did, but he is not happy. Something about covert operations in his jurisdiction did not make him a happy camper. It's really all going to work out fine, though, since he thinks you two work for us now. I cannot imagine how he got that impression, but I did not correct him. He should leave you alone, but please do not give him a cause upon which to act."

Ramon smiled, "Hey Chico! The sheriff thinks we are spies! Cool!"

Tad grumbled, "Just ducky."

Murphy continued, "That's about it. Any questions?"

"How's Baker?"

Dixon said, "Who's Baker?"

"Just fine," Murphy said, "…and recuperating getting ready for his next assignment. Mr. Dixon would like to speak to you two now."

Dixon turned to Tad and Ramon, aware that no one was going to tell him who Baker was. "Gentlemen, as you know, I used to represent Mr. Forbish. I am conducting my final business for him now. I have for each of you a check for twenty-five thousand dollars."

Dixon handed Tad and Ramon each an envelope. Tad held onto his, but Ramon opened his and whistled. "Wheeeww! Hey, Chico. It's fat city now! This is gonna help!"

Tad said, "Dixon, this is too much. The agreement was twenty-five thousand total, not each."

"Yeah, well, consider it a bonus. This large brown envelope is even more important. Please open it and read it."

Ramon brightened up, "Hey, that reminds me of a joke – What do you call a contortionist from the Philippines?"

Tad stared at Ramon in embarrassment. Dixon looked at him like he was turd in a punchbowl. Murphy never flinched, "That would be a manila folder. Can we get on with this?"

"Sheesh!" Ramon said, "No one appreciates good jokes anymore."

Tad opened the envelope and removed the thick stack of documents. He scanned each page and flipped back and for the documents.

Tad exhaled and shook his head, "No way."

"Way." Murphy said.

Ramon said, "What's up, Chico? What's that say?"

"He gave us the boat."

"The *Wild Hair*? The MacGregor? Cool! Why? I thought they liked that boat."

"No, Ramon. Not the *Wild Hair*, they gave us the *Who's Your Daddy?* That can't be."

Dixon explained, "Forbish bought that boat for this operation. In light of the sacrifices you two made and based on the fact that you got both his daughters back safely *and* terminated the parties responsible for killing his other daughter, he was grateful. The boat has been donated to the Conch Island Yacht Service, more specifically, their youth sailing outreach program."

"We don't have a youth outreach program."

Murphy piped up, "As long as Ramon is around, you certainly do."

Tad and Ramon sad, silent and dazed.

"Well," Murphy said, "…don't you think a Thank You is in order?"

"Thank you, Mr. Dixon. Thank you." Tad sat in silence and then said to no one in particular, "This is a seven hundred thousand dollar Morris Yacht. How in the world are we going to pay the taxes on it? We can't even pay the *taxes*!"

"Relax, Thaddeus!" Murphy said. "I have a feeling we can help you out with that!"

"Oh shit." Ramon said, "Here it comes."

"There may come a time in the future when we need you to run an errand, do a small task. Nothing big, just a favor." Murphy explained.

Tad shook his head, "No thank you."

Murphy continued, "I know you do not want to do this as a career. But we need capable men and women who can help us periodically. What we do is *necessary*. I know you understand what I am saying. Thaddeus, I respect you and surprisingly enough Ramon enough to not to try to recruit for full time operations. But we might need your unique talents one day. It is like I said earlier. You are never really out. I will not call you unless I really need you. I promise. Now go and enjoy your boat, your newfound freedom and your paycheck"

Tad and Ramon shook hands with Dixon and Murphy and left the room. Tank was sitting outside, waiting on them. "You ladies ready to go?"

"I think so. How did you know to come get us?"

"That Murphy guy called the marina and I answered the phone. He told me to get you at the jail and to bring you here."

Tad asked, "Where was George?"

"Oh," Tank answered, "He was at the motel."

Ramon chimed in, "So you live at the hotel and were at the marina answering phones and George lives at the marina and was at the hotel. That makes sense."

Tank said, "It will."

"Care to elaborate?" Tad asked.

"No."

"Why the mystery?"

"It's the way of the Hawaiian. An enigma"

"Enigma? That reminds me of a joke!" Ramon said.

"Shaddup" said both Tank and Tad in unison.

The ride home was quiet and uneventful. As they rode by the sign advertising the Mandalay, Tad was pensive. He was grateful he survived the encounter with the she-terrorist Hayes, but he genuinely missed Sandy. He knew he could not possible sort out the emotions yet. He would have the time.

When they pulled into the marina parking lot, they saw George out back by the water, lighting the grill. He was smiling and waving. Tank's mother, Annie, was putting table cloths on the picnic table. The mood was festive. Several of the people on the liveaboards were helping out, bringing coolers and setting up fish cookers.

George walked up to Tad and hugged him, "You're back! I knew you would be. But you smell like crap so go and shower. Hurry up! Take that criminal Ramon and tell him to hose off also. We'll be getting started soon!"

Tad looked around. "What will be getting started soon?"

"The engagement party, you moron!" George said, "We're tying the knot! Jumping the broom."

Tad swallowed a big lump, braced himself and said, "With BethAnn? George, I hate to be the one to tell you this, BUT she's…"

"BethAnn? BethAnn! You boob! To Annie! Annie and me are getting married! BethAnn my ass. Whatsamatter with you?"

Tad was for the second time in the last hour dumbfounded. "You're marrying Annie? That's great! That's…how did this happen? When…I don't understand…What's going on, George?"

George took Tad's elbow and led him away from the crowd, making sure Tad stayed downwind. "The day you left, I kicked BethAnn's ass right outta here. Told her to hit the road. She pitched a fit, but she left. I'm not a young man any more and I was acting like a idiot. I can see what she could see in me, you know, being a bullhunk of a man that I remain. But I decided to go for it. I been liking Annie for quite some time. I just never thought she would like me. She's a real catch, you know. A tiger in bed also."

"Ahhhh! Too much information, George!" Tad said.

George continued as if Tad had not interrupted, "So I go over and ask her over for coffee. The next thing you know, we're doing the horizontal tango…"

"Umm, Umm, Umm, I'm not listening!"

And I got the courage up to ask her to marry me. I asked her yesterday. I went to the jewelry store and got a ring and all. I got down on one knee and took her hand and said, "Annie Taneikaika, will you marry me? And you know what? She said yes. I said good, now help me up. My freaking back was killing me. So now we're having the engagement party! This is good stuff! Go get cleaned up and wash off that jail funk and come on down."

Tad thought a few seconds, "You're engaged to Annie? Cool. That's really good, George. I mean it. Congratulations. Engagement party tonight. Ought to be fun. When is the wedding?"

"Tomorrow."

"Tomorrow? You got engaged yesterday, had the engagement party today and you're getting married tomorrow?"

George looked at Tad as a wizened professor might gaze upon a particularly stupid student, "Well, Duh! Isn't that what you young people say? Duh? Duh! Poolside ceremony tomorrow at sundown. I need a best man. You got anything going on at say…sundown?"

The emotions swelled within Tad. George was like a father to Tad. "Yes, George. It would be an honor."

"Yeah? Good. Well honor me by showering and changing clothes. The shrimp go in the cooker in fifteen minutes. We got sausage, corn, potatoes, dolphin on the grill. We got cold beer and margaritas. You two hooligans hurry up."

As George was walking away, he heard a loud squeal come from near the office. "Omigod! Ramon! You're back!" She ran and hugged him, almost knocking him down. "Omigod! It's so good you're back. George and Annie…EWWW! You stink. Nevermind, George and Annie…EWWW! You have got to go…shower or something."

Ramon smiled, "Give me ten minutes! I shall return and sweep you off of your feet yet again!"

Tad and Ramon walked toward their apartment, each deep within his own thoughts, each smiling. Life was good. .

• • •

The following evening came quickly. Tad, Ramon, Tiffany, Tank and several of the residents of Conch Island Marina pooled together their efforts and decorated the pool behind the King Kamehameha's office.

Ramon saw Tank covering the picnic tables, "Hey Tank! Where'd you get all those tablecloths?"

"They're bed sheets. Same thing. Kinda."

"You wash them? There's no curlies on them are they?"

"Tad, is it OK if I kill your friend? It'll be quick."

"Sure Tank. Go ahead."

Ramon made sure to keep the pool between him and Tank. Ramon was stringing up lights around the fence and in the palm trees. Some of the lights had little red peppers hanging from them. Others had palm trees, sailboats, hula girls, parrots and other various shapes. The boat people had a distinct sense of style in their lights. There were many, many strings with plain lights donated to ceremony by the liveaboards in the marina. There was a festive feel in the air.

Two different groups were mixing together, laughing and joking. The people who lived on the sailboats and trawlers in the Conch Island Marina were mixing with the dangerous, black leather Harley Davidson crowd that generally claimed the ownership of the King Kamehameha pool. The liquor store down the street had just delivered a keg of draft beer, which was being submerged in ice in a garbage can.

Something suddenly struck Tad, "Hey Tank! What about the minister? Who's going to perform the ceremony?"

Tank broke into a slight grin, which for him was an amazing show of emotion. "We have that all taken care of. He'll be here in plenty of time. He's a friend of mine. Actually a friend of Mom's."

"What about marriage licenses? Blood tests? All that stuff?"

"They are not worried about that. They intend to enter a state of matrimony in direct violations with the laws of the State of Florida so that they can be cheated of any fruits legal domesticity. Additionally, since a marriage is a covenant with God, they figure their vows to God probably overrule any non-etheral legal codes." Tank explained.

Ramon said, "For real? Cool. Didn't think George had it in him."

Tank looked exasperated. "You idiot. They got all the paperwork in order. It's going to be legal. It's going to be in accordance with the teachings of the church. It's going to perfect for my momma. Got it?"

"Got it, Tank." Ramon said, knowing that messing with Tank's mother was a highly sensitive enterprise that could only lead to pain and suffering. "How you feel about your Momma and George marrying? I'm serious. No fooling around. You OK with that?"

Tank sauntered over to the keg that was on ice. He pulled three plastic cups off of a stack and pumped the keg up. He expertly poured three cups of amber, cool beer. He handed one to Ramon and one to Tad.

"Well, it's like this. That's my Momma and you both know how I feel about her. She's smart and tough, but she's still a lady. She always has liked George, though heavens know why. I guess I like him OK too. He was always good to us. So I like the match. If Momma likes him, that's good enough for me. And you two are like George's sons. At least that's what he tells Momma..."

Ramon butted in, "He said that? I'm his son? Oh man, I must be the one he don't talk much about. Imagine a Greek Cuban ..."

"...As I was saying," said Tank, "George treats you two like you are his sons. That means you two and I are going to be like...brothers. So I've been thinking about that. That's pretty cool, since I don't have any other brothers. I am thoroughly convinced both of you will be in prison soon doing long stretches, so I would like to start this family thing correctly."

He handed Ramon and Tad a cup of beer.

"To my new family. Cheers!" Tank held his cup up.

"To new family!" Tad said and held his cup up to toast.

"Live long and prosper!" Ramon said and held his cup up.

They all touched glasses and downed the beer. Then Tank grabbed Ramon and lifted the squirming mass over his head. "Time for our Cuban brother to go swimming."

Splash!

Tank smiled broadly, "I'm liking this family thing already!"

At precisely thirty minutes before sundown, the evening calm was shattered by the roar of motorcycles approaching. Twenty Harleys pulled into the parking lot. Each parked in line, backing in and dress right dressed on the nest. Brother Wheelie Jack Jenkins got off his bike and walked over to Tank.

"Tank, where can I find Annie? Is everything set?"

"Yes it is, Brother Jack. She's in the office. Can't come out because George might see her."

"Then I'll go see her there."

Tad walked up to Tank, "A preacher riding a Harley? In a leather jacket? For real?"

"Tad," Tank said patiently, "It's the message that is important, not the clothes or transportation. Brother Jack has ministered to the needs of many who just don't feel…welcomed in some churches. He's one of the good guys."

Tad was becoming more and more impressed by the depth and intellect of his new giant Polynesian brother. "I never knew."

"Sometimes," Tank continued, "…there is more to a person than meets the eye."

Ramon butted in, "Like a big, dumb-looking galoot being a dentist? Like that?"

Tank eyed Ramon, causing him to back away a step, "Yes, Ramon. Exactly."

Five minutes before sundown, Tank invited everyone to gather around the pool. Someone in the back pushed the play button on a portable CD player and a beautiful Hawaiian song wafted through the evening air. George was standing in front of Brother Jack, looking spiffy in his faded khakis and Hawaiian shirt. Tad and Ramon stood to his side. The door to the office opened and Tank emerged with Annie on his monstrous arm. He beamed as he presented the bride to the group.

The tiny woman smiled and looked across the pool to George. She and Tank slowly made their way down the sidewalk, around the pool and stopped in front of Brother Jack. Someone had the presence of mind stop the music.

Brother Jack began, "Brothers and sisters, we are gathered here today in the presence of our lord…" The service was about five minutes, but Tad thought it was the most moving wedding he could imagine. He hoped his wedding, if he ever had one, would be as auspicious.

Ramon was praying that Tiffani was not getting any ideas.

Before Brother Jack pronounced the couple husband and wife, each read their vows. George took out a scrap of paper from his pocket, put on his reading glasses and began.

"Hmmph. Annie Taneikaika, I vow to you the following things: Let me see…Oh yeah…" George had never been a smooth talker, but he hit his stride. "…Annie, you are the woman I want to spend the rest of my life with. You are my ray of morning sunshine and the cool breeze in my hair. You make me smile when there's nothing to smile about. I vow that I will never leave you. I vow you will be the first thought in my head when I wake up and the last thought when I go to sleep. Dreams of you while I am asleep and having you near me while I am awake will make me a man without want. I vow to you that I will spend every remaining day on this Earth making you happy and showing you how much I love you."

The crowd ooohh'd and aaahhh'd. Ramon raised his right eyebrow to Tad in a silent message, *"Hey, that's pretty good!"* Two bikers in the front row were dabbing tears from the corners of their eyes.

Annie stared into George's eyes and smiled. She began.

"George Giani, you honor me by choosing me. Though it took time, I knew you would come to me eventually. I vow that you will never be alone for the rest of your life. I'll always be by your side. I will be by your side during all times, both good and bad. Neither poor health, bad luck, nor the actions of your idiot sons will come between us. You can ride my Harley, but only after you have been properly trained. This I vow."

Tad snuck a look at Ramon who was looking at Tiffani and making a *Yeah! She mentioned me* face. Tiffani winked back. The two bikers in the front row began to sob uncontrollably.

Brother Jack said, "I now pronounce you Husband and Wife! You may kiss the bride." The crowd roared their approval and the celebration was on! Someone dropped a Buffett CD in and the tropical sounds filled the pool area. The marina residents had started putting out an enormous spread of food, conch fritters, bar-b-que chicken, hot wings, chips and dip and much more.

The celebration continued until far into the night. Tad found Tank, who was having a debate with a FSU coed who happened to be staying at the Kamehameha as to whether Flagler's interest in the keys was mostly philanthropic, purely commercial or a personal challenge that defied labeling and defining. This while they guzzled hunch punch.

"Hey, Tank, you seen George and Annie?"

"Brianna, this is Tad. Tad, meet Brianna. She's a philosophy major at FSU."

"Oh, sorry! Hi there, Brianna. Tank, Do you know where George and Annie are? I want to say something before I leave."

"Tad, Brianna brings up a very interesting point. Actually, it's sort of a philosophical dilemma, if you think about it. If the Pope craps in the woods, does it make a sound? When it falls? What do you think?"

Brianna smiled broadly at the big Hawaiian. He looked back at Tad, "I'm just kidding. Yes, I do know where they are. They are gone. Actually, that would mean that I don't know where they are, right, kitten?"

Tank put his finger on Brianna's lips. "There, there. You don't have to answer that. Let me read your eyes. The answer is…"

"Gone? What do you mean gone? Where are they?" Tad asked.

"Venice. Like you didn't know that."

"Venice? Like in Italy? What are you talking about?"

"No, Venice, South Dakota. Of course, Venice, Italy."

Tad stared at Tank, "I give up. Divulge your information, please. I know nothing."

"Didn't Mr. Murphy tell you? When I talked to him on the phone, I must have let it out that George and Momma were getting married. You know, he did ask a lot of questions. Nosy fellow, he is. He said that he would be sending a gift shortly and for Momma and George to enjoy it with his compliments. So, this morning at about nine o'clock, the lady from Largo Travel showed up here at the hotel. She had a package for Momma. Two tickets to Hawaii.

Momma told her she had already been there and done that and was not planning on going back. The lady made a phone call and then, while still on the phone, looked up at Momma and said 'Venice?' Now that made Momma happy. She left and came back about an hour later with plane tickets, hotel accommodations, everything. They are staying at some ritzy place on the square, near the Grand Canal. Cool, huh? As the travel agent lady left, she said, 'This is from Mr. Murphy'"

Tad was having a difficult time finding words. "How long will they be gone?"

"I don't know. I think two weeks. I guess George will be looking to you to run the marina. I'll come over and help, if you need me."

• • •

The two weeks passed quickly. Tad and Ramon threw themselves into their work. They had a hundred different odd fix-up jobs that needed taking care of around the marina. Tad emptied out the office and re-painted it, a task that had been needing doing for years.

He and Ramon cleaned the *Who's Your Daddy* out from bow to stern, removing the debris from travel, Jimbo's blood and the bad memories. The blood cleaned up well, but the memories seemed to still linger heavily. They installed all the electronics that Jimbo/Walter had brought. The big Morris was truly ready for any sea passage.

Tiffani left a week after the wedding. She took Ramon out on the dock one afternoon while the sun was going down and had a long talk to him. Tad watched it all from a distance. Ramon never mentioned it, other than saying, "…She had to go." Tad figured Ramon would talk about it in his own time, though he did seem more quiet than usual.

Tank had been spending his evenings at the marina, which pleased Tad greatly. Tad discovered each day new depths to the big Hawaiian that now claimed Tad to be his brother. Ramon continued to bait Tank with comments, both funny and stupid. Tank counseled Ramon often. They would walk down the dock to the same spot where Tiffani announced her leaving. Tad watched, again, from a distance. The two talked for over a half-hour, though mostly Tank listened.

Again, Ramon did not say much, but did get back to his original form in picking at Tank. Tad hoped no one would have to take him down that dock for a talk.

George and Annie returned on a Saturday afternoon, a full day early. *"We did it this way so you knuckleheads wouldn't make fuss."* George moved in with Annie at the King Kamehameha. He cleaned out everything from his two-room apartment that connected to the marina office. He said that it "…wasn't right to keep two places at once. It didn't show much faith in the relationship." Tad agreed.

George would have his poolside coffee in the morning and walk over to the marina office. By eight o'clock, Tad already had the office open, though it was rare for anyone to be in that early.

Tank was preparing to head back to dental school to finish out his remaining year. His Momma could not have been more proud of him. Even Ramon showed an interest, "Hey Tank, you want me to come spend a weekend with you? You think you can hook me up? You probably need me to hook you up!"

Tad and Ramon would often spend afternoons sailing the big Morris up and down the coast. They continued to get their fledgling yacht service off the ground by working on boats, doing bottom jobs, and making occasional deliveries. *Somehow* they managed to get customers who had *somehow* gotten the word that Conch Island Yacht Service was for them. Tad smelled Murph in the background, but like always, he could not and did not want to prove it. No matter, business was business.

The evening before Tank left for school, they all went to the Mandalay for a farewell dinner. Tad glanced once at the fateful slip where the showdown occurred, but found that he didn't need to look at it any more. Ancient history.

And so the family was together one more time. Tad and Ramon. George and Annie and Tank. They all watched the sun go down behind the trees, enjoyed the cool breeze and gave thanks for one more day in Paradise.